# Burden of Proof

Based on a true story

Balbinder Chagger

# Burden of Proof

Based on a true story

This first edition published in 2020 by Balbinder Chagger

Copyright © Balbinder Chagger 2020

All rights reserved

The moral right of the author has been asserted

The right of Balbinder Chagger to be identified as author of this work has been asserted in accordance with the Copyright, Designs and Patents Act 1988

Without limiting the rights under copyright reserved above, no part of this publication may be reprinted or reproduced or utilised in any form or by any electronic, mechanical or other means, now or hereafter invented, including photocopying and recording, or in any information storage or retrieval system, without the permission in writing from the author.

Cover photograph, design, typesetting, and art by Balbinder Chagger

www.burdenofproof.co.uk
balbinder.chagger@burdenofproof.co.uk

ISBN 979-8-677-20878-2

*For*

*Sumitran and Harbhajan*

# ABOUT THE AUTHOR

*Burden of Proof*, a work of fiction based on a true story concerning unfair treatment at work, is Balbinder Chagger's second book. Balbinder has many years of employment history across several international investment banks. His first book, *Options Explained Simply: The Fundamental Principles Course*, is a work of nonfiction based on his financial knowledge.

# CONTENTS

| | | |
|---|---|---|
| 1 | Quick Private Chat | 1 |
| 2 | Appraisal | 8 |
| 3 | Announcements | 18 |
| 4 | Consultation | 23 |
| 5 | Unfairness | 37 |
| 6 | Bonus | 48 |
| 7 | Difference of Treatment | 54 |
| 8 | Ranjit Singh's Testimony | 70 |
| 9 | Neil Hobson's Testimony | 100 |
| 10 | Simon Ong's Testimony | 146 |
| 11 | Veronica Cotton's Testimony | 171 |
| 12 | Jackie Monroe's Testimony | 181 |
| 13 | Colin Marr's Testimony | 191 |
| 14 | Adam Sirinathan's Testimony | 198 |
| 15 | Nathan Wilcox's Testimony | 201 |
| 16 | Adrian Brent's Testimony | 212 |
| 17 | Respondents' Case | 218 |
| 18 | Claimant's Case | 227 |
| 19 | Judgement Day | 244 |

# 1

# QUICK PRIVATE CHAT

~ Tuesday 22nd November 2005, 3:00 p.m. ~

'Would you be interested in taking up voluntary redundancy?' my line manager, Neil Hobson, puts to me in a plush glass-walled meeting room, having just taken me inside for a quick private chat.

His proposal hits me completely by surprise. The bank hasn't announced any plans of redundancies in our department. Why is he asking me this, I wonder sitting opposite him at a small circular-shaped meeting table with a vacant chair on either side of us. This seems to be coming out of the blue.

'Well, Ranjit?' he prompts me.

'No,' I answer firmly.

I love my job. I know it intimately. I'm very good at it. My job performance appraisals, which occur half-yearly, confirm it officially. Neil has been my line manager for about a year now. He conducted my last two appraisals, the 2005 mid-year and the 2004 year-end appraisal. He gave me glowing assessments on both occasions.

'If you are interested,' he follows through, 'I could have a word with HR and see what package is available'.

I know the bank's policies don't permit voluntary redundancies. The bank precludes them. Its workforce is its biggest resource and it manages it proactively, retaining complete control over determining what its staffing needs are and deciphering whom it must retain and whom it may let go. It does not delegate the decision to its workers and risk walking out of the door people critical to its needs. If Neil is asking me, then he must have cleared it with HR already, and he would not dare have done that without firstly obtaining his own line manager's approval. What is this about?

'No, thanks, I'm not interested,' I reply firmly.

'If you think you can get another job pretty quickly,' he says, 'you could be quids in'.

If his line manager and HR are both in on it, then something must be going on that I'm not aware of. Suddenly, the thought hits me that redundancies are going on in our department. Feelings of insecurity, uncertainty, and helplessness overwhelm me. I find solace, though, in recalling the bank's policies state it will let us know our jobs are the subject of a redundancy as soon as it knows it, and that it has not announced any plans of redundancies affecting our department.

'No, I'm not interested, not even in the slightest bit,' I reply clearly.

I glance through the room's glass sidewalls into the adjoining meeting rooms. In the room on my right, a middle-aged lady stands beside a flipchart presenting to five people seated around an oval-shaped conference table. In the room on my left, a young man paces about slowly while talking on his mobile phone.

'Do you want some time to think about it and then get back to me?' he persists.

Why doesn't he accept my answer? Could it be that he wants me to leave? Why? I do a good job. I serve him well. I make him look good.

'No. I can tell you right now,' I say. 'I'm not interested'.

'Okay,' he says as though he has tried as much as he could and the quick private chat is over.

'Anyway,' I follow through, 'why do you ask?'

'Oh, I just want to sound you out in case there're redundancies in our area,' he replies. 'You know, since Eurocredito bought us last year, it's been making redundancies left, right, and centre to save costs'.

He's right. We are a UK bank operating in the retail banking sector. That is, the bank runs branches on high streets up and down the UK selling products like bank accounts, mortgages, and loans to millions of customers. This is the bank's primary business. It deploys thirty thousand staff in it, being ninety-eight per cent of its total workforce. The bank's business activities are regulated by the UK's Financial Services Authority, which we more commonly refer to by its initials as the FSA. Eurocredito, the colossal European banking group worth two hundred billion euros in share value, bought us about a year ago to gain ready access to the UK market via our customer base. Since buying us, it has been rebranding the branches with its name, blue and yellow colour scheme, and stars logo. It has also been streamlining the retail business and shedding staff in large numbers there.

'Yes. But, that's all been on the retail banking side, not in investment banking, where we work,' I clarify.

The bank also runs a tiny investment banking business employing the other two per cent of its workforce, being some six hundred people. The investment banking business is based in the bank's head office on London Wall, in the City of London. The head office also houses on its top floor the bank's executive management suite, where the Chief Executive Officer and other executive board members reside. In contrast to the retail business, the investment business has no customers. Essentially, it is the bank trading financial instruments on its own behalf, like equities, currencies, bonds, futures, and options. Retail and investment banking are completely different and separate businesses.

'The bank hasn't announced any plans of redundancies in our department, right?' I ask him.

'No,' he replies.

'Are you aware of any plans?' I press him.

'No,' he says.

His answers are consistent with the bank's policy of

letting us know our jobs are at risk as soon as it knows it.

Through the room's glass front wall with the door, I see our open-plan office, which is on the first floor, with its clusters of work desks with computer screens and staff working away. Each cluster comprises eight desks pushed together, such that four people sit adjacently facing one direction with four other people sitting on desks opposite mirroring them. The clusters are arranged in straight rows creating a grid of pathways between them for people to move about the floor. A couple of rows away, I see the other three members of my team sitting on the four adjacent desks allocated to us. Our team's name is Market Risk Control. At one end of the row of four desks sits Katia Mykonola. She and I are the senior members of the team. We're seasoned professionals with many years of work experience and subject matter expertise in the field of market risk. Our job titles are Market Risk Controllers. She also reports into Neil. Immediately to her left sits Mary Richardson and then, Anthony Grenfell. Mary and Anthony are the junior members of the team. We hired them around April and May. Their job titles are Market Risk Associates. Katia is Mary's line manager and I'm Anthony's. My desk is at the other end, next to Anthony's.

'Shouldn't you be asking the whole team this kind of thing openly in a team meeting?' I put to him. 'Why are you isolating me and asking me privately?'

'Because only you,' he replies, 'have ever requested voluntary redundancy'.

'What?' I say shocked. 'When did I do that?'

'Back around July last year,' he answers.

'That was no request for redundancy,' I assert remembering the context. 'I raised voluntary redundancy then in a team meeting as a follow through to what you had just said to us all. We were highlighting a business issue to you. But, you refused to acknowledge it existed because, you said, none of us had resigned over it. Why should we have to sacrifice our jobs to make you see? It was frustrating. So, I asked you whether you support your stance with any voluntary redundancy option'.

'It was a personal request for voluntary redundancy,' he rebuts.

'Why would you say that?' I ask alarmed by his view. 'Nobody would see it like that'.

'It was a personal request,' he reiterates firmly.

'It most certainly was not,' I protest. 'It was a reaction to you, to try to make you sit up and think about what you were saying to us. I knew the bank doesn't entertain voluntary redundancies'.

'But, you agree you asked about voluntary redundancy,' he puts to me.

'Yes, but during a team discussion and as a follow through to what you had said,' I clarify. 'If I had wanted voluntary redundancy, I wouldn't have requested it openly in a team meeting. I'd have raised it privately and confidentially to my line manager, who wasn't you at the time,' I assert.

At the time, the Market Risk Control team consisted of three people. There was Katia and I, and a Head of Market Risk Control, into whom we both reported. He reported into Neil.

'Hmm,' he muses as though contemplating how to surmount this fact.

The head of our team eventually left the bank to take up employment elsewhere. Neil, then, became our direct line manager. Katia and I were the only members of the team for the next six months, until the two junior Associates joined.

'That was one and a half years ago,' I add. 'I never pursued it or even mentioned it ever again'.

'That's your view,' he says as though his view outranks mine.

'Well, we can ask Katia for an independent view. She was present at the meeting,' I reply in an effort to make him see objectively. 'Anyway,' I continue, 'now that you've asked me, I suggest you ask everyone else in the team too. Otherwise, it'll be unfair. Besides, why wouldn't you want to sound them out too?'

We vacate the meeting room and return to our desks. He sits at the desk directly opposite mine. Our computer screens obstruct our views of each other. The three desks to his left belong to the Market Risk Reporting team, which also reports into him. Hence, he has the job title, Head of Market Risk Control and Reporting, being an amalgamation of the two teams' names. His line manager is Simon Ong, the man in charge of our department. His job title is Director of the Market Risk Department. He has a private office in the executive management suite. He has a handful of heads of teams reporting into him, Neil being one, through whom he manages his staff of fifty.

Behind me is a glass wall running the whole width of the floor. On the other side of it is the trading floor. It bustles with the bank's trading staff going about its business of trading financial instruments. Their business activities expose the bank to market risks, being the amount of money it could lose as financial markets move up and down.

Our team's job is to monitor and control the traders' activities so the levels of risks the bank is exposed to remain within the agreed risk limits. It's a skilled and specialised job. It requires expert knowledge of financial instruments and financial markets, and of risk measurement and risk control techniques. It involves standing up to traders who exceed their risk limits and telling them to cut their positions. It also involves making sure the trading conditions the FSA imposes on the bank are complied with.

One FSA condition is that none of the traders may access the controllers' working areas. The glass wall satisfies this condition, while also enabling us to sit near the traders so that we have the ready access we need to them to be able to do our jobs efficiently. Our security passes allow us access through the glass wall to the trading floor side, because the FSA permits us to go there. But, the traders' deny them access to our side.

Another FSA condition is that the bank notifies it of its trading activities and risk matters according to the rules it imposes on us, which are formalised and set out in an official document. There are some activities that the FSA is happy for the bank to get on with without it being notified about them. There are other activities that it is happy for the bank to get on with, but it wants to be post-notified about them. Then, there are other activities that it does not want the bank to do at all without firstly pre-notifying it about them and getting its explicit permission to proceed, which it could take up to thirty days to give. Notification failures can result in the FSA imposing sanctions on the bank. To reduce the risk of errors, Katia and I discuss matters and crosscheck each other's decisions. We also keep Neil informed of what we're doing so he can have a say and is well positioned to be able to update his peers and Simon. Each week, we have regular individual one-to-one meetings with him, a regular collective team meeting, and as many ad-hoc meetings as required. We maintain records of discussions and decisions for future reference and for audit and regulatory purposes.

Katia and I are good at our jobs. We've never made a mistake. Three months ago, Eurocredito sent a team of its internal auditors to review and check our work. To the envy of all the other teams in our department, they found no issues at all and gave us a completely clean audit report.

Neil's quick private chat undermines my peace of mind. I have a gut feeling that I have been targeted and something against me is afoot behind my back.

# 2

# APPRAISAL

~ Friday 16th December 2005, 3:30 p.m. ~

'So, Ranjit, how do you think you performed this year?' Neil asks conducting my 2005 year-end appraisal meeting with me in a private meeting room.

'Really well,' I say to start off. 'I had a really good mid-year assessment and I carried on pretty much the same way during the second half of the year. I had more responsibility this year because I took on the responsibilities of the departed former Head of Market Risk Control, and I had an Associate to manage too. I performed above and beyond all of the objectives the bank set me,' I say blowing my own trumpet. 'I was proactive. I generated initiatives and drove them forward. I worked effectively with colleagues and was a positive influence on them,' I go on with great enthusiasm. 'I showed strength of character and stood firm against the traders when they wanted to take excessive risks. I strengthened and enhanced the risk control environment by identifying issues and implementing improved procedures and processes'. To round off, I say, 'I, in collaboration with Katia, achieved a completely clean Eurocredito audit report'.

'Yes, I agree with all of that,' he says without even a trace of enthusiasm in his voice. 'Here's your appraisal document. I've completed it already. If you could just sign it off at the bottom, then we can wrap up quickly here and I can be off on my Christmas break,' he says.

'Oh, I thought we were going to complete it together,' I reply. 'No matter. I'd better read it first, though'.

I start reading. As I expect, he reflects the things I just mentioned to him. Additionally, he praises me for benefiting the department with the experience and expertise I gained in my previous employments at other banks. He says, looking ahead, my challenge over the next year is to control the traders' increased desire to take greater risks to try to hit their increased revenue targets. It all seems good. But wait, what's this he's written at the end?

'Er,' I mumble looking perplexed. 'Neil, what do you mean by, *"Occasionally, Ranjit needs to take greater account of the regulator's requirements and embrace change more positively"*?' I ask. 'Where did that come from? And, why is my appraisal score reduced? It's much lower than it was at mid-year! Why? What happened from July onwards?' I ask bewildered.

'Calm down,' he says. 'It's nothing serious,' he adds casually. 'Just *occasionally*,' he says playing it down. 'It's nothing to be concerned about'.

'I beg to differ, Neil,' I reply. 'To the contrary, it's very serious. It'll impact my annual bonus and my future prospects. I'm not signing off on that! It's false. Please remove the criticism and revise my score up,' I request.

'It is true,' he asserts. 'My assessment stands'.

'It's not true,' I reply. 'Besides, appraisals aren't meant to contain any surprises. You're meant to highlight and discuss issues throughout the year, as and when they arise, so corrective action can be taken to keep performance on track,' I remind him of the bank's policy on performance and appraisals. 'This is the first I've ever heard that I've underperformed, and pretty seriously, at that. It's a complete shock, and it's come in an appraisal meeting. If it were true, you'd have said something before. Why didn't you ever say anything before?' I challenge him.

'This is my assessment of you, as your manager,' he asserts.

'But, your assessment is arbitrary,' I reply. 'It's meant

to be objective. It's meant to be based on facts and supported by evidence. Where's your evidence to back it up?'

'What evidence do you need?' he says. 'I'm your line manager and this is my assessment of you. That's evidence enough,' he asserts.

'What sort of attitude is that?' I reply. 'Neil, your comment is untrue. Please remove it and revise my score upward,' I request, 'because it's serious. It will impact me negatively for years to come'.

'No,' he replies resolutely.

'If you won't do it, then I'll need to appeal against your assessment,' I reply. 'In which case, I need you to explain the basis of your assessment'.

'So be it,' he says.

'Okay, then. Let's start with your criticism that I need to take greater account of the regulator's requirements. Give me some examples of when I failed to do that,' I challenge him.

'There are a few things you failed to notify the FSA about,' he replies vaguely.

'Which things? When?' I press him for specifics.

'I can't remember off the top of my head,' he answers.

'If I really had failed, there would have been some sort of comeback on me as soon as the failures were detected, right?' I put to him. 'But, you've never said anything to me before'.

'As I said, I don't remember off the top of my head,' he replies.

'Well, could you look into it after this meeting and email me the examples with supporting evidence please?' I ask.

'Yes, I could do that,' he replies.

'I appreciate you're heading off on annual leave today, but please don't forget to do it before you go,' I urge him. 'I need the information to write up an appeal'.

'I won't forget,' he assures me.

'Let's look at your other criticism, that I need to embrace change more positively. Give me some examples of when I failed there,' I challenge him.

'Er, let's see,' he says. 'Back in October, someone proposed a change to the Risk Limits Policy. You didn't support the proposal on the basis that the policy works fine as it is,' he says.

'That's right,' I confirm. 'There's nothing wrong in that. In fact, you, Katia, and I discussed the proposal together and we collectively agreed to reject it because we all concluded it wasn't needed'.

'Hmm,' he mumbles. 'I don't think so. I don't remember Katia and I doing that,' he asserts.

'You certainly did. You're included on an email with the minutes of the meeting. They show that the three of us did exactly that,' I reply. 'Any other examples?'

'In September, Simon instructed you and Katia to change the line of delegated authorities to include me,' he says. 'You highlighted issues concerning the change'.

'That's right,' I confirm. 'Katia did too. We both did. It's our job to do so. You know it's our job to advise Simon on risk matters. I was doing the job the bank expects me to do. But, I also told you that although I'm highlighting concerns with the change, I am getting on with implementing it as Simon instructed'.

'I don't recall Katia raising any concerns. Only you did,' he says.

'So what, if only I did? It's my job' I reply. 'Are you really criticising me for doing the job the bank expects me to do? By the way, you're copied in on emails that show Katia raised concerns too. Any other examples?'

'Yes, but not off the top of my head,' he says. 'I'll email them as well to you'.

'Neil,' I say, 'your negative comment on my appraisal is totally arbitrary. Please remove it and revise my score up. You're my manager. You're under a duty of trust to treat me reasonably and fairly. But, your assessment is unfair and detrimental to me'.

'I am treating you reasonably and fairly,' he rebuts. 'My assessment is objective,' he asserts refusing to budge.

'But, you haven't supported it with any evidence,' I reply.

'I have. I'll email it to you. Then, you'll see,' he says. 'But, you can appeal my decision, if you want to,' he adds as though he knows it will be a futile effort on my part.

'Neil, is there something going on here that I don't know about?' I ask.

'No,' he replies bluntly.

'Okay. Please do let me have your email before you leave today so I can appeal off the back of it,' I remind him.

Disagreeing fundamentally, we return to our desks. It's 4:00 p.m. I unlock my computer screen and send him an email putting on record that I dispute the appraisal he just gave me. I ask him to send me examples and evidence to support his assessment before he leaves the office today for his long break. He will not return until Tuesday 3rd January.

I look up on the bank's intranet site its procedure for appealing appraisals. It says before lodging any formal appeal, the individual should first try to resolve the dispute informally with the line manager. Failing to achieve a resolution informally, a formal appeal articulating the full grounds of the appeal must be lodged within ten days from the date of the appraisal meeting. Neil will be out of the office for the next sixteen days. I must have his email before he leaves today to be able to lodge the appeal within the ten-day time limit.

Feelings of job insecurity and uncertainty weigh me down. I try to lift up my mood by recalling that Neil also commented that my challenge over the next year is to control the traders' increased desire to take greater risks. I strive to convince myself that this bodes well, that my position is secure. Still, though, I feel anxious that some detriment is heading my way.

An email alert pops up in the bottom right hand corner of my screen. With a great sense of urgency, I rush to check if the email is from Neil. To my dismay, it's not. I let out a sigh and then, start reading it. It's from a trader asking for my approval to trade an exotic equity option that is beyond his mandate. I review the details he's given and deicide I need more information to give my answer. I head off to see him. I pass through the door in the glass separation wall and traverse my way on the trading floor to his desk. We discuss the trade in detail. On my return to my desk, some forty minutes later, I see that Neil has left the office. I rush to check if he sent me the email.

~ Tuesday 3rd January 2006, 11:00 a.m. ~

Having left the office sixteen days ago, Neil is back today. He looks very pleased with himself. He had left without sending me the email, I believe, intentionally to deny me the chance to act in his absence. I spent the entire Christmas period agitated. I harbour grave concerns about my position, annual bonus, and prospects rooted in his sudden unexplained criticism on my appraisal and lowering of my score. The fact that he went off without giving me the information I needed to lodge a formal appeal only frustrated me and added to my anxiety. His return gives some relief to my feelings because he is available to chase up, which I do right away by email so it is on record.

It's 5:00 p.m. The first business day of the new calendar year, and also the bank's financial accounting year, is drawing to a close. People are starting to drift out the office. But, I still haven't received Neil's reply. I rise off my seat and look down at him from over the tops of our computer screens.

'Neil,' I say to get his attention. 'Could you let me have

that email, please?'

'Oh,' he replies, 'er, I'll try to get back to you on that by the end of the week'.

He's dragging his feet intentionally, I believe.

'Can you send it to me as a matter of urgency please, ideally today?' I say. 'You promised you'd let me have it before you went off on holiday. It's been two and a half weeks now. I need it urgently'.

'I'll try my best,' he says in disinterested tone with his eyes fixed on his computer screen and his fingers typing away.

~ Monday 9th January 2006, 9:00 a.m. ~

I can't believe the weekend passed by so fast and it's Monday again. Arriving at my desk and logging on, I see that Neil finally emailed me on Friday evening after I had left the office. He intentionally waited till after I left, I surmise opening his email, so the weekend would add two more days of delay. It's been three and a half weeks since the appraisal meeting, far in excess of the ten-day time limit to appeal.

I read the points he makes and reply by email refuting each and every one with my justification and supporting evidence.

Regarding the Risk Limits Policy example, which he gave during the appraisal meeting, he says I admitted that I did not support the proposed change. I reiterate there is nothing wrong with what I did and that he, Katia, and I all agreed to refuse the change.

On the delegated authorities example, which he also gave during the appraisal meeting, he attaches an email from me raising issues about the change. He clarifies that he is not saying I did not implement the change, but that my attitude of highlighting issues about it evidences my reluctance to embrace change. I reiterate that it is my job to highlight issues and there is nothing wrong in what I did.

Regarding his criticism that I need to take greater account of the regulator's requirements, on which he could not recollect any examples off the top of his head during the appraisal meeting, he now gives two.

Firstly, regarding the Managed Income Portfolio on which the risk calculation methodology was changed in January, he says I told him I would tell the FSA about the change at our next meeting with it, in April. He says that without informing him, I changed my mind and decided not to tell the FSA at all, which is the wrong thing to do. He says the FSA should have been post-notified of this change. I reply that I did not change my decision behind his back, as he alleges, and that I made the correct notification. I attach an email evidencing that I kept him and Katia informed all along as to what I am going to do and that he was on board with my decision, as was Katia. I add that if he realised in April that I made an error, then why did he not shout it out in April, or May, or record it as an issue in my mid-year appraisal in June? I ask why he waited eight months till my year-end appraisal to say anything?

Secondly, regarding the Single Equities Portfolio on which the traders' mandate was expanded in April to allow the trading of more stocks and shares, he says I did not pre-notify the FSA about the change. He says the FSA should have been pre-notified and I am remiss because I post-notified. He says he only realised my error in September when the FSA, at our September meeting with it, told him it wants to be pre-notified about such changes in future. I reply that what the FSA said in September signifies a change in its preference. It used to want to be post-notified. Going forward, it wants to be pre-notified because that is the preference of the new officer it has assigned to regulate us. I attach an email evidencing that the FSA's requirement before September was post-notification. I attach another email from Katia confirming this. I explain that I did not commit a notification error, as he alleges. I assert that I notified the FSA in April in accordance with the rule applicable in April. Again, I add that if he realised in September that I had made an error, then why did he not shout it out in September, October, or November? Again, I ask why he waited three months till my year-end appraisal meeting to say anything?

I end my reply by appealing to his senses to be reasonable, to remove his criticism from my appraisal, and revise my score up.

~ Tuesday 10th January 2006, 9:00 a.m. ~

*I see no reason to remove the criticism and I believe it is important that I provide feedback to one of my subordinates to guide him to improve his behaviour appropriately*, Neil's email reply reads, which he sent me yesterday, again after I had left the office.

My effort to resolve the dispute informally with him directly is exhausted and has been in vain. I have no option now but to appeal formally. I refer to the bank's procedures and check to whom I should lodge a formal appeal. To my dismay, I discover it is my manager's manager. I recall Neil saying, *"you can appeal my decision, if you want"*. He and Simon must have this sewn up between them. Having cause for concern about Simon's independence, I doubt the fairness and effectiveness of an appeal to him. Regardless, I have to do something. I forward all of the email correspondence on the dispute to him for the record, while I consider how to surmount my concerns.

It's 5:00 p.m. The business day is drawing to a close. I'm about to leave for the day when I receive an email from Neil instructing me to attend a meeting in the morning at 9:00 a.m. in Syndicate Room 2 on the ground floor. How unusual, he hasn't said what the meeting is about. I rise off my seat and look down at him from over the tops of our computer screens.

'Neil,' I say to get his attention. 'What's this meeting tomorrow morning about?'

'Oh, that,' he says casually. 'I just want to brief you about something. It can wait till the morning'.

# 3

# ANNOUNCEMENTS

~ Wednesday 11th January 2006, 9:00 a.m. ~

Why is Veronica Cotton here, I wonder as I enter Syndicate Room 2 and see her sitting beside Neil?

'Thank you, Ranjit Singh, for coming to this meeting,' Neil starts reading aloud from a sheet of paper. 'With me is Veronica Cotton, the HR Business Partner to the Market Risk Department,' he continues. 'I'm reading from a script, of which I will let you have a copy after to keep'.

Oh! How formal and unusual! What's this about?

'You'll know that Eurocredito is on an efficiency drive and looking to make cost savings,' he continues. 'It has identified roles within the Market Risk Department that are unnecessary. The workload in the Market Risk Control team no longer requires two Controllers'.

Fear that I'm being made redundant stuns me. Don't panic, I tell myself recalling the bank's policy of letting us know our jobs are the subject of a redundancy as soon as it knows it. He's not going to tell me I'm redundant, he's going to tell me a redundancy process is about to kick off.

'The bank has decided to reduce the number of Controllers from two to one,' he goes on.

What! When did it decide that? What about letting us know our jobs are the subject of a redundancy as soon as it is known?

'I have carried out the redundancy process myself,' he continues. 'I have applied the bank's standard redundancy process and criteria, which is agreed with its in-house union'.

But, we're supposed to be able to have a say about all

of that. We weren't told there are redundancies going on in our department. We haven't been consulted. We haven't been given a chance to give our input. This is improper.

'I have assessed people for the remaining Controller role based on their skills, experience, and performance,' he continues. 'Unfortunately, you were not selected for the role and are now at risk of redundancy'.

Oh no! My heart sinks as, suddenly without any warning, my worst fear comes true.

'A two-week individual consultation period between you and the bank commences today,' he continues, 'in which you will have the chance to attend a one-to-one meeting to ask questions and discuss your situation. If nothing changes by the end of the two-week period, you will be issued your termination of employment notice. I will now hand over to Veronica'.

'Ranjit,' she says, 'what are your immediate thoughts?'

'Huh,' I mumble in a state of shock. 'Er, sh-shocked, I, er, I-I'm shocked,' I manage to say. 'I, er, I can't believe it. No warning was given, not even yesterday afternoon when I asked Neil what this meeting's about. No notice was given that redundancies are going on in our department. What about the bank's policy of letting us know as soon as it knows?'

'We understand this might be shocking and that you might need some time to take in what you've heard,' she says. 'You need to look after yourself. Go home and come back in tomorrow. We'll arrange a one-to-one meeting for tomorrow where we can go through all of your questions'.

'Okay,' I mumble sombrely.

'You can bring along a colleague or a representative from the bank's union,' she adds.

'I'm not a member of the bank's union,' I say.

'Well, you can bring a colleague,' she replies. 'Before you go, here's a Redundancy Information Pack,' she says handing me a wad of printed A4 papers stapled together in the top left hand corner. 'It contains a lot of useful information and answers to frequently asked questions'.

'I'm going to talk to the rest of the team now,' Neil says picking up the receiver of the phone resting on the circular-shaped table between us, and dialling out. 'Hi Katia,' he says into the mouthpiece. 'It's me, Neil. Can you grab Mary and Anthony and come down to Syndicate Room 2 on the ground floor right away please'. Hanging up and addressing me, he says, 'I'd appreciate if you didn't mention this to them or to anyone else. See you tomorrow, now'.

I leave the room feeling sombre and head up the stairs back to my desk. Katia and the two Associates pass me by on the stairs on their way down to see Neil. I compose myself and try to appear normal.

'Hey, Ranjit,' Katia says. 'I need to discuss a trade with you when I get back to my desk'.

'Okay,' I reply.

'See you in a bit,' she says continuing down the stairs.

I arrive at my desk, log off, grab my coat, and head out of the office into the cold winter air. Feeling downbeat, I stop off at my regular café situated just around the corner from the office to sit and console myself over a cup of tea. The warmth from the cup comforts me somewhat. As I reflect on what happened, my mobile phone rings. It's Anthony.

'Where are you?' he asks.

'In our café,' I reply.

'We're coming,' he says.

The three of them arrive within a few minutes.

'I'm really sorry to hear the news,' Katia says.

'Me too,' Mary and Anthony say simultaneously.

'Are you okay?' Katia asks.

'Well, I'm shocked and shaken, but I'm okay,' I reply. 'It was so sudden. No notice or warning at all'.

'Yeah, I had no idea there were redundancies going on

in Market Risk,' Katia says.

'We're shocked too,' Anthony says. 'We had no idea either, until just now when Neil told us we're all safe'.

'What did he tell you?' I ask them all.

'That they've decided to cut a Controller role and that everyone in the room is not at risk, that we're all safe,' Anthony replies. 'He read out a script to us titled Not At Risk'.

'He didn't say anything about you explicitly,' Katia explains. 'But, we deduced you're being let go because you weren't in the room'.

'Yeah,' Mary interjects. 'We're shocked that it's a Controller they decided to cut. Anthony and I told Neil to let the two of us go instead. It doesn't make any sense to let go of you, with all your knowledge and experience, and keep us'.

'But,' Anthony adds, 'he said it's all been decided'.

'Thank you both for offering to go in my place,' I say to Mary and Anthony. 'I'm really touched you did that. I might need to propose that to him formally, if it's okay with you'.

'Yes, I'm fine with that,' Mary replies.

'Me too,' Anthony says.

'Thank you,' I say. 'I believe he'll just dismiss it out of hand anyway. The decision seems to be set in stone'.

'We'd better get back before we're missed,' Katia says.

'Okay. Thanks for coming,' I say.

I remain in the café and continue reflecting on what happened. Some recent events strike me as being improper. I alone was asked to take up voluntary redundancy. My appraisal score was lowered suddenly and implausibly. I wasn't given the information I needed to draft up a formal appeal against the appraisal.

I become suspicious. I dwell on the fact that it is one person who did all of these things, Neil. I factor in that he said he carried out the redundancy process himself. My suspicion grows. I wonder whether the process is such that he could have fixed it to ensure I am the one who is selected for redundancy. I go a stage further and contemplate whether it is such that he could even have engineered a bogus redundancy situation with the exclusive surreptitious purpose of removing me.

# 4

# CONSULTATION

~ Thursday 12th January 2006, 2:00 p.m. ~

'Thanks for coming to this one-to-one meeting,' Neil says with Veronica sitting beside him. 'It's part of the two-week redundancy individual consultation period. Its purpose is to explain to you how you were selected for redundancy and to address any concerns and answer any questions that you might have. What are your immediate thoughts?'

'Neil,' I reply. 'I was completely shocked and taken aback yesterday by your announcement. Having recovered somewhat overnight, my thoughts are as follows. No warning was given at all. No notice was given that redundancies are going on in our department, contrary to the bank's policy of letting us know as soon as it knows. I had no chance to give any input into what the redundancy process and selection criteria should be. Clearly, the process is unfair and doesn't comply with the law. I believe it was predetermined right from the outset that I'd be the one who'd be selected for redundancy. I'm shocked to learn that you told Katia and the Associates that they're all safe and not at risk. That act seals and completes my fate. This two-week period is consultation in name only. With my fate already sealed, what is there to consult about?'

'About how you were selected,' he replies.

'I've been selected. It's happened. It's in the past. Consultation should be about things that are yet to happen,' I asserts.

'Well, you can still avoid redundancy by managing to

get redeployed elsewhere in the bank,' he says.

'I'd love it if I get redeployed. That'd be great,' I reply. 'But, the possibility of redeployment does not make this a consultation. Consultation is about being given the chance to give input on things, like what the redundancy process will be, who will be in the redundancy pool, and what criteria will be used to select people. Those kinds of things were all decided behind my back. The decision to make me redundant has, in all practical sense, been made. Furthermore, Katia and the Associates told me yesterday that you and Veronica announced to them that they're not at risk, that they're safe. All of these things happened before today, being the start of the so-called consultation period. So, how is this a genuine consultation period?'

'Perhaps the rest of the team made the assumption that they're safe,' he replies.

'Come on, Neil. You read out a Not At Risk script to them,' I rebut. 'There's no assumption about it'.

'You're not redundant yet,' Veronica interjects. 'We followed the bank's standard procedure. We consulted with the bank's union. It represents you and your interests. It fulfilled the part that you would have fulfilled yourself. So, you see, Ranjit, you were consulted, via the union'.

'Then, the standard procedure is unfair and unlawful,' I reply. 'Besides, I'm not a member of the union. I called the union yesterday to ask if someone would accompany me today to this meeting. They told me they only represent their members. They confirmed that I'm not a member and that they don't represent me. They said no, they won't accompany me to this meeting. They said they can't discuss anything further with me'.

'The bank recognises only its union for collective consultation,' she says. 'The whole redundancy process is agreed with it. It was your choice not to have joined it. How are we supposed to know who is or isn't a member?'

'I find it very hard to believe that a union that tells me

it only represents its members would agree a process on behalf of non-members too,' I reply. 'It'd be the easiest thing in the world for you to do to ask me if I'm a member. If you wanted me to know there's a redundancy going on, if you wanted to give me the chances I should have had, then you would have asked me. It's obvious to me that it was predetermined that I'd be the one selected for redundancy. No wonder,' I say addressing Neil, 'I'm the only one you asked to take up voluntary redundancy. Clearly, you wanted me out specifically'.

'That's not true,' he rebuts. 'The department needs to make cost savings. It was decided that one Controller role is surplus to needs. I assessed the people in the redundancy pool completely objectively against the selection criteria. The person with the lowest redundancy score was selected. That just happened to be you, unfortunately'.

'Who are the other people in the pool?' I ask him. 'What are their scores?'

'Er, well, we're not at liberty to disclose that information to you,' he replies. 'We need to respect people's confidentiality'.

'Okay, I understand that. Then, don't give me their names. Just tell me the number of people in the pool and the scores,' I follow through.

'We're not at liberty to disclose that information either,' he replies.

'When did you consult me and get my view as to what criteria will be used to select the person to be made redundant?' I ask.

'We consulted the union, which is the same as consulting you,' Veronica interjects.

'The total redundancy score is made up of two parts,' Neil moves on. 'The first part consists of eight competencies, seven of which I chose from a list of standard ones agreed with the union, and one which I created myself'.

'You made one up yourself?' I interject. 'So, you didn't actually apply the standard process, like you say you did'.

'The standard process allows me to make some up myself,' he rebuts. 'Each competency is scored a 2 if it is met fully, a 1 if met partially, or a 0 if not met. You scored full marks on six competencies and 1's on two of them. Hence, your score is 14/16 on the competencies part of the redundancy score. Are you with me so far?'

'Yes,' I reply. 'What about the second part?'

'The second part,' he goes on, 'is the year-end appraisal score. Yours is 4/8. Hence, when you add the two parts together, that's 14/16 plus 4/8, your total redundancy score comes to 18/24'.

He hands me a copy of my competencies scorecard. I notice he's signed it off as completed. I read his assessment comments against the two competencies that he didn't award me full marks for.

'Firstly,' I say, 'I see you scored me down on the competencies for the same reasons that you lowered my appraisal score, which I'm in the process of disputing. So, naturally, my dispute automatically extends and applies to these competencies scores too. Secondly, I see you make three additional criticisms on the competencies, which you never raised in the appraisal or anywhere else. They're false. I dispute them too'.

'This is my assessment of you,' he asserts. 'You have the opportunity in this consultation period to provide evidence against it and to try to change it'.

'The time limit for appealing the appraisal expired long ago, though,' Veronica interjects. 'You can only dispute the competencies scores now, not the appraisal score also'.

'I couldn't appeal the appraisal within the time limit because Neil intentionally denied me the opportunity,' I reply. 'He went off on annual leave without giving me what I needed to be able to draft up an appeal. He didn't return until after the time expired. Even upon his return, he didn't give me the information until a week later. But, he knows very well that I was disputing the appraisal right from the appraisal meeting itself. I refused to sign it off. I still haven't signed it off. It's not finalised'.

'If you want to appeal against your redundancy score,' Neil says, 'you can to do it to me during this consultation period. If I don't overturn my decision and you haven't managed to achieve redeployment elsewhere in the bank, then the bank will issue you a termination notice. Then you can raise a formal grievance to dispute the redundancy'.

'There's no way you're going to overturn your own decisions,' I reply. 'You're not independent. I've already appealed to you to re-assess my appraisal properly, but you haven't. You may as well tell me what's the procedure for lodging a formal grievance'.

'You have to raise a formal grievance in writing, stating the grounds of your grievance,' Veronica interjects. 'Simon Ong will hold a hearing meeting and will decide on the grievance'.

'But, Simon also isn't an independent person,' I reply. 'He's Neil's line manager. He must have been involved in the redundancy somehow'.

'That's the bank's procedure,' she asserts dogmatically.

'Wouldn't it be better for everyone if someone who's not been involved at all in my redundancy judges the grievance?' I ask.

'The bank's procedure is that Simon judges it,' she reiterates. 'You'll have the right to appeal against his decision, which will be heard by a panel of three judges. Their decision will be final. You'll have no right of appeal thereafter. The process will end there'.

'We've run out of time,' Neil interjects. 'I need to move to my next meeting'.

'But, we haven't covered everything yet,' I reply. 'This is important to me. Could you just stay and delay your other meeting please'.

'I wish I could,' he replies. 'But, unfortunately, I can't'.

'In that case, I need a continuation meeting,' I reply.

'Okay, but I'm rather busy,' he says. 'It'll have to be sometime next week. We'll let you know when'.

I view the delay into next week a brazen tactic to run down the clock. The thought vexes me that they regard the consultation merely a nuisance formality in which they intend to stand their ground by any possible means and get it over with.

~ Wednesday 18th January 2006, 2:00 p.m. ~

'Before we hand over to you in this continuation one-to-one consultation meeting,' Veronica says sitting beside Neil, 'I want to address the concern you expressed in our last meeting a week ago, that the redundancy process is unfair and doesn't comply with the law. I took the time to look into it. I also discussed it with my HR colleagues. I can confirm that the process is fair and lawful. We've followed the bank's standard procedure and the bank's union does indeed represent you in collective consultation'.

'I find that hard to believe when the union told me directly that it doesn't represent me,' I reply.

'Okay, I don't want to enter into an argument about this. Let's move on to the other things you want to discuss,' she says.

Addressing Neil, I say, 'I'm looking at the copy of my competencies scorecard that you gave me last time. I see you signed and dated it the 15th of December, which is the day before you conducted my year-end appraisal meeting'.

'Actually,' he interjects, 'I completed your appraisal on the 15th, at the same time as I completed the competencies scorecard. I held the appraisal meeting with you the next day only to communicate your result to you'.

'But, the appraisal is meant to be done together by the manager and the individual during the appraisal meeting, so that both sides can discuss the performance and reach an agreed assessment,' I reply.

'We needed to have it finalised by the 15th for our meeting with the union,' Veronica interjects.

'Firstly,' I reply, 'that's no excuse for not doing it the way it should be done. Secondly, the bank's standard procedure says that it will let me know my role is the subject of a redundancy as soon as it knows. If you knew by the 15th that I'm selected for redundancy, then you must have known before the 15th that my role is the subject of a redundancy. Why didn't you tell me before the 15th, or on the 15th at the very latest? Why did you wait until the 11th of January to tell me?'

'We knew before the 15th that there's a redundancy,' she replies. 'But, we couldn't tell you until the 15th because it's only then that we knew it's you specifically who's affected. We wanted to tell you on the 15th. But, the union told us to hold off and wait till the 9th of January'.

'Really? Why would the union tell you to breach the bank's policy of letting me know as soon as the bank knows?' I ask. 'Especially when you say the union and the bank agreed the redundancy policy together. What you're saying sounds odd'.

'Well, it did tell us to wait,' she asserts.

'I don't think it told you to wait,' I reply. 'I think you chose to wait until after the time limit to appeal the appraisal expired, so the appraisal becomes set in stone'.

'Not at all,' she asserts.

'It's little wonder,' I say to Neil, 'that, having finalised and presented my appraisal score to the union, you couldn't budge on your arbitrary assessment of me when I presented you with objective evidence to the contrary. You had already made the redundancy decision, signed it, sealed it, and gotten the union to approve it and move ahead with it. You needed the appraisal to remain static, set in stone the way you had presented it to the union. That's why you disappeared off on holiday straight away without giving me the information I needed to appeal it. You wanted to make sure I couldn't appeal it. And on your return, even though it was after the time to appeal had elapsed, you still delayed in giving me the information because you didn't want to take any risks. You intentionally planned things to deny me my right to appeal. This just reinforces my belief that my redundancy was predetermined before you even approached me in November with an offer of voluntary redundancy'.

'That's not true,' he replies.

'Ranjit,' Veronica interjects, 'do you have any evidence to change your scores?'

'Yes,' I answer. 'I've given it to Neil already and asked him to revise my appraisal. Surely, he told you?'

'No,' she replies. 'I'm not aware of anything like that'.

'Your appraisal meeting was on the 16th of December,' Neil says. 'You had ten days to challenge your appraisal formally. You didn't raise any formal appeal. End of!' he asserts.

'Neil,' I reply. 'Please be reasonable and revise my appraisal so that it's an objective assessment of my performance'.

'My assessment of you is objective and well founded,' he asserts.

'At the very least, Neil, please remove your comment saying that I need to take greater account of the regulator's requirements and embrace change more positively,' I request.

'No,' he says resolutely. 'I see no reason to remove it. As your line manager, I believe it's important for me to give you feedback to let you know the areas where you need to improve'.

'Veronica,' I say, 'what's the bank's policy on giving references to prospective employers'.

'The bank is very careful about supplying references because it doesn't want to say something that might make it liable,' she replies. 'So, only the HR department is allowed to give out references. It does so in a strictly controlled manner. The bank's policy is that we communicate the individual's latest appraisal score and the manager's comments'.

'You communicate the manager's comments to prospective employers?' I ask.

'Yes,' she replies.

'That's exactly what I read in the Redundancy Information Pack that you gave me,' I say. 'If a prospective employer asks the bank for a reference on me, the bank will tell it that I need to take greater account of the regulator's requirements and embrace change more positively, because that's part of the manager's comments on my latest appraisal, right?'

'Yes,' she answers.

'Which right-minded employer will hire me after receiving a reference saying that?' I ask them both. 'That is a career-ending reference. Is that what you want to do, to end my career,' I ask Neil, 'to make me unemployable, to destroy my livelihood?'

'Of course not,' he replies.

'Then, at the very least, remove that comment from my employment record,' I request again.

'No,' he says. 'The comment is justified. It stays'.

'I can't continue my career with that comment on my employment record,' I reply trying to make him see the grave significance of it. 'If you won't remove it, you'll leave me no option but to escalate the matter'.

'As we've told you already,' he replies, 'you have the right to appeal formally against the redundancy'.

'I'd rather resolve it here with you,' I reply. 'That would be best for everyone. I don't want to fight tooth and nail, which is the only option you'll leave me if you squeeze me into a corner with no other way out. Veronica,' I say, 'please advise him to be reasonable?'

'He's the line manager here,' she replies. 'It's his decision'.

'We've beaten the appraisal subject to death,' he says. 'We've run out of time again. I need to move to my next appointment. Are you finished with consultation now?'

'No, I have more things I need to discuss,' I reply.

'Fair enough,' he says. 'We'll arrange another meeting for tomorrow'.

'Please give serious thought overnight to what I said,' I impress upon Neil. 'I can't leave standing this unjust and fatal employment record that you're trying to foist on me'.

~ Thursday 19th January 2006, 2:00 p.m. ~

'I want to deal with the three criticisms you make about me under the competency called Conversion,' I say to Neil to start the third one-to-one consultation meeting. Veronica sits beside him. 'The first criticism is that I consider praise from my line manager patronising. Can you explain to me why the way I take praise from you is a competency?'

'It's relevant,' he says.

'But, can you explain why it's a competency?' I ask again.

'The criticism is valid,' he says. 'I have an email from you telling me to stop patronising you when I praised you once'.

'Yes, I know, I did say that,' I confirm. 'But, it's not a competency. It's unfair to reduce a competency score on the ground of something that isn't a competency'.

'I think it is a competency,' he asserts.

'Veronica,' I say, 'you're the HR expert here. Can you tell us the expert view please?'

'I've already told him it's not a competency and told him to remove it,' she replies. 'But, he wants to leave it in'.

'Neil, doesn't it bother you that you're going against the advice of the bank's HR expert?' I ask.

'I think it's relevant,' he replies firmly.

'Veronica,' I say, 'doesn't it bother you that he's going against your expert advice? The bank's assigned you here as it's HR expert and advisor to our department. The bank expects you to protect its interests'.

'He's the line manager here,' she replies. 'I can advise him, which I've done, but the decision is his to make'.

'That's a bit of a lame answer,' I reply. 'Shouldn't you escalate to someone that he's going against your expert advice?'

'As I said, it's his decision,' she replies. 'Let's move on'.

'Okay. Neil,' I say, 'the second criticism you make is that I rarely discuss issues with you and that if I had discussed more often, you could have helped me achieve my objectives. Which objectives did I fail to achieve?'

'You committed FSA notification errors on the Managed Income Portfolio and the Single Equities Portfolio,' he replies.

'Firstly,' I respond, 'I didn't commit any notification errors. Secondly, I discussed things with you in our weekly one-to-one meetings, in our weekly team meetings, and throughout the week, face-to-face and over emails. That amounts to discussing things with you regularly, not, rarely. You never told to me that I didn't discuss things with you enough'.

'You did commit the errors and they prove that you didn't discuss things with me enough,' he asserts.

'Let's move on,' I say, 'to the next criticism you make. You say that I had difficulty accepting the restructure at the end of 2003, where our team's reporting line was changed from Simon Ong to you. You say that I regularly raised the issue that the team should report directly into Simon. Can you explain how any of this is a competency?'

'They are competency matters,' he asserts.

'If my acceptance in 2003 was genuinely an issue, why wasn't it recorded as an issue in my 2003 year-end appraisal?' I ask.

'I don't know,' he replies. 'I wasn't your line manager

then. I didn't do your 2003 year-end appraisal'.

'The fact that my line manager at the time didn't record any issues means that there weren't any issues,' I reply. 'On becoming my line manager in October 2004, why didn't you record it as an issue in my appraisals? It's because it never was an issue. Veronica,' I say, 'is it correct that the appraisal meeting is meant to contain no surprises. That is, all issues should be raised during the year, as and when they arise, so they can be addressed and performance is managed proactively?'

'Yes,' she confirms. 'That's the bank's policy on performance and appraisals'.

'Neil, all the criticisms you make of me, in the appraisal and on the redundancy competencies, come as complete surprises to me,' I assert. 'You never mentioned any of them before. Clearly, none of them are genuine. One of them is about something that happened two years ago. It has no relevance to the current assessment period. I'm asking you once again, Neil. Please remove the criticisms from my employment record and re-perform the redundancy fairly'.

'The criticisms are genuine and legitimate. My assessment is objective. The redundancy is fair,' he asserts.

~ Monday 23rd January 2006, 2:00 p.m. ~

'Today is the last day of the so-called individual consultation period,' I say to Neil and Veronica, both of whom sit opposite me across a circular-shaped meeting table in what I believe will be my last meeting with them. 'You've consistently maintained your position that my selection for redundancy is completely fair and lawful, despite evidence to the contrary'.

'It is fair, Ranjit,' Veronica interjects rolling her eyes.

'Anyway,' I continue. 'I'd like to propose an alternative to avoid my redundancy, which I ask you to consider seriously'.

'Okay, let's hear your alternative suggestion,' Neil says.

'I propose that instead of making a Controller role redundant, you make either one or even both of the Associate roles redundant,' I say. 'This alternative is more beneficial to the bank because it retains the most experienced and knowledgeable members of the team. The team has operated successfully before for periods of six months at a time with just two Controllers. So, it's not as though it's a risky configuration. It's been tried and proven to work'.

'I'll reiterate what I've already told you,' Neil replies. 'To achieve efficiency and cost savings, the decision to cut a Controller position and transfer the less complex work to the two Associates has already been made. The reason we decided to cut a Controller role, rather than the Associate roles, is because the team's workload going forward requires one Controller and two Associates'.

'But, the workload carried out by the two Associates can be transferred to two Controllers instead,' I put to him. 'After the Head of Market Risk Control left in October 2004, Katia and I were the only two team members for the next six months, until the Associates were hired. The two of us managed completely successfully by ourselves'.

'I believe the way I've reconfigured the team represents the most efficient and cost effective use of resources,' he asserts. 'If you feel strongly about it, I suggest you raise it as part of any formal grievance you decide to lodge'.

'Fine,' I reply. 'That's what I'll have to do then'.

'Do you have anything else you want to discuss?' Veronica asks.

'No,' I answer.

'Then, I'm sorry to say the consultation period has ended without any change to your situation,' she declares. 'I'll instruct HR to issue your notice of termination. Your notice period is three months. It starts today. Your last day of employment will be the 18th of April'.

'On that note,' Neil interjects, 'I've decided you shouldn't come into the office anymore. I'm putting you on Gardening Leave for the whole of your notice period. You're to remain at home. Please surrender your security access pass to me now'.

# 5

# UNFAIRNESS

~ Monday 6th February 2006, 10:00 a.m. ~

'Welcome, Ranjit, to this grievance hearing,' Simon Ong says from behind his desk in his office. 'This meeting is convened to hear your grievance about your redundancy. As required under the statutory grievance procedure set out in the 2004 Dispute Resolution Regulations, this hearing is in response to the bank receiving your grievance concerns formally in writing. Also with us today is Janet Shipley of HR. Please state your grievance'.

'My grievance,' I start, 'is about the way I have been treated in the redundancy carried out in the Market Risk Department. I have been treated unfairly, particularly in that I was selected for redundancy before any consultation was carried out'.

'On Wednesday the 11th of January,' I continue, 'in a very brief meeting, Neil told me that I'm at risk of redundancy. He said a decision had been made to reduce the number of Market Risk Controllers from two to one and a selection exercise was performed, which resulted in me being selected for redundancy. As this was the first I ever heard of it, then clearly I was selected for redundancy before being told there is a redundancy situation affecting my role'.

'Neil says the bank's union represents me and that it was consulted with,' I continue. 'I'm not a member of the union. I contacted the union to check if it represents me. It told me quite clearly that it doesn't because I'm not a member. I don't know why Neil didn't simply ask me if I'm a member before getting on with the redundancy behind my back'.

'I also believe,' I continue, 'that it was predetermined right from the outset that I'd be the one selected for redundancy. Back on the 22$^{nd}$ of November, Neil approached me in isolation with an exclusive invitation to take up voluntary redundancy. He never approached anyone else with any similar offer'.

'Immediately after telling me that I'm at risk,' I continue, 'he told everyone else in the team that they're not at risk, that they're safe. If everyone else is safe, then my fate is complete and I'm not really at risk of redundancy, I'm at certainty of it'.

'The whole process was carried out unfairly and with particular detriment to me,' I continue. 'I was selected before being consulted. I wasn't given a chance to say what criteria should be used. My views weren't sought. I had no chance to give any input. All the critical decisions were made behind my back and without me knowing they were being made. The process doesn't comply with the bank's own policy, which says that no individual can be selected for redundancy without knowing a selection is going on, let alone comply with the law'.

'Please note that I didn't sign-off on my year-end appraisal,' I continue. 'I dispute the appraisal because my score is reduced completely arbitrarily. Despite the appraisal being incomplete and in a disputed state, it is used in the redundancy selection as though it is finalised and agreed'.

'During the two-week individual consultation period,' I continue, 'I provided Neil evidence which proves that my appraisal and competencies scores are unfair and arbitrary. I asked him to re-perform the redundancy process fairly. But, he simply rejected my case out of hand'.

'Also during the two-week period, I made credible alternative suggestions to avoid my redundancy,' I continue. 'I proposed that one or both of the Associate roles be cut instead of a Controller role. This alternative that I suggested is tried and tested. It's been proven to work successfully. Furthermore, it's better because it has the benefit of retaining the most experienced and knowledgeable members of the team. But again, Neil simply rejected my proposal out of hand'.

'Neil dismissed everything I said without any good explanation,' I assert. 'The consultation period is consultation in name only, in which Neil and Veronica essentially paid lip service to my concerns and to the issues'.

'Thank you for listening,' I say to end.

'Okay,' Simon says. 'Thank you for airing your concerns. What is it that you'd like to see happen?'

'I'd like to see the position reviewed and redressed so that I'm no longer the subject of unfair treatment and of an unlawful redundancy. Perhaps the redundancy can be re-performed fairly'.

~ Wednesday 15th February 2006 ~

Simon's apparent lack of engagement and questioning at the grievance hearing gives me the impression that he too regards my grievance merely as a nuisance formality in which he intends to go through the motions to give a surface appearance of independent consideration, but ultimately rubberstamp the decision already made. The bank's letter regarding its judgement of my grievance arrives, by second-class post. With no expectation of a decision in my favour, but with the keenest eagerness to know the reasons, I open the letter. It's dated 9th February and signed by Simon. He says the follows:

> *Collective Consultation:* The bank recognises its union, and only its union, for the purpose of collective consultation. The union represents all employees, whether they are its members or not.

The union was consulted ahead of the selection being performed. It represented you and your interests. It fulfilled the part that you would have fulfilled yourself directly. This is consistent with the bank's procedures.

*Individual Consultation:* Having been informed on 11th January that you are at risk of redundancy, there followed a two-week individual consultation period in which there were four meetings between yourself, Neil, and Veronica to address your concerns. This amounts to meaningful and effective consultation. There is no evidence to support your claim that Neil and Veronica were merely paying lip service, as you put it, to your concerns.

*Predetermined Selection:* Neil approached you exclusively because of a previous discussion you had with him asking him if he could arrange voluntary redundancy for you to leave the bank. At the time there was no such opportunity. When one arrived, he thought it sensible to present the opportunity to you. No one else had ever expressed any interest in voluntary redundancy. Nevertheless, no decision had been made at that point. His approach had no bearing on you being selected for redundancy. I'm aware you were disputing a negative manager's comment on your appraisal. However, you raised no formal challenge. Neil is confident his assessment is valid. Even if his comment is removed, your score will remain the same. Hence, there would be no difference to the selection process and you would still be selected for redundancy.

*Alternatives to Redundancy:* I believe Neil has reasonable business reasons for the team reconfiguration he proposed and implemented. Your alternative proposal of two Controllers with one or no Associates is an inadequate configuration in comparison. Regarding your claim that your proposal would retain the most senior experience and knowledge, I am comfortable that Neil has taken into account what is required to support the bank.

*Grievance Outcome:* I find no evidence to support your claim that you were treated unfairly. Consequently, I dismiss your grievance. You have the right to appeal my decision within ten days of the date of this letter.

~ Monday 20th March 2006, 9:00 a.m. ~

'Ranjit, welcome to this appeal hearing,' says Jackie Monroe, the bank's Head of Employment Cost Management, sitting on a panel with two other judges. 'We are convened to hear your appeal about your redundancy. I will be chairing today's hearing. Assisting me on the panel is Jennifer White, the bank's Director of Complaints Management, and Charles Burns, the bank's Director of Cost Management. Also present is Neil Hobson, your line manager, and Kylie Hales, the bank's Appeals Co-ordinator. Please state the grounds of your appeal'.

'I appeal against Simon Ong's dismissal of my grievance concerning my redundancy,' I say to start. 'He dismissed my grievance saying that there is no evidence supporting my claim that I have been unfairly treated in being selected for redundancy. My concerns are as follows: I'm selected for redundancy without knowing the bank's union represented me in collective consultation; I'm selected before being consulted; and I'm told I'm at risk of redundancy while the others in the redundancy pool are told they're not at risk, the reality of which is that I'm at certainty of redundancy, not at risk of it. Thank you for listening'.

'Thank you for airing your concerns,' Jackie says. 'I want to begin by asking you what you understand you were at risk of?'

Handing the panel a copy of the At Risk script that Neil read out and gave me in January, I answer, 'the At Risk script refers to a Controller role being at risk of redundancy. However, the decision to cut a Controller role had already been made by the time of the announcement. Hence, the role was not at risk of being cut, it had already been cut'.

'What it actually means,' she says, 'is that the role will cease to exist. It does not mean that your employment will be terminated necessarily. You could still be redeployed elsewhere in the bank. So, your termination is not certain. Hence, you are at risk. I do, however, understand that you have a highly specialised skillset and I do appreciate that your redeployment would be rather difficult'.

'That, in all practical sense, means that my termination is a certainty,' I reply. 'Even more so because the others are all told that they're safe'.

'Hmm,' she muses.

'I would also like to highlight,' I continue, 'that I was selected for redundancy even before the union was consulted. Neil confirmed, during the so-called individual consultation period, that he finalised the redundancy selection exercise in time for the meeting with the union on the 15th of December'.

'Only when the names of the individuals who will be affected by redundancies in an area are known are those individuals told of the redundancy,' she says.

'Well, it was known on the 15th of December that I am affected, but I wasn't told then. I was told in January,' I reply.

'Although it was known then,' Neil interjects, 'when we consulted the union, it told us to wait until the 9th of January to make the announcement'.

'Ranjit, how do you think the process should have gone?' Charles asks.

'The bank's policies say that changes will be discussed with employees and their views will be sought and taken into account,' I reply. 'They state that no employee will be selected for redundancy without the employee knowing there's a redundancy process going on. That's how the process should have gone,' I answer. 'We should all have been told there's a redundancy situation affecting the Market Risk Department. The change should have been discussed with us. Our views and feedback should have been sought'.

'But, if we did that,' Neil interjects, 'then many people would be unsettled and panicked, rather than just the redundant one. So, we didn't tell anyone until we knew who is selected for redundancy. This way, we only unsettled one person'.

Addressing Neil, Jackie asks, 'who was in the redundancy selection pool?'

'Just the two Controllers, Ranjit and Katia Mykonola,' he answers.

That's what I thought, but didn't know it as a fact. I recall that previously, when I asked him for this information during a one-to-one consultation meeting, he declined to disclose it to me on the basis that he needs to respect people's confidentiality. This is the first time I know as a matter of fact who is in the redundancy pool alongside me.

'How was Ranjit selected?' she asks him.

'The standard criteria were used, eight competencies and a performance appraisal,' he answers.

'Who was involved in the selection process?' she asks.

'Just me,' he answers.

'Did Ranjit challenge the process?' she asks.

'He wasn't happy with the appraisal score that I'd given him. But, he didn't appeal it formally,' he answers. 'But, even if he had, and even if his appraisal score is increased to the same as Katia's, it doesn't make any difference to the selection exercise. He'd still be the one chosen for redundancy because he has lower scores on the competencies. You see, on the appraisal, his score is 4/8 and Katia's is 6/8. On the competencies, his is 14/16 and hers is 16/16'.

What! Did I just hear correctly? My mind goes into a state of bewilderment knowing that he scored me down on the competencies based on criticisms that apply equally to Katia, but he awarded her full marks. I struggle to remain connected mentally to the proceedings around me as I try to get a grip on the implications of what he just revealed.

'What outcome would you like to see form this hearing?' Jackie asks me.

'Huh, er,' I mumble. 'Sorry, what did you say?' I ask trying hard to come out of deep thought and bring my awareness to the hearing.

'What outcome would you like to see form this hearing?' she repeats.

'Er, hmm, I'd like to see the situation reviewed and, er, redressed so that I'm no longer the subject of, er, hmm, unfair treatment and, er, of an unlawful redundancy process,' I answer with half my mind still on the implications of what Neil revealed. He didn't score her down at all. He didn't treat us the same. He treated me less favourably. Why? 'Er, for example, the process could be re-performed fairly'.

'Re-perform the redundancy?' Jennifer asks. 'But, the others have been told they're safe'.

'Er, yes,' I reply. 'Even though the At Risk and Not At Risk announcements were made simultaneously, everyone tells me that the two-week period that followed is consultation. If it genuinely is consultation, then there should be no issue in going back and telling the others that they're no longer safe'.

'Hmm,' she contemplates.

'Ranjit, is there anything further you'd like to take this

opportunity to say?' Jackie resumes.

'Yes,' I reply. 'From what I've heard here, it's clear that I'm selected for redundancy without knowing the bank's union represented me in collective consultation. It's also clear that I'm selected before being consulted. The union tells me it doesn't represent me and it won't talk to me. I'm told I'm at risk while the others are told they're safe. For all these reason, the process is unfair and unlawful'.

'Okay,' she says. 'We'll let you have our decision as soon as we can'.

'Please could you make sure it's soon,' I add. 'The bank's procedures say that you should have held this hearing within two weeks from when I lodged my appeal. But, it's taken you five weeks to hold it. The situation the bank's put me in is very stressful. I am doing my best to contain my anxiety and to achieve a resolution amicably through constructive dialogue with the bank. The purpose of the grievance procedures and the time limits stipulated in them is to help keep stress levels low as possible. When the bank exceeds the time limits and stays silent, it keeps me in the dark and increases my anxiety. When I chase it to get a move on, I get the impression it is disinterested in resolving the issues and is dragging its feet on purpose. Simon's decision letter being sent by second-class post exemplifies its contempt for this matter. I also see the slower mail delivery service as another attempt by the bank to deny me my opportunity to appeal, by running down the appealing time'.

'I understand your point,' Jackie replies. 'I'm sorry to hear there have been delays. But, I'm sure there must be good reasons and that any delay is unintended'.

~ Saturday 25th March 2006 ~

Since the appeal hearing meeting last Monday, the same concern awakes me each morning that keeps me from falling asleep at night. Why didn't Neil treat Katia and me equally? Why did he treat me less favourably than her? I keep ruminating on the difference of treatment. I would understand it if there is some plausible explanation for it. But, neither he nor anyone else has given one yet.

The appeal panel's obvious obsession with the bank's standard procedures, and its absolute conviction that they are applied to my redundancy, inform me that its mind is made up and is closed even to compelling arguments to the contrary. The bank's letter with its decision about my appeal arrives. With no confidence of the decision being in my favour, I open the letter. It's dated 22nd March and signed by Jackie. She says the follows:

> *Regarding your concern that you were selected for redundancy without knowing the bank's union represented you in collective consultation:* The bank has agreed a collective consultation procedure with its union. The union is your elected representative. It has the right to challenge and influence redundancy proposals and acts in your interests. The bank followed the agreed procedure in your redundancy.
>
> *Regarding your concern that you were selected before you were consulted:* This is not the case. The bank consults with individuals as soon as there is the possibility that their roles will be put at risk. It consults with individuals as soon as they are considered to be at risk of redundancy. It is possible that while an individual is at risk, he or she is redeployed in another job at the bank and the notice of termination is prevented. In your case, the two-week consultation period gave you the opportunity to challenge the restructure proposed by Neil.
>
> *Regarding the fact that you were told you are at risk while the others were told they are not at risk:* Individuals whose jobs are not likely to be put at risk are told

at the same time as those whose are.

*Appeal Outcome:* The panel agrees that the redundancy process applied to your position is in line with the agreed procedures and is applied fairly. Consequently, the panel dismisses your appeal. The panel's decision is final. The appeal process has ended. The bank considers the matter closed.

The bank's manner of handling the issues lets me down utterly and causes me much distress. It said I should firstly try to resolve the issues informally with my line manager. When I did that, he was disinterested and wholly unreasonable. It said next, I should give it formally the opportunity to resolve the issues. I did so in good faith and in the belief that cooperation will benefit all parties and lead to an amicable resolution. But, it played me. After dragging its feet for an excessively long time, finally, it denies me justice and slams the door shut in my face, leaving me out in the cold to live with the adverse consequences of its actions upon my life.

To my great distress, my false poor employment record concerns me gravely, and rightly so. Already, it's featured in a redundancy process and rendered me jobless, all of a sudden. But, its potential to harm me is not spent by the dismissal. It does not end here. My future prospects are jeopardised seriously by the bank's policy of communicating the manager's comments in references to prospective employers. It threatens to end my career. The thought pains me deeply that Neil's unjust and arbitrary comments, which took him only moments to make and which he will soon forget, can inflict on me a permanent, life changing effect and lay to waste my life's precious years and hard work at building a career. I have no choice. I'm compelled to try to do whatever I can to set the record right, even if I fail, lest I wish to live afflicted by regret.

# 6

# BONUS

~ Thursday 6th April 2006, 2:00 p.m. ~

'Welcome, Ranjit,' says Colin Marr, the bank's Head of Trading Credit, sitting opposite me at a circular-shaped table in a meeting room in the bank's headquarters. 'This hearing is convened to hear your grievance about your 2005 bonus award. I will be chairing today's hearing. Also present is Neil Hobson, your line manager, and Veronica Cotton of HR. Please state your grievance'.

'My grievance,' I begin, 'is that my 2005 bonus award, which the bank notified me of on the 9th of February, is significantly lower than the amount that I was awarded the year before. Having discussed the matter informally with Neil,' I continue, 'I understand that the reduction is due to my 2005 year-end appraisal score being lower than the previous year's. I believe I am treated unfairly and unreasonably in the allocation of my 2005 bonus award'.

'My grievance is not just about the amount of the bonus,' I continue. 'It's also about the slow, biased, and improper manner in which the bonus issue has been dealt with so far. As soon as the award was announced, I began trying to achieve a resolution informally with Neil directly. But, he appeared to be disinterested in my concerns. I had to chase him again and again to get him to respond. Thus, it took almost a month to get to a position where I could conclude that I'm getting nowhere with him and that I must escalate the matter by way of a formal grievance, which I then did on the 9th of March. This hearing should have happened within two weeks from that date. But, the bank has taken four weeks to hold it. Initially, the bank most ridiculously assigned Neil to hear the grievance despite he quite obviously not being an independent person in the matter, and he accepted to hear it. Given that he appraised me and dismissed my informal attempts to resolve this issue, obviously there's no chance that he is going to decide against himself'.

'Over the four and a half years that I worked at this bank,' I continue, 'my actual performance was consistently high. My responsibilities increased year-on-year. No matter how the bank performed in terms of profitability, my bonus award always increased year-on-year. The fact that I was given a lower appraisal score for 2005 is highly odd in itself. It's a matter for which I have not received any plausible explanation. I dispute the appraisal. I did not agree it. I did not sign it off'.

'I appreciate that the bonus is discretionary,' I say, 'but, the bank is under an obligation to exercise its discretion in a way that is non-detrimental to me and to take all relevant factors into account. In 2005, the year of work for which the bonus is awarded, my responsibilities were the highest they ever were. I had additional trading businesses to control and I also had a junior team member to manage. Alongside that, the bank had a bumper profit year. Despite all of this, my bonus is twenty per cent lower than the previous year's. It should have risen, but it decreased. The bank exercised its discretion in an arbitrary and unfair manner'.

'Never before in my entire twelve-year career in investment banking did my bonus fall compared to the previous year,' I continue. 'I can't help but link the way I am treated in the bonus with the unfair way that I have been treated in my redundancy'.

'Thank you for listening,' I say to end.

'Okay, thanks for airing your concerns,' Colin says. 'What is it that you would like to happen?'

'I'd like my bonus award reviewed and redressed such that I'm not the subject of unfair and unreasonable treatment,' I reply. 'In the interest of resolving the issue amicably and pre-empting the need for escalation, I urge you to investigate this matter properly and objectively'.

~ Wednesday 17th May 2006 ~

The bank's handling of the bonus issue is snail-paced, despite it promising officially in its policies to deal with disputes and decide their outcomes in a reasonable time frame. It should have gotten back to me with a decision within five days of the grievance hearing, according to its procedures. But, only today, six weeks on, has its letter arrived. Its official outward rhetoric seems to have no inward effect of committing itself to the standards it speaks of. It instils no confidence in me that it has dealt with my grievance properly. With no expectation of a decision in my favour, and every expectation that I will have to appeal, I open the letter. It's dated 12th May and signed by Colin. He says the follows:

> *Investigation:* I performed a detailed analysis on a no-names basis of the bonus awards in the Market Risk Department for the years 2004 and 2005. I then reviewed the results to see if there are any significant inconsistencies apparent. There were two. I sought clarifications on them from Simon Ong, the person who made the bonus allocations. I am satisfied with the explanations he gave.
> 
> *Grievance outcome:* I conclude that the bonus allocations are fair and equitable. I do not believe you are treated unfairly in the allocation of your bonus award. Therefore, I dismiss your grievance. You have the right to appeal my decision within ten days of the date of this letter.

Colin's trivial and shallow investigation, which could

hardly have taken him thirty minutes to perform but took the bank six weeks to inform me the results of, insults my intelligence.

~ Monday 3rd July 2006, 11:00 a.m. ~

Having lodged an appeal on 17th May against Colin's decision, the bank should have held a hearing within two weeks. But, it's holding it today, five weeks later than its own deadline. It could not declare more boldly its disinterest in resolving the issues and its intention to mock me into submission by dragging its feet for exceedingly long periods before eventually dismissing the issues out of hand. It is little wonder then why, on my arrival at the bank at 9:45 a.m. for the 10 a.m. scheduled meeting, the receptionist informs me the hearing is postponed to 11:00 a.m.

'Welcome to this meeting, Ranjit,' says Adam Sirinathan, the bank's Chief Credit Officer, from behind his desk in his private office situated a few rooms along from Simon Ong's. 'We are convened to hear your appeal about your 2005 bonus award. Also present is Janet Shipley of HR. Please state the grounds of your appeal'.

'The ground of my appeal,' I start, 'is that so far, the bank has not investigated my claim regarding my 2005 bonus award properly and thoroughly. Colin Marr's investigation is, at best, trivial and shallow. It doesn't seem that he took important factors into account. He doesn't seem to have even verified the explanations that Simon Ong gave him. He seems to have simply accepted them at face value'.

'I did not sign off on my 2005 year-end appraisal, which is one of the inputs to the bonus allocation process. How was the fact that I was disputing the appraisal taken into account in Colin's analysis?' I put to him.

'In 2005, I had greater responsibilities than before,' I

continue. 'I had additional trading businesses to control and also a junior team member to manage. Alongside that, the bank had a bumper profit year. How were these matters factored into the investigation?' I ask. 'If anything, my bonus should be higher than the previous year's, not lower'.

'I told the bank that I can't help but link the way I'm treated in the bonus award with the unfair way that I was treated in my redundancy,' I continue. 'Where is the bank's investigation into this claim?' I ask.

'I believe the bank exercised its discretion in an arbitrary and unfair way in awarding me a bonus,' I continue. 'I would like the bonus reviewed and redressed such that I'm not the subject of unfair and unreasonable treatment'.

'My grievance is also about the unreasonable way the bank has dealt with my claim so far,' I add. 'It's failed to do a thorough and proper investigation. It took ten weeks to deal with the first stage of this grievance when its policies state it will complete it in four. Today's hearing meeting should have happened within two weeks from when I lodged my appeal. But, it's taken seven weeks to occur. On top of that, when I arrived here today for the scheduled time, I was told the meeting is postponed by an hour'.

'Thank you for listening,' I say to end.

'Yes, I apologise about the hour's delay today,' he says, 'but, something came up last minute'.

'Fine, apology accepted,' I say. 'It's in the past. Looking forward, in the interest of resolving the issue amicably and pre-empting the need for escalation, I urge you to investigate this matter properly and within a reasonable timeframe'.

'Okay,' he says. 'I understand your concerns. I'll look into them and get back to you as soon as possible'.

## ~ Wednesday 19th July 2006 ~

The bank's letter on its decision about my appeal arrives. In the belief that it is intentionally abusing its privileged decision-making position to ridicule me, I open the letter. It's dated 13th July and signed by Adam. He says the follows:

> *Appraisal:* Whilst you dispute your 2005 appraisal, the appraisal is only one of the factors amongst many others that the bonus award depends on.
>
> *Determining Factors:* In addition to the appraisal, the following factors are also taken into account in determining the size of the bonus award: the bank's overall profitability for the year; the size of the bonus pot allocated to the department; the individual's performance relative to others' in the department; and the individual's market value, being the amount necessary to retain the individual in his role.
>
> *Increased Responsibilities:* Only the factors listed above are taken into account in determining the bonus award. Your increased responsibilities are irrelevant because your salary level accounts for them.
>
> *Peer Group:* We are not able to disclose details of your peers for confidentiality reasons. But, I have looked at them and conclude that you are treated fairly.
>
> *Appeal Outcome:* Having analysed the data and interviewed Simon Ong, I find that you are treated fairly in your bonus award. Therefore, I dismiss your appeal. This decision is final. The appeal process has come to an end. The bank considers the matter closed.

# 7

# DIFFERENCE OF TREATMENT

~ Tuesday 4th July 2006, 10:00 a.m. ~

'Welcome, Ranjit,' says Nathan Wilcox, the bank's Head of Fraud, sitting opposite me at a circular-shaped table in a meeting room in the bank's headquarters. 'This meeting is convened to hear your grievance about the difference of treatment that you allege to have occurred during your redundancy. I will be chairing today's grievance hearing. Also present is Janet Shipley of HR. Please state your grievance'.

'My grievance is about the way I've been treated during the redundancy exercise carried out in the Market Risk Control team in the Market Risk Department,' I start. 'I believe I am the subject of difference of treatment by being treated unfairly and less favourably than Katia Mykonola, whose circumstances were virtually the same as mine and who was the only other person in the redundancy pool'.

'Firstly,' I continue, 'back on the 22nd of November last year, Neil approached me exclusively with an invitation to take up voluntary redundancy. He never made any such similar offer to Katia. This is a difference of treatment that has not been explained plausibly'.

'Secondly,' I continue. 'The criteria used to distinguish between Katia and me in the redundancy selection exercise were the competencies and the appraisal scores. During the selection exercise, Neil made a number of criticisms about me on the basis of which he reduced my scores. All of the criticisms apply equally to Katia'.

'Now, firstly, he gave her full marks on her

competencies scorecard, that's 16/16,' I continue. 'I'm not privy to the details of her scorecard. I only know that she got full marks. But, it's logical to deduce that while he scored me down based on a number of criticisms that apply equally to her also, he didn't similarly criticise her and score her down. It's like he looked for reasons to mark me down, overlooked the fact that those reasons apply to her also, and didn't even look around for other reasons that might apply to her'.

'Secondly,' I continue, 'he must have done the same on our appraisals. There, he reduced my score down to 4/8 based on a number of criticisms that apply equally to her. He gave her a score of 6/8. Again, I'm not privy to the details of her appraisal. But, it's logical to deduce that while he scored me down based on criticisms that apply to her also, he didn't similarly criticise her and score her down'.

'I will give you examples of the criticisms he made about me and show you how they apply to her also,' I continue.

'Regarding his criticism that I don't embrace change positively,' I continue, 'he says that I didn't support a change to the Risk Limits Policy on the basis that the policy already represents good practice. I have emails showing that Katia and I discussed the proposed change with him and that all three of us, that's him included, agreed not to support the change for the said reason. All three of us didn't support the proposed change,' I reiterate. 'Yet, he scored me down for not embracing change positively and doesn't seem to have scored Katia down similarly'.

'Also on the same criticism,' I continue, 'he says that I raised concerns and issues about the change to the line of delegated authorities that Simon Ong instructed us to implement last September. I have emails showing that Katia also raised issues to Neil and to Simon regarding this change. Yet again, I'm scored down while she seems not to be'.

'Staying with the embracing change criticism,' I go on, 'he says that I had difficulty accepting the restructure at the end of 2003 where our team's reporting line was changed from Simon Ong to him. He says I regularly raised the issue that our team's reporting line into him is inconsistent from the line of delegated authority, which excludes him and is directly into Simon Ong. Again, I have emails showing that Katia and I both flagged up such issues. Yet again, I'm scored down while she doesn't seem to be'.

'Moving on to his criticism that I do not take the regulator's requirements seriously,' I continue. 'He says I told him that I would tell the FSA in April that the methodology for calculating the risk on the Managed Income Portfolio was changed in January. He says that without informing him, I changed my mind and decided not to tell the FSA at all, which he says was the wrong thing to do because the FSA should be post-notified about it. I have emails showing that I kept him and Katia informed all along as to what I'm going to do and that they were both on board with it. Yet, I'm scored down while Katia doesn't appear to be. I did not change the decision behind his back, as he alleges, and no notification error was committed. If he genuinely believes I failed to post-notify the FSA, then why hasn't he ever taken it upon himself to tell the FSA and put the error right? The reason he's never done that is because he knows there's no error to rectify,' I assert.

'Also on the same criticism,' I continue, 'he says that in April I expanded the traders' mandate on the Single Equities Portfolio to allow them to trade more stocks and shares, and that I did not pre-notify the FSA about the change. He says the FSA should have been pre-notified and I am remiss because I only post-notified it. He says he only realised my error in September when the FSA told him it wants to be pre-notified about such changes in the future. I have an email from Katia agreeing with me and confirming my decision to post-notify. But, yet again, I'm scored down while she doesn't seem to be'.

'He also criticised that I find praise from my line manger patronising,' I continue, 'because once, when he said well done to me, I told him not to patronise me. I have witnessed Katia on a few occasions make it clear to him that she finds him patronising. Yet again, I'm scored down while she doesn't appear to be. On one occasion, she came over to me looking very frustrated and annoyed. She showed me an email he had sent her. It was telling her to do something that is trivial and obvious that she'd do anyway. He had copied in a number of other people in the department. She told me she finds his email very patronising and asked what I think. I thought she was within reason to find it patronising. She asked me if I'd accompany her while she confronts him. I agreed. She approached him and took him into a private meeting room. There, she told him off angrily. She scolded him. She asked him why is he patronising her by telling her to do something quite obvious, and by email on which he's copied in numerous third parties? She asked him is it to give others the impression that she doesn't know what to do? She asked him can he not manage her without having to rely on the weight and support of third parties?'

'He also criticised that I rarely discuss issues with my line manager,' I continue. 'The fact is that I discussed things with him often, in our weekly one-to-one meetings, in our weekly team meetings, and throughout the week. I discussed things with him directly face-to-face and over emails. All of this amounts to discussing things with him regularly, not, rarely. Katia discussed things with him in the same manner. We behaved the same way. Yet again, I'm scored down while she doesn't seem to be'.

'These differences of treatment that I've brought to your attention haven't been explained plausibly,' I assert. 'I believe the difference is based on race. I believe it's a matter of race discrimination,' I claim. 'I believe the lax manner in which the bank handled my grievance about my 2005 bonus award is also motivated by race'.

'Thank you for listening,' I say to end. 'For your convenience, I've brought along with me printouts of the emails I referred to. They evidence and prove my case,' I say proffering Nathan a folder containing the printouts.

'Er, thanks, but that won't be necessary,' he says declining to take it.

'But, they'll be useful to you to verify what I'm saying,' I reply trying to persuade him.

'That's quite okay. If I need them, I'll request them,' he says.

'Okay,' I reply wondering why he would decline to take them. 'The only claim I can't support with email evidence,' I say, 'is that Katia also found Neil patronising. But, you can interview her directly about that, she still works for him'.

'Okay. Thanks for letting me know,' he replies. 'I want to ask you some things. Have you ever experienced any hint of race discrimination at the bank prior to your redundancy?'

'No, not before the redundancy,' I answer.

'Would you have any evidence of any race discrimination prior to your redundancy?' he asks.

'No,' I answer. 'I just said I never experienced any before my redundancy'.

'Would anybody else have any evidence?' he asks.

'I don't believe so,' I answer. 'As I said, I don't believe I experienced any race discrimination before my redundancy'.

'Why didn't you raise the issue of race discrimination earlier? Why didn't you raise it in your redundancy consultation or in your grievance about the redundancy?' he puts to me.

'Because I didn't know it then,' I answer. 'I didn't have enough information then to know that I'm the subject of race discrimination. I was told very little. I was kept in the dark. When I asked Neil and Veronica during the consultation period who else is in the redundancy pool and what their scores are, they told me they couldn't disclose that information because of confidentiality reasons. I was kept in the dark and told only what the bank decided it wanted to tell me. It was not until the 20th of March, during the redundancy appeal hearing, that I became aware of the facts that evidence the race issue. It was there that Neil disclosed that Katia is the only other person in the redundancy pool and revealed what her scores are. It was only at that moment that I became aware of evidence pointing to race discrimination. Only from that time onward was I in a position to be able to determine rationally that there is a race issue at play, and I raised a grievance about it within a reasonable time'.

'What was the relationship between you and Neil like?' he asks.

'It was professional,' I answer. 'It was challenging at times in a professional sense because of the nature of the work we did. There are often matters on which it's possible to have professional differences of opinions. But, there weren't any personal issues. The relationship was just like the ones I had with other members of staff'.

'Okay. Thanks for airing your concerns,' he says. 'I'll investigate and let you have my decision'.

~ Monday 24th July 2006 ~

Every day since the grievance hearing has been a day of pessimism. Nathan's outright refusal to look at the emails I had brought him instils no confidence in me that the bank is dealing with my grievance properly. To the contrary, it gives me the impression that it's conducting the investigation with one eye on the outcome it desires, consciously steering the investigation down the path that allows it to dismiss the issue, recognising the evidence that supports its decision and turning a blind eye to opposing proof.

The bank's letter on its decision arrives. With no expectation of a decision in my favour, and every expectation of an improper and biased investigation, I open the letter. It's dated 18th July and signed by Nathan. He says the follows:

> After meeting you, I interviewed Neil. Both of you describe your relationship as professional. Neil explained his rationale for why he scored you and Katia differently.
>
> *Voluntary Redundancy:* Neil explained that you were approached exclusively because only you had previously requested voluntary redundancy.
>
> *Risk Limits Policy change:* Neil confirmed that Katia also questioned the change. But, he says that she was more pragmatic in accepting it while you were reluctant.
>
> *Delegated Authority change:* Neil says that while both you and Katia were not supportive of the change, once the change was implemented, Katia accepted it and got on with the job while you continued to be critical.
>
> *2003 Reporting Line change:* Neil is not aware of any issues from Katia, only from you.
>
> *Managed Income Portfolio:* Neil agrees that no notification was required. But, he believed you would tell the FSA about it informally. It was not till much later that he learned that you had not told the FSA. As the change did not need to be formally notified to the FSA, he never subsequently took it upon himself to tell it. He did not score you down for not notifying the FSA, but for not standing by the agreement you had with him to tell the FSA about it informally.
>
> *Rarely Discusses Issues:* It is my conclusion that

there was a level of information and communication missing from you to Neil, like not letting him know that you would not inform the FSA about the change regarding the Managed Income Portfolio. There, he believed you would tell the FSA. But, it was not till much later that he learned from the FSA itself that you had not told it.

*Grievance Outcome:* Based on what I heard from both of you, I do not find that you are treated unfavourably on the basis of race. The redundancy process is fair and was applied fairly. Hence, I dismiss your grievance. You may appeal against my decision within ten days of the date of this letter.

The investigation Nathan purports to have conducted mocks me. He's simply taken Neil's word over mine without even trying to verify independently what either of us said. A bank's Head of Fraud, of all people, surely knows better than this. How brazen he is to purport to have done such a shallow and biased investigation.

~ Thursday 10th August 2006, 12:30 p.m. ~

'Welcome to this meeting, Ranjit,' says Adrian Brent, the bank's Head of Compliance, from behind his desk in his private office situated a few rooms along from Simon Ong's. 'The purpose of this meeting is to hear your appeal against Nathan Wilcox's decision about the alleged difference of treatment during your redundancy. Also present is Amanda Thompson of HR. Please state the grounds of your appeal'.

'My appeal is on the ground that the difference of treatment that Katia Mykonola and I received has not been explained plausibly,' I start, 'and that the only logical explanation is that it is due to race discrimination. The main issues are as follows: I am treated less favourably than Katia; the less favourable treatment includes my selection for redundancy, where I lost my job while she kept hers; the bank has so far failed to investigate the difference of treatment properly and has failed to give any plausible explanation for it; and in the absence of any plausible explanation, the reason for the difference can only be discrimination on the ground of race'.

'Nathan Wilcox did not investigate my claims properly and thoroughly,' I continue. 'He seems to have simply taken Neil Hobson's word over mine. Neil is not likely to just own up to his wrongdoings when asked about them. Nathan seems to have made no attempt to verify what each of us said. I even brought him evidence to verify it with, but he declined to look at it'.

'In fact, on some matters, Neil told Nathan a different version of events to what he had said originally. He changed his story,' I continue. 'Nathan would know this if he had bothered to investigate what Neil told him. He would know if he bothered to look at the evidence that I had brought him. As well as changing his story, Neil made several misrepresentations, which Nathan would also know if he bothered to look at the evidence that I had brought him'.

'Regarding voluntary redundancy,' I continue. 'Neil made the misrepresentation that I had requested voluntary redundancy. This is completely false. I have explained many times on record the context in which I raised the matter of voluntary redundancy. I refer you to that explanation'.

'On the Risk Limits Policy change,' I continue, 'Neil made the misrepresentation that Katia was more pragmatic in accepting the change while I was reluctant. This also is completely false. There is email evidence showing we both did not support the change'.

'Moving on to the change in the line of delegated authorities,' I continue. 'Neil changes his story here.

Originally, at the time of the redundancy, he said that I wasn't supportive of the change and Katia was. Now, he changes his story, acknowledging that Katia also wasn't supportive of the change and saying that once the change was implemented, she accepted it while I continued to be critical. Not only is this a change in his story, but also it is completely false. I have email evidence showing that we both told him we were getting on with implementing the change. Once the change became effective, we both complied with it'.

'On the subject of the change in the team's reporting line in 2003,' I continue, 'Neil misrepresented that he is not aware of any issues raised by Katia. But, there is email evidence proving that he is aware'.

'Regarding the Managed Income Portfolio,' I continue. 'Again, Neil changes his story. Originally, at the time of the redundancy, he said there is a requirement to post-notify the FSA and that I made a notification error because I didn't do it. Now, he says a different thing. He acknowledges there was no need to post-notify. I can only presume he changed his story because he got caught out by me pointing out that if he truly believes I made an error, then why has he never taken it upon himself to post-notify the FSA and put the error right. So now, he says I didn't make any error but I had an agreement with him that I would tell the FSA about this matter informally. He says I didn't stand by the agreement. Not only is this different to what he said originally, but also it is completely false. I was not party to any such agreement. I notify the FSA according to the FSA's rules and regulations, not according to agreements with third parties on what we will or won't tell the FSA about. Furthermore, Neil also made the misrepresentation to Nathan that it wasn't until much later that he learned from the FSA itself that I hadn't told it about this change. I have emails showing that I kept him and Katia informed all along of every decision I made on this matter. He knew all along that I hadn't informed the FSA. This explanation also applies to the next point I make, about me rarely discussing issues'.

'On the matter of me rarely discussing issues,' I continue, 'Neil made the misrepresentation to Nathan that I hadn't told him that I would not tell the FSA about the Managed Income Portfolio. He claims that he learned from the FSA that I hadn't told it about this matter. As I just explained in my last point, this is completely false'.

'Once again, I stress the bank hasn't investigated the difference of treatment properly,' I continue. 'Nathan makes no mention in his response to me of investigating whether Katia found Neil patronising. It seems he didn't even interview her. If he did, then he makes no mention of it in his letter. Why would he not mention he interviewed her if her evidence supports his decision? He also makes no mention of investigating the matter about the Single Equities Portfolio'.

'I raised my grievance in the spirit of cooperation and in good faith, to give the bank a chance to resolve this matter properly, amicably, and privately, with a view to pre-empt any need for escalation,' I continue. 'But so far, the bank hasn't cooperated back and hasn't taken me seriously at all. I urge you to investigate the issues properly and fully. Thank you for listening'.

'Okay,' Adrian says. 'Thank you for explaining the grounds of your appeal. To start with, can you give me any examples of where you were racially discriminated against at the bank prior to your redundancy?'

'No. I don't believe I suffered any race discrimination prior to my redundancy,' I answer.

'Would anyone else have any examples or evidence of you being racially discriminated against prior to your redundancy?'

'I don't believe so,' I answer. 'I already said I don't believe I suffered any race discrimination prior to my redundancy'.

'Okay. Moving on, then. Did you request voluntary

redundancy back in 2004?' he asks.

'No,' I answer. 'I've already explained the context in which I mentioned voluntary redundancy. I raised it as a follow on question to what Neil had said to us all in a team meeting. I raised it as a reaction to his action'.

'Regarding the change in the line of delegated authorities, you say that once the change became effective you accepted it and complied with it. Can you prove that you always complied with it?' he puts to me.

'Yes, I can,' I reply. 'The fact that there's no evidence to the contrary proves that I always complied with it'.

'But, can you prove that you never not complied?' he asks.

'What? What sort of question is that?' I reply bemused. 'You're asking me to prove a negative. That's preposterous. There's no evidence that I failed to comply. There's no evidence that I ever breached it. Hence, I always complied'.

'But, you can't actually prove with any tangible evidence that you always complied, is that correct?' he asks.

'The fact that there's no evidence to the contrary is tangible evidence proving that I always complied,' I answer.

'That's not the same thing,' he asserts. 'That's a different thing. It seems you can't prove that you always complied'.

'It's exactly the same thing,' I rebut.

'No, it isn't. Anyway, let's move on,' he says. 'Why would Neil say that you find praise from him patronising?'

'Because I told him so,' I answer. 'But, Katia also told him she finds him patronising. I witnessed it. You can check with her directly yourself. We both told him he is patronising. But, he criticises only me and scores only me down for it, not her also'.

'Why would Neil say you rarely discuss things with him if it didn't ring true?' he asks.

'It doesn't ring true,' I answer. 'So, the only plausible explanation I can think of is because he is racially motivated to say it'.

'Why would he say you failed to notify the FSA if it isn't true?' he asks.

'He said that about the Managed Income Portfolio and the Single Equities Portfolio,' I answer. 'On the Managed Income Portfolio, he's changed his story, as I've explained to you. Now, he says there was no notification failure there. He contradicts what he originally said at the time of the redundancy. The truth is there was no need to notify the FSA on either portfolio. There never was any notification error. Again, the only plausible explanation I can think of why he'd say I failed to notify the FSA is because he's racially motivated to say it'.

'I have no more questions,' he says. 'Is there anything more you'd like to add?'

'Yes,' I reply. 'I have again brought along with me printouts of the emails I referred to. They evidence and prove my claims. Nathan wasn't interested in looking at them. Would you be interested?'

'I'd rather not have hard printouts,' he says. 'Could you send me soft copies by email?'

'Yes, of course. I'll do it as soon as I get home, in about an hour,' I reply.

'Okay, thanks. I'll let you have my decision soon,' he says.

~ Tuesday 12th September 2006 ~

It is clear from Adrian's preposterous investigation style of asking me to prove a negative at the appeal hearing that his mind was pre-fixed on finding ways to dismiss my grievance. The bank is, as usual, taking a brazenly long time to get back to me. It's been over a month since the appeal hearing. Each day has been a day of anguish.

Finally, its letter on its decision arrives. Without a hope of a decision in my favour, I open it. It's dated 7th September and signed by Adrian. He says the follows:

> Having met with you on 10th August, I interviewed Neil and spoke with Nathan. I also considered the emails you supplied me.
>
> Both you and Neil confirmed that there was no racial prejudice during the time you worked with each other. In fact, both of you confirmed that the relationship between yourselves was professional.
>
> The redundancy process in your case is agreed with the bank's union and is applied fairly.
>
> *Voluntary Redundancy:* I believe it was appropriate for Neil to approach you exclusively about taking up voluntary redundancy because only you had approached the bank before, in 2004, and requested voluntary redundancy.
>
> *Delegated Authority change:* I do not believe you fully embraced the change once it became effective. I believe Katia did.
>
> *FSA Notification failures:* Having interviewed Neil and considered your evidence, it is clear to me that you did not notify the FSA on the Managed Income Portfolio and the Single Equities Portfolio, and that you did not inform Neil that you had not done so.
>
> *Rarely Discusses Issues:* Having interviewed Neil and considered your numerous emails, which you say evidence your case, I do not consider that your view is supported.
>
> *Grievance Outcome:* I find no evidence that the grounds of your redundancy are racially motivated and do not believe you are treated unfairly. Consequently, I dismiss your appeal. My decision is final. The bank considers the matter closed.

Truth fails where oppression prevails, I tell myself. In the belief that cooperation would be mutually beneficial, I gave the bank every opportunity to resolve the issues amicably and quickly. It slowly, mundanely, and systematically, over a long period of nine months, dismissed every one of the issues. Its manner has been a source of great anxiety, wearing me down mentally and depleting my resources. Suppressing me into submission is clearly its strategy for then, it will have no one to answer to and its improper, self-serving manner of handling the issues becomes moot and irrelevant. I have exhausted every channel that was available to me to resolve the issues with it directly. It leaves me without any reasonable form of closure.

It possesses full information and knowledge about my employment. It knows what the truth is. In its own domain, it has complete power to decide what I am told, whether it's a truth or a lie. It has absolute right of judgment over itself and over me. My cooperation has benefited it significantly, allowing it to glean from me the full details of my case against it and the evidence I possess. Meanwhile, it has given me nothing, except, perhaps inadvertently on Neil's part, revealed that Katia is the only other person in the redundancy pool and what her scores are.

I want to walk away, to put my dismissal behind me, and move on to pastures new. But, the matter of a false career-jeopardising employment record causes me grave concerns. Stand up or put up are the only options the bank boldly leaves me. Drop the issues and live with the adverse consequences, or dare to escalate them to the higher authority of the courts, are my only choices now.

Having never sued anyone before, the idea of taking legal action against someone generally scares me enough. But, litigating specifically against this immensely powerful corporation terrifies the hell out of me. It has very deep pockets. It can afford to throw as much money at disputes as it takes to get its way. On top of that, it is an experienced expert at handling them. Expecting to encounter them from time to time during the course of its business, it is set-up and prepared to take them on in its stride with retained HR and legal professionals at the ready. The inevitable expense, personal commitment, and stress fighting an adversary of such formidable advantages and strengths will entail intimidates and deters me.

By contrast, I'm puny. I'm naive at handling disputes. I have no legal knowledge that amounts to anything meaningful. I can have access to the necessary legal expertise only as far as I can afford to pay costly lawyers from my precious savings, which are already depleted significantly by expenditure on legal services to date. Crucially, I'm a person, not a corporation. I could not and did not prepare and set myself up to take in my stride the extremely rare, highly costly, and inessential life event of litigating against a powerful corporation worth billions. The thought petrifies me that the overwhelming amount of money, time, and energy that will be necessary to take on the bank will impact me severely. The bank's behaviours to date leave me in no doubt that it will exploit to the maximum each and every single opportunity to be awkward and uncooperative in the knowledge that it will cope comfortably while I struggle under the cosh. It can quash me simply by prolonging expensive legal proceedings with the aim to squeeze me into severe financial hardship where I run out of savings and struggle to live, unable to meet the imperative expenses of food, rent, and bills. I feel helpless against its power and might, like a lone pawn against all sixteen opponent chessmen.

The only meaningful advantage I possess is the precious truth, which is of little solace. The bank will use its every advantage ruthlessly to manipulate and obliterate it to get its way.

Stand up or put up, either way, the outlook is bleak.

# 8

# RANJIT SINGH'S TESTIMONY

~ Tuesday 5th December 2006, 10:00 a.m. ~

'Mr Singh, is that your signature on the witness statement and is that the evidence you wish to give the tribunal?' my counsel asks immediately after I finish swearing to tell the truth.

I sit isolated and exposed at the witness stand in an employment tribunal before three judges looking down on me. They sit at their bench on a raised platform at the head of the courtroom, emphasising that they are the power and the authority in this domain. The judge sitting in the centre with the chair whose back protrudes twelve inches above the other two is the chairman. At a desk two paces away to my right sits my counsel with her assistant. On another desk symmetrically to my left sits the respondents' counsel, representing Neil and the bank, with her assistant. Two paces behind me is the public gallery, full with spectators. Neil, Simon, Veronica, and a number of the bank's other officers sit together in the public gallery immediately behind their counsel.

'Yes,' I answer firmly.

My predicament gave me no choice but to escalate the issues to the employment tribunal. I registered a formal complaint against the bank and against Neil personally at the London Central Employment Tribunal situated on Kingsway. Against the bank, I allege that it dismissed me unfairly, racially discriminated against me, and breached my employment contract in relation to my 2005 bonus award. Against Neil, I allege that he racially discriminated against me.

They both formally deny the allegations against them, claiming that they did not racially discriminate against me, the reason for my dismissal is redundancy, and my dismissal is entirely fair and lawful. They have brought along six witnesses to testify against me. But, they do not include Katia, a firsthand witness on many of the matters, which suggests her evidence is a risk to their case and an asset to mine.

The respondents and I together have presented the tribunal with over one and a half thousand pages of documentary evidence that is pertinent to the issues at hand. I have presented the tribunal my statement on the matters at hand, which includes the following details:

> I am the claimant in this case. I have spent most of my career working in the field of Market Risk Control, which is the activity of ensuring business trading activities at the bank remain within predefined risk limits. Controlling market risks entails identifying the risks the bank is exposed to, measuring them, analysing them, and reporting them to management and other stakeholders.
>
> I started working for the bank in November 2001 in the Market Risk Control team alongside two colleagues. Our job titles were Market Risk Controllers. Up until December 2003, each of us reported individually directly into Simon Ong, the Director of the Market Risk Department. He was our line manager and also the head of the department.
>
> In December 2003, Simon reorganised our team. He moved one member out and placed her in another team. Thus, the team shrank in number from three to two people. He made the other member the head of the team and gave him the job title of Head of Market Risk Control. My reporting

line was reset into him. His reporting line was reset into Neil Hobson, who already reported into Simon and managed another team in the department. Thus, the management reporting line ran from Simon to Neil and then, to our team. The line of delegated authority, however, was different. It excluded Neil. Simon delegated his authorities to manage risks to our team directly, bypassing Neil. Thus, whilst Neil had the responsibility to manage us, he did not have the powers necessary to do our job, like to make market risk related decisions.

There were two businesses, though, on which I continued to report directly into Simon. They are the Wealth Management business and the SPAYN business. On these businesses, Simon held one-to-one meetings with me directly, without my line manager, the head of our team, and Neil being involved in anyway.

Six months later, in May 2004, we hired Katia Mykonola as a Market Risk Controller alongside me. Thus, we became a team of three.

Ever since the reorganisation, our team head engaged Neil in discussions regarding business issues that arose from the inconsistency between the team's management reporting line and the line of delegated authorities. The inconsistency caused issues in the workplace because although it was visible to everyone that Neil is our manager, it was invisible that he does not have the same authorities and powers as we do. The inconsistency caused confusion for people because they assumed he, being our manager, had at least the same powers as we. The confusion created operational inefficiencies and issues in the workplace, like people going to him for matters he did not have the authority to decide on instead of coming to us directly. The inefficiencies introduced delay into work processes and increased the level of operational risk. Our team head updated us regularly on his discussions with Neil.

In June 2004 though, our team head started including us directly on workshop meetings with Neil to address this subject. All three of us, Katia included, highlighted the same concerns and issues to Neil. The meetings were unproductive, though. Neil simply refused to acknowledge that there are any issues. In one workshop meeting in July, he went as far as telling us that there is no need to implement any of the solutions we proposed to deal with the inconsistency because nobody in the team has resigned over the issues and hence, there are no issues. I was very frustrated by his stance of dismissing the issues on the basis that none of us had resigned. It was wholly unreasonable of him to expect us to sacrifice our jobs to make him see that there are business operational issues. So, as he made it clear that he is not willing to recognise the issues until someone in the team resigns over them, I immediately followed up by asking him whether he supports his stance with a voluntary redundancy option. My question was a reaction to his antagonistic stance. I was feeling frustrated. Asking him about voluntary redundancy was the only way I could think of there and then to try to make him sit up and take notice of what he had just said to us. Several weeks later, he approached me in isolation and told me there is no voluntary redundancy option attached to his stance. I thought nothing of his comeback. I already knew the bank's policies preclude voluntary redundancies.

The respondents are trying to characterise what I said at the team meeting as a major personal request for voluntary redundancy, which is completely false and wholly disingenuous. If I had wanted to leave the bank, which I did not, I would have taken the initiative to discuss it privately with my line manager at the time, which was not Neil. I would not have discussed it with Neil openly in front of other team members and spontaneously off the back of something that he had just said. It would suit the respondents to characterise my question as a personal request for voluntary redundancy because it would help to justify their unfair and discriminatory treatment of me when in November 2005, before any redundancy scoring had taken place and in breach of the bank's policies, Neil approached me privately and asked me whether I would be interested in taking up voluntary redundancy. He never made any similar offer to Katia, my comparator, who is Greek and white. I submit that he offered voluntary redundancy to me exclusively because if I accepted, then there would be no need to carry out a sham compulsory redundancy exercise with a prejudged outcome.

Around September 2004, the bank was taken over by the European banking group Eurocredito. Also around that time, the head of our team resigned and left the bank. On his departure, Simon re-allocated all of his responsibilities and authorities to Katia and me directly, still bypassing Neil, and assigned Neil to be our line manager. He retained my reporting lines directly into himself on the Wealth Management and SPAYN businesses.

Katia and I were the only two members of the team for about the next six months until we hired two junior team members, Mary Richardson and Anthony Grenfell. They both had the job titles Market Risk Associates. Katia managed Mary and

I managed Anthony.

On 19th September 2005, Simon changed the line of delegated authorities to include Neil. Hence, from then onwards, the authorities and powers to control market risks flowed from Simon to Neil and then, from Neil to Katia and me.

I submit that the decision to dismiss me was predetermined by Neil by 22nd November because that is when he approached me with an offer of voluntary redundancy. The compulsory redundancy exercise that followed is a sham where he fashioned the assessments to support his predetermined decision. No reliance can be placed on the assessments because they were used as vehicles to ensure my departure after the voluntary redundancy route failed to achieve it.

The appraisal is one of the two redundancy selection criteria. Yet, Neil informed the union that I am the redundant person before my appraisal was even started, let alone completed. This is evidenced clearly in the following two ways. Firstly, he submits *Breakdown of Duties* schedules to the union on 15th December, being the day before my appraisal was started. The *Proposed Duties* schedule that he submits shows no work allocation under my name while under Katia's, it shows her original workload plus my workload transferred to her. Thus, the schedule informs the union that I am the person selected for redundancy and Katia is not. Secondly, the *Redundancy Rationale* papers that he drafted up and submitted to the union on the same day state, *"the At Risk manager has been off work and the workload has been managed well"*. He is referring to me in this statement because I had been working from home while recuperating from a broken leg. It is apparent from these documents that I was selected for redundancy before my appraisal was even begun. How could he identify me as being the person at risk before one of the selection criteria, the appraisal, is completed without having predetermined it? Clearly, he predetermined it and subsequently fixed the selection criteria scores to support his decision. The scores are not bona-fide.

Neil has given unsatisfactory reasons for the lowering of my assessment scores. My scores were lowered but Katia's were not when she and I had acted exactly the same way, held the same views, and were in the same situation. The reason Neil is unable to explain satisfactorily this difference of treatment is because there is no satisfactory explanation. He reduced my scores because it suited his personal goal of selecting me for redundancy.

The bank justifies not notifying me that there is a redundancy process in progress by saying that its in-house trade union consulted in the process on my behalf. It says the union supported my interests and fulfilled the role that I myself would have fulfilled had I known a redundancy is in progress. I reject this explanation. I was never a member of the union. The union did not inform me of anything.

On 12th January 2006, I attended a meeting with Neil and Veronica Cotton, which the bank refers to as the first one-to-one individual consultation meeting. I explained to them that, actually, I am no longer at risk of redundancy because my redundancy is now a certainty. Therefore, the two-week consultation period is entirely bogus. I highlighted that my appraisal is not completed. I have not signed it off because I am disputing it. I asked them how could the redundancy exercise be finalised when one of the components it depends on is not finalised? I explained to them that because I am disputing my appraisal score and my competency scores are lowered on exactly the same basis, then my appraisal dispute automatically extends and applies to the competency scoring too.

My overall point is that the process is unfair, discriminatory, and prejudged.

The feebleness of the points put forward by the respondents and the inadequacy of their explanations to justify the process reinforced my view that my selection for redundancy is predetermined and fixed by Neil. I am being accused of mistakes that I never made and of things I do not deserve to be accused of. The explanations given are untenable.

Because I have never known that I have been the victim of race discrimination before in my career, it did not occur to me immediately that the respondents' inexplicably unfair and unreasonable conduct might be motivated by race. It was only later on, when I took stock of matters, looked at the sequence of events, compared my treatment with Katia's, and reviewed the process in full, that it became clear to me that there is no other plausible explanation for their conduct except race discrimination.

The race discrimination I suffered is not overt. I was not racially abused openly, excluded, or subjected to name-calling or derisory comments based on race. This makes the discrimination all the more pernicious. The discrimination perpetrated consists mostly of less favourable treatment in the form of an obviously unfair redundancy, which I believe was engineered to get rid of me. It is also in the form of obvious unfair and less favourable treatment regarding my bonus award and other matters, and a dismissive attitude towards my legitimate grievances, which were handled exceedingly slowly and in a prejudged manner. As a result of the race discrimination perpetrated by the respondents, I have lost my job and have been extremely distressed.

I was born in India to Indian parents. I am Indian and Asian in ethnic and national origins, and in appearance. I have lived in the UK since I was one year old. I am British.

I had not encountered race discrimination in the workplace before. I would not normally attribute matters to race and have never played any kind of race card. I do not bring this legal action of race to the employment tribunal lightly, nor do I relish the consequences of doing so. However, I honestly believe that I am the victim of race discrimination in this case. I believe my grievance regarding race discrimination was not dealt with fairly. With the respondents dismissing the issues out of hand and regarding matters closed, I had no option but to escalate matters to the tribunal, where all parties will be granted a fair hearing.

On 26th September 2006, I received the bank's response to my Race Relations Act Questionnaire, which I had served upon it. During the eight weeks that it had the questionnaire, it never disputed the validity or reasonableness of the questions I asked in it. I was therefore surprised and concerned at its point blank refusal to provide answers to some key questions. It deprives me of critical facts to which I am entitled.

I believe I was dismissed unfairly, both substantially and procedurally. Substantially, I do not believe there was a genuine redundancy situation. Neil engineered the situation with the surreptitious purpose of removing me. Procedurally, I do not believe the procedure followed is fair and reasonable. I say the process is a sham to remove me.

I believe my selection for redundancy is motivated by the colour of my skin. The selection criteria scores were prejudged and fashioned against me on the grounds of my Indian and Asian race.

My grievances and appeals were not dealt with fairly and properly. There was a repeated failure by the bank to provide proper and full explanations. The improper manner and the extremely slow pace the bank conducted its investigations also evidence the direct race discrimination that I experienced. I believe the lowering of my 2005 bonus award is also motivated by race discrimination.

Addressing the chairman, my counsel says, 'Sir, I wish to bring up some supplementary issues'.

'Do so now so the respondents' counsel may have the chance to cross-examine the claimant on them,' the chairman replies.

'Thank you, Sir,' she replies. Addressing me, she says, 'you are marked down regarding the Managed Income Portfolio on which Neil says that, although there is no need to notify the FSA, you had an agreement with him that you would tell the FSA. He says that you did not follow through on the agreement. Is this correct?'

'It is correct that there is no need to notify the FSA,' I answer. 'However, it is incorrect that I agreed with him that I would tell the FSA about it. At the time, it was Katia's and my job, not Neil's, to decide whether the FSA needs to be notified and if so, what kind of notification is required. If the wrong notification is made, then Simon Ong would hold Katia and me to account, not Neil, who I'm sure would then do his best to distance himself from accountability. I assess the kind of notification that needs to be made based on the FSA's rules and regulations, not according to any agreements with third parties, like Neil, as to what we will or will not tell the FSA about. I made no such agreement with him'.

'Did you inform Neil what you are going to do in terms of notification on the Managed Income Portfolio?' she asks.

'Yes,' I answer. 'I discussed it with him face-to-face and included him on all email discussions about it, along with Katia and about five other members of our department. He knew exactly what was happening the whole time. Notifying the FSA is a serious matter. Incorrect notification can result in the bank being penalised in some way by the FSA. So, to prevent errors from occurring, Katia and I would discuss and check each other's notification decisions. We'd also keep Neil in the loop so that he could have a say and would be in a position to update his peers and Simon'.

'Did he reply on those email discussions?' she asks.

'No,' I answer firmly.

'What would he do if he disagreed with what you were doing?' she asks.

'He'd say something, shout out, as would Katia also. FSA notification is too important a matter to sit back and stay quiet on. Plus, if either one of us makes a mistake, then it will reflect poorly on the whole team. The whole team will look bad and lose credibility,' I answer.

'You and Katia both took the same view?' she asks.

'Yes, and Neil too took the same view as us,' I reply.

'What are the practical effects of pre-notification and post-notification?' she asks.

'Well, there are actually three kinds of notification, as follows: no-notification, pre-notification, and post-notification. There is no practical effect on business activities regarding no-notification and post-notification. The FSA has given its approval to the bank to trade some kinds of things without the bank ever needing to bring them to its attention. Those things fall into the no-

notification category. The bank can just get on with that kind of business activity. So, there is no practical impact on business in the case of no-notification. Then, there are some kinds of trades that the FSA is happy for the bank to get on with, but it wants to know about them after the event, at its next scheduled meeting with us. They fall into the post-notification category. Again, the bank can just get on with that kind of business activity too. So, there's no practical impact on business in the case of post-notification either. Then, there are other kinds of things that the FSA does not want the bank to do at all without first obtaining its explicit permission to do them. They fall into the pre-notification category. The bank must inform the FSA about them and obtain its approval before it goes ahead and does them. The FSA says it can take up to thirty days to give its decision. So, pre-notification can cause a significant delay to business activity, of up to thirty days'.

The chairman interjects, 'Mr Singh, how do you know what kind of notification to make?'

'The FSA provides us with a mandate document spelling out the notification rules and requirements. We comply with the documented rules and notify accordingly,' I answer.

The chairman signals my counsel to continue.

'If you do not pre-notify,' my counsel resumes, 'but, the FSA thinks you should, would there be any consequences?'

'Yes. The consequences can vary depending on the situation from just a slap on the wrist to something quite harsh, like a fine or a penalty,' I answer. 'In cases of severe failures, the FSA could stop us trading in some businesses. So, it's important to notify correctly. We can always be super cautious and pre-notify the FSA on every single thing. That way, we'd never get in trouble. But, we'd unnecessarily overwhelm the FSA with things it doesn't want to know about and we'd grind our business activity down to a snail pace because the FSA can take up to thirty days to respond. So, we need to notify correctly and efficiently, meaning that we should not impact business activity unnecessarily'.

'Moving on to the Single Equities Portfolio,' she says, 'which you are marked down for also. You post-notified. But, Neil says the matter should be pre-notified. Did you and Katia both take the same view?'

'Yes, we did. We both decided the requirement is to post-notify,' I answer.

'What view did you form regarding Neil agreeing or disagreeing with your approach?' she asks.

'That he agrees with it,' I answer firmly.

'Moving on to the line of delegated authority,' she says. 'Neil took you with him to a meeting with the bank's legal team regarding the delegation. What was your role in the meeting?' she asks.

'This was Neil's second meeting with the bank's legal team. He had one before by himself. But, what he reported back to Katia and me didn't make sense to us. So, there was a second meeting to which I went along with him,' I answer.

'At the meeting, the legal team clarified that Neil is excluded from the line of delegated authority and that he does not have the decision-making powers that you and Katia have, is this correct?' she asks.

'Yes, it's correct,' I answer.

'In August 2005, Simon Ong sends you and Katia an email instructing you to implement a change to the line of delegated authorities, to include Neil in the line. At this stage, is the email implementing the change?' she asks.

'No,' I answer. 'The change is not effective yet. The email informs us what the change will be and instructs us to kick off the process to bring about its implementation'.

'Where are you when the email is sent?' she asks.

'I was working from home. I was recuperating from a broken leg,' I answer.

'Were you consulted about the change?' she asks.

'No. This email is the first that Katia and I heard about it,' I answer.

'Did you think not consulting you is a good idea?' she asks.

'No. It was Katia's and my job to advise Simon about such changes and to make recommendations to him about them,' I answer. 'So, not consulting us was highly unusual. It bypassed the job the bank gave to us to perform. It bypassed our expertise and our responsibility'.

'You raise concerns about the change?' she says.

'Yes. It was my job to do so,' I answer. 'However, I told Neil by email that whilst I'm flagging up concerns, I'm also working with Katia on implementing the change as Simon instructed us'.

'What was Katia's view?' she asks.

'The same as mine,' I answer. 'She was in the office and I was at home. We discussed the matter over the phone. We held the same view'.

The chairman interjects, 'Mr Singh, you say you should have been consulted about the change. Why?'

'Because it was our job to propose, advise, and make recommendations to Simon regarding the risk procedures. We should be consulted so the job the bank gave us to do and wants done, can be done,' I answer.

'But, it was not your decision to make whether the line of delegated authority changed, correct?' the chairman puts to me.

'Correct,' I answer. 'It was Simon's decision. Simon is the Director of the department. He owns the risk procedures. The actual decision was his to make, not Katia's and mine. We were his experts in market risk control. Our job was to maintain and develop the risk procedures on his behalf. Our job was to propose, advise, and recommend changes to him. Normally, he only acted on our advice and recommendations. This was the first and only occasion where he didn't'.

'What concerned you about the change?' the chairman asks.

'Lots of things,' I reply. 'It was Katia's and my responsibility to ensure the bank's procedures are fit for the purpose of controlling market risks. The bank's procedure is that we propose changes and Simon makes decisions to implement them based on our advice and recommendations to him. Here, he was circumventing this established procedure, which is a concern in itself, especially when the bank and the FSA believe the procedure is being performed and are placing reliance on it. In addition to that, we thought the change is unnecessary and that it weakened the procedures by introducing inefficiency and risk of errors'.

'Is your objection to the change in the line of delegated authority to the fact that Mr Hobson is being included in it?' the chairman asks. 'If it were another person instead, would you not have the same concerns?'

'Simon admitted that the procedures are not broken in anyway and that they do not need fixing,' I answer, 'and that the change is not any reflection on how Katia and I perform our duties. So, my primary concern was that the change itself is unnecessary and is introducing the inefficiency of an additional step into the procedures, regardless of it being Neil or someone else. Regarding the fact that it is Neil specifically, Katia and I have a proven track record and experience in managing and controlling market risks whereas Neil doesn't. By inserting Neil, I had the secondary concern that a risk of errors is being introduced into the procedures'.

The chairman signals my counsel to continue.

'When the change came into effect,' my counsel resumes, 'to what extent did you accept or not accept it?'

'From the moment it came into effect, I accepted it fully and complied with it fully,' I answer firmly.

'You are also marked down for failing to embrace change with respect to the team's management reporting line that was implemented in December 2003. There is a workshop meeting in June 2004 between you, Katia, Neil, and the then head of your team. You write up an email summarising what was agreed in the workshop and email it to everyone who was present. At the bottom of the email you say, *"Please let me know of any errors or omissions or alternations required"*. Does anyone get back to you on the email?' she asks.

'Yes. Neil got back to me with a point he wanted included,' I reply. 'I added in his point and re-issued the email. After that, no one got back to me'.

'What was everyone's mood about the workshop, including Katia's?' she asks.

'That we all had reached agreement on what the issues caused by the inconsistency between the management reporting line and the line of delegated authorities are,' I answer.

'Moving on,' she says. 'You say there is an occasion where Neil sent Katia an email which sparked her off and resulted in her telling him she finds him patronising'.

'Yes,' I reply.

'How did she communicate to him that she finds him patronising, was it by email or was it orally?' she asks.

'Orally,' I answer. 'She came over to me huffing and puffing and looking very annoyed. She showed me his email. He was telling her to do something quite obvious and trivial. She's a senior, experienced, seasoned professional. She told me she finds it very patronising and asked what I think. I agreed. She asked me if I would accompany her to go to see him about it. I accompanied her. She took him into a private meeting room. There, she proceeded to give him a piece of her mind. She scolded him, asking him why is he patronising her by telling her to do something quite trivial and obvious by email on which he's copied in numerous third parties? She asked him is it really necessary, is he trying to give others the impression that she doesn't know what to do, can he not manage her without having to rely on the weight of others?'

'Thank you, I have no more questions,' she says.

The chairman signals the respondents' counsel to cross-examine me. It sends a chill down my spine. I know I have nothing to fear because I'm innocent and I will tell the truth. But still, I feel fear knowing that it is her job to trip me up and make me appear guilty, and knowing that she is an experienced expert at it. I brace myself for a grilling.

'Thank you, Sir,' she replies. 'Mr Singh,' she starts, 'your enquiry about voluntary redundancy in July 2004 is not in Katia's presence, is it?'

'It was in her presence,' I reply.

'It is not made spontaneously, as you say. It is, in fact, made to Neil in a separate meeting with just the two of you present,' she asserts.

'That's incorrect,' I reply. 'It was a spontaneous reaction to what he had told us all in a team meeting'.

'Having made the enquiry, Neil gets back to you later on about it,' she says.

'Yes,' I reply.

'You do not ask him why is he getting back to you? You do not make clear to him that you were just letting off steam. So, how can he know that you were not being serious?' she puts to me.

'Because I made the point in an open team meeting in response to something he had said. It would have been obvious to any reasonable person that it is a reaction to his action,' I reply. 'He got back to me in isolation saying there is no such option. I wasn't at all surprised because I knew the bank's policies don't allow voluntary redundancies. I thought nothing of him getting back to me. I had moved on. I didn't give his response any attention'.

'The fact that he gets back to you indicates that he thinks it is a genuine enquiry,' she asserts.

'No reasonable person would have thought it is a genuine enquiry,' I reply. 'I was making a point in a team meeting as a follow on to what he had said. If I really wanted to enquire about voluntary redundancy, then I would have done it privately, not openly in a team meeting, and I would have done it to my line manager, which was not Neil at that time, it was the Head of Market Risk Control'.

'Katia never enquired about voluntary redundancy,' she says.

'Not that I'm aware of,' I reply. 'But, I wasn't privy to every conversation she ever had'.

'So, when Neil approaches you regarding voluntary redundancy in November 2005, there is a reason why he approaches you exclusively,' she asserts.

'Over-ruled!' the chairman interjects. 'Submission, not a question'. Addressing me, he says, 'after Mr Hobson got back to you in July 2004 and informed you there is no voluntary redundancy option, were there ever any subsequent discussions about voluntary redundancy in the one and a half year period to the time when he approached you in November 2005?'

'No, never,' I answer.

The chairman signals the respondents' counsel to continue.

'When Neil approaches you in November 2005,' she continues, 'you tell him you are not interested'.

'That's correct,' I reply.

'In his approach, he does not use the phrase *you could be quids in*, does he, Mr Singh?' she says in harsh tone.

'He did say it,' I reply.

'I put it to you that he did not say it,' she asserts.

'He did,' I reply.

'I put it to you that he did not,' she repeats.

'Objection!' the chairman interjects addressing her. 'You cannot keep repeatedly putting the same construct to him when he has given you his answer quite clearly. If you have evidence contradicting what he says, then show it. Otherwise, move on,' he orders.

'Moving on,' she says. 'There were specific pieces of work on which you reported directly to Simon Ong'.

'That's correct,' I reply.

'But, Simon Ong was not your line manager. He was not responsible for your appraisals. You just reported directly to him on those pieces,' she asserts.

'That's correct,' I reply. 'But, he managed me directly on those pieces of work as though he is my line manager'.

'Let us turn to the matter of the reorganisation in December 2003,' she continues, 'where Neil becomes your team's line manager. This reorganisation leaves you so discontented in your job that you look for alternative employment elsewhere,' she puts to me.

'That's incorrect,' I reply. 'I was happy in my job and I wasn't proactively looking for another job'.

'Ah, you say not, Mr Singh,' she says gleefully. 'But, at the beginning of 2005, you attend an interview at another bank arranged by a recruitment agency,' she says.

'It wasn't a formal interview for any specific role,' I reply. 'It was an informal meeting to get to know each other. It was networking'.

The chairman interjects, 'how did that come about, Mr Singh?'

'The recruitment agency representing the bank contacted me and asked if I'd be interested in having an informal chat with its client. I agreed. The agency arranged the meeting. I attended one evening after work,' I answer.

'Was it to discuss the possibility of working for them?' the chairman asks.

'Potentially, but there was no specific role on the table. No specific job was discussed,' I reply.

'So, you were headhunted by the agent,' the chairman says.

'Yes, that's correct. They approached me. I didn't

approach them,' I clarify.

'What happened after the meeting, how were things left?' the chairman asks.

'Nothing happened,' I answer. 'The agent never contacted me again and I never contacted them'.

The chairman signals the respondents' counsel to continue.

'On the 20th of September 2005, Simon Ong makes a change to the line of delegated authorities,' she continues. 'Before, the delegation was from himself directly to you and Katia, bypassing Neil. He changes it to include Neil so that the delegation flows from himself to Neil and then, to you and Katia. Is this correct?'

'Yes, it's correct,' I reply.

'Katia sends out the email to notify the relevant stakeholders of the change. She sends it because you are not on board with the change, are you?' she puts to me.

'Once the change was implemented, we both were on board with it. We drafted the email together. But, it can only be sent out from one person's email account. It's impossible to send it out from two people's,' I reply. 'The email tells the recipients to contact me, as well as her, if they have any queries. She sent it out of her account on both our behalves. We couldn't both send it. The same goes for all other changes that occurred. The emails went out of one of our accounts, sometimes hers, sometimes mine, on behalf of both of us'.

'But, a week earlier you sent Simon Ong an email raising concerns and issues with the change,' she says.

'Yes, that's correct. A week earlier the change was not effective. Katia and I were still working on implementing it,' I reply. 'It was our job to review the change and raise any concerns and make recommendations to Simon. Yes, I sent Simon an email with my concerns. I was doing my job'.

'You were unsupportive of the change,' she says.

'There were concerns and issues. I flagged them up. It

was my job to flag them. Katia raised concerns and issues too. It was her job also. We both were unsupportive,' I answer.

'But, the email is from you only. There is no such email from Katia,' she says.

'We both discussed the matter together and flagged our concerns separately,' I reply.

'There is no evidence in the documents before the tribunal that she flagged up any concerns,' she asserts.

'There is,' I reply.

'Katia did not oppose the change to the extent that you did,' she says.

'We both opposed it to the same extent,' I answer.

'From the evidence, it is clear that you believe you have genuine reasons to challenge the change. But, you must accept that it looks like you resist the change?' she puts to me.

'We could not support the change prior to its implementation because there were concerns and issues surrounding it. If the issues could be addressed and resolved satisfactorily, then we would support it,' I reply.

'You point to a series of seven emails and claim they evidence that Katia also did not support the change,' she says. 'However, they do not evidence what you say, do they, Mr Singh?'

'They do evidence it,' I reply. 'Those seven emails are a sample series of seven consecutive changes to risk procedures, in chronological order, that were implemented in the department over a period of time. The emails are to Simon. They are from Katia and me. The email in the middle of the series, the fourth one, is about the change to the line of delegated authorities, which we both didn't support. When we support a proposed change, we explicitly recommend Simon to approve it by including in our email the wording, *"Market Risk Control recommends you approve the change"*. That is our standard practice,' I explain. 'We do it for the record, to leave an audit trail, so the FSA and auditors can see clearly that the established process is being followed. You can see that for all the other six changes in the series, our emails include this phrase. That's because we supported those changes. But, the phrase does not appear on the email regarding the change to the line of delegated authorities. We didn't write it on that one because we didn't support that change'.

'But, these emails do not show that Katia expressed the same concerns as you,' she says.

'They show that both Katia and I didn't support the change by the fact that we made no recommendation to Simon to approve it, like we normally do,' I reply.

'Just because the phrase is missing from the email, it does not prove that Katia had the same concerns as you,' she rebuts. 'It's a big leap to conclude that Katia had the same concerns because the phrase is missing,' she says.

'Objection!' the chairman interjects. 'What significance should be attached to the phrase is a matter for the tribunal to judge'.

'Yes, Sir,' she replies. Addressing me, she continues, 'you say your redundancy is a sham. Do you accept that there was a large-scale cost cutting exercise in progress at the bank?'

'I'm aware there was cost cutting going on in the bank's retail business, but not in the investment banking business, which is where I worked,' I answer.

'Do you accept losing a Market Risk Controller is part of that cost cutting?' she asks.

'No, I don't,' I answer. 'I wasn't aware of any cost cutting affecting our department and I believe our team was already lean and efficient'.

'Do you accept that Neil had discussions with the union regarding your redundancy?' she asks.

'Objection!' my counsel interjects. 'Out of Mr Singh's scope of knowledge'.

She acknowledges the objection and continues, 'do you accept that the situation that led to the redundancy of a

Market Risk Controller is part of a large-scale redundancy process?'

'No, I do not,' I answer. 'As I've already said, I wasn't aware of any redundancies affecting our department and I believe our team was already lean and efficient'.

'Do you accept that you are given an explanation for the approach of voluntary redundancy, even though you do not agree with the explanation?' she asks.

'Yes, I accept that I was given an implausible explanation with which I do not agree,' I reply.

'You say that the only plausible explanation for the voluntary redundancy approach is race discrimination. But, there is no evidence of race discrimination,' she says.

'Well, I've never been given any other plausible explanation,' I reply.

'During your redundancy individual consultation meetings with Neil and Veronica Cotton, you raise issues on the basis of unfairness only. You do not raise any issue of race discrimination then,' she says.

'That's correct,' I reply.

'It is a very big leap to make, then, that you were approached for voluntary redundancy due to race discrimination,' she says.

'During the individual consultation period, I thought the issue is of unfairness only, based on the evidence I was aware of at the time,' I reply. 'I was kept in the dark and told only what Neil and Veronica decided to tell me. As time went on, further evidence emerged, on the 20th of March, which made me realise that racial discrimination is the basis of the approach. So, it's not a big leap to make because it's based on evidence. It's not made arbitrarily'.

'You were challenging only the manager's comments on your appraisal, not the appraisal score also,' she says.

'The score is based on the manager's comments. My score is lowered because of the comments. The fact that I am challenging the comments means that the score is also being challenged. They are linked. The comments need to be addressed and removed first. Then, the revision in the comments needs to be reflected in the score'.

'You are aware of the process for appealing the appraisal,' she says.

'Yes. The first stage is to seek resolution informally directly with the line manager. If this turns out to be unproductive, then the next stage is to appeal formally within ten days of the appraisal meeting,' I reply.

'You make no formal challenge,' she says.

'Firstly, I didn't sign-off on my appraisal. Therefore, I didn't agree and finalise it. Secondly, I was denied the opportunity to lodge a formal appeal,' I reply. 'Immediately after Neil conducted my appraisal meeting on the 16th of December, he disappeared off on holiday for sixteen days without giving me the information I needed to draft up and articulate the grounds of a formal appeal. On his return on the 3rd of January, he continued to delay giving me the information I need. He only sent it to me two days before I am told I'm at risk. Even then, he sent it in the evening after I had left the office for the day. So, I actually received it just one day before. I believe he delayed on purpose, to run down the clock, to deny me the chance to launch a formal appeal. I escalated the dispute to Simon on the day before I am told I'm at risk. Then, Neil and Veronica told me the redundancy consultation process takes over and is the place to dispute the appraisal'.

'You do not make it clear to Simon Ong that you are formally appealing?' she asks.

'According to the bank's procedures,' I reply, 'the formal appeal is to be made to Simon. But, he didn't seem to be an independent person here, given that he's Neil's line manager. I escalated the dispute to him anyway so he'd know that I dispute my appraisal while I consider how to appeal to someone independent'.

'Being selected for redundancy does not stop you from launching a formal appeal, does it?' she says.

'I continued to appeal the appraisal with Neil and Veronica in the individual consultation period. They told me that's where I need to do it,' I reply. 'The consultation period is a formal process. So, I disputed it formally because I disputed it inside a formal process'.

'Do you accept that the bank followed its own redundancy procedures?' she asks.

'No,' I reply. 'It did not follow them. I brought up the areas of deviation to Neil and Veronica, and to the people who participated in my grievances'.

'Do you accept that the process in relation to your redundancy was discussed with the union by Neil?' she asks.

'I don't know what was or was not discussed with the union,' I answer. 'I had no idea discussions were taking place. I was not privy to them. I wasn't a member of the union'.

'There is documentary evidence of discussions that took place with the union,' she asserts.

The chairman interjects, 'if he is not a member of the union and was not present at the discussions, then how can he know a redundancy is going on? It must be the case that he was not consulted with before he is chosen for redundancy. Move on,' he orders.

'Moving on then,' she says. 'In November 2004, Neil sends you an email saying, *"Well done",*' she says.

'That's correct,' I reply.

'You respond saying, *"I do not appreciate patronising comments like this. Please stop",*' she says.

'Yes, that's correct,' I reply.

'So, Neil is accurate in saying you find praise from your line manager patronising,' she puts to me.

'This is in relation to a piece of work that I reported directly to Simon on,' I reply.

'But, Neil is your line manager, not Simon,' she says.

'Yes. But, this is work I was doing directly for Simon,' I reply. 'Simon was managing me directly on it as though he's my line manager. He held one-to-one meetings directly with me alone. In all practical sense, he was effectively my line manager on this work'.

The chairman interjects, 'Mr Singh, why did you find Mr Hobson's comment patronising?'

'This is an area in which I have expert knowledge and Neil doesn't,' I reply. 'The task was trivial and easy for me. It was well within my comfort zone. It really was a piece of cake. I thought a *"well done"* from someone who doesn't know what the task entails is patronising. It's a bit like me, having no knowledge or experience in law, saying well done to someone like you for judging a case. A *"congratulations"* might be the more appropriate thing to say'.

'Did Mr Hobson reply back saying he was not intending to be patronising?' the chairman asks.

'No,' I answer. 'There was no reply back'.

The chairman signals the respondents' counsel to continue.

'Katia does not find praise from Neil patronising?' she says.

'I know she found him patronising in some respects,' I reply.

'Patronising in relation to praise specifically,' she clarifies.

'I don't know about praise specifically,' I answer. 'I wasn't privy to all the communication between them. But, it wouldn't surprise me at all if she found him patronising in relation to praise also. I know she found him patronising in other respects. He scored me down for finding praise from him patronising. He could have marked her down for finding other aspects patronising. There is no reason why patronising should apply to praise exclusively'.

'Moving on,' she says. 'On the 10th of April, you make a last ditch attempt at trying to put across your points to Neil, protesting that your redundancy is unfair'.

'Yes,' I reply.

'This is the first time you mention race as an issue,' she says.

'That's correct,' I answer.

'So, up to this point, you do not think your redundancy is on the grounds of race,' she says.

'Up to the 20th of March, I didn't think race is an issue because up to then I had very little information to go on and I wasn't aware of any evidence of a race issue,' I reply. 'I was kept in the dark by the bank and told only what it decided to tell me. But, on the 20th of March, during the course of a grievance hearing, evidence surfaced that made me think race could be the grounds. The seed of a race issue became planted in my head at that point'.

'When do you first think race is an issue?' she asks.

'I became aware of the evidence of a race issue on the 20th of March, at the grievance hearing meeting,' I answer. 'I knew that Katia had behaved the same as I had on matters that Neil criticised me about and lowered my scores for. At the grievance meeting, he revealed her scores. He awarded her full marks. He didn't reduce her scores even though the criticisms he made of me and reduced my scores for apply equally to her. I became suspicious that he didn't criticise her similarly. This is the first time I thought there might be some kind of difference of treatment at play'.

The chairman interjects, 'when did you first think it is on the grounds of race?'

'Some time soon after that meeting,' I reply. 'I gave myself some time to cool off, to make sure I'm not reacting in the heat of the moment to what I heard there, to make sure I think objectively about it'.

The respondents' counsel resumes, 'the first time you raise race formally as an issue is on the 14th of June'.

'No, it's not,' I correct her. 'As you pointed out just a few minutes ago, the first time I mention race is in my letter of the 10th of April. It takes time to draft up and finalise a letter. So, obviously, I thought it's race before the 10th of April, before I even started drafting the letter'.

Addressing the respondents' counsel, the chairman interjects, 'also, what about the letter of the 12th of May from his lawyer to the bank? Race is also very clearly mentioned as a ground there'.

'I apologise, Sir,' she says apprehensively as though she knows she has been caught out.

'Do not try to mislead the tribunal,' the chairman warns her, 'to the idea that he did not raise the issue of race within an acceptable time period. It is not the case that he first realised it is race in March and did not raise it until June. Although he did not raise it immediately, he did raise it within a few weeks from when he realised it, which is well within a reasonable time'.

'Yes, Sir,' she replies. 'Moving on,' she continues. 'You point to an email documenting a discussion in relation to the Risk Limits Policy on which you say Neil scored you down for not supporting a change, but did not score Katia down for doing the same. But, Neil has told you that the Risk Limits Policy is not the instance for which he scored you down'.

'He's told me no such thing,' I reply. 'He made it very clear he scored me down in relation to the Risk Limits Policy'.

Reviewing the said email, the chairman interjects, 'Mr Singh, how does this email show that you and Miss Mykonola took a different stance jointly from everyone else? It shows that everyone agreed not to support the change'.

'That's correct, and that's exactly my point,' I answer. 'It shows that everyone, including Katia and Neil, agreed not to support the proposed change. Yet, I'm exclusively criticised for not embracing change in relation to it and my score alone is reduced. The same treatment is not applied to Katia'.

'You, Miss Mykonola and Mr Hobson agreed not to

support the change?' the chairman asks.

'That's correct,' I reply.

'So, the email shows that both you and Miss Mykonola did not support the change,' the chairman says.

'That's correct,' I confirm. 'And Neil criticises me and scores me down for not supporting it, but not Katia,' I add.

The chairman signals the respondents' counsel to continue.

'Moving on,' she resumes. 'In relation to the bonus entitlement, do you accept that you were a member of a wholly discretionary bonus scheme?'

'Yes,' I answer.

'The size of a bonus award is not only tied to performance appraisals, correct?' she asks.

'Correct,' I reply.

'Do you accept that Colin Marr is independent of the race and the redundancy matter?' she asks.

'Yes,' I answer.

'Do you accept that he is independent of Neil?' she asks.

'Yes,' I reply.

'There is no evidence that your appraisal is scored down on the basis of race,' she says.

'I have presented ample evidence that shows my appraisal score could only have been lowered on the basis of race and nothing else,' I reply.

'The tribunal has been presented bonus allocation records in your department. They clearly show that another person in the department also got a lower bonus, even though his appraisal score increased. Therefore, you getting a lower bonus because your score decreased is not out of kilter,' she says.

'It is out of kilter,' I reply. 'The records shows that only two people suffered a decrease in their bonuses. I'm one and the other is the one you refer to. No one else suffered a decrease. Even if they got a lower appraisal score, their bonus either remained the same or increased. Clearly, the two of us are treated differently from everyone else, and there's an interesting observation relating to the difference of treatment'.

'Hmm,' she ponders and then, says, 'I have no more questions'.

Addressing my counsel, the chairman asks, 'would you like to re-examine the claimant?'

'Yes, Sir,' she answers. Addressing me, she says, 'from the bonus allocations records, we can tell that the other person who gets a lower bonus is Jai Khanna. What race is Jai Khanna?'

'Well, he's not white,' I answer. 'He's brown. I'd say he's of Asian ethnicity'.

Looking startled, the chairman asks the respondents' counsel, 'is it Jai Khanna?'

She turns around to Simon, sitting behind her, and confers with him in whispers. Then, she answers, 'yes, Sir'.

'What is his race?' the chairman asks.

Again, she confers with Simon and then, answers, 'Asian, Indian'.

# 9

# NEIL HOBSON'S TESTIMONY

~ Wednesday 6th December 2006, 10:00 a.m. ~

'I do solemnly, sincerely, and truly declare and affirm that the evidence I shall give shall be the truth, the whole truth, and nothing but the truth,' Neil says swearing in sitting isolated and exposed at the witness stand before the judges' bench.

I sit in the public gallery immediately behind my counsel with a clear side view of him. He has presented the tribunal his statement on the matters at hand. It says the following:

> I am one of the respondents in this case. I joined the bank ten years ago, in 1996. I have been in my current role, the Head of Market Risk Control and Reporting in the Market Risk Department, since December 2003.
>
> Up to December 2003, the Market Risk Control team consisted of three people, each separately reporting directly into Simon Ong, the Director of the Market Risk Department. In December 2003, Simon transferred one team member into another team in the department. Thus, the team shrank in size to two people, Ranjit Singh and the other member. Simon made the other member the head of the team, giving him the job title of Head of Market Risk Control. Simon reset Ranjit's reporting line into him, and his reporting line into me. Ranjit and the head of the team were unhappy with the change in the team's reporting line from

Simon to me. They believed it should continue to be directly into Simon.

In May 2004, we recruited Katia Mykonola into the team. Ranjit was involved in interviewing and selecting her.

In June 2004, the head of the team facilitated round table meetings to discuss the issue of the team's management reporting line, which included me, being inconsistent with the line of delegated authority, which excluded me. The whole team and I participated in the meetings. Katia did propose possible better reporting lines, but she did not criticise or object to the reporting line into me. It is incorrect to say that she objected as Ranjit did. I scored Ranjit down for having difficulty in accepting the change in the team's reporting line. Katia did not have this difficulty because she never worked under the previous reporting line into Simon. She never experienced the change of reporting line. She joined the bank under the team's reporting line into me. Hence, she was by default accepting of it because if she were not, then she would not have taken up employment with us.

Although the minutes of the workshop meeting evidence that the team were not happy with the management reporting line, they do not show that Katia failed to embrace the change positively. My opinion is that whilst there were times when Katia had issues with changes that were proposed or implemented, she was much more accepting of the changes than Ranjit. He was much more critical. The change to the team's reporting line in December 2003 is an example of this. The change had been implemented in December 2003. Yet, he was still unhappy about it in June 2004. His unhappiness continued into 2005 where, again, he suggested the team should report directly into

Simon. This validates my assessment in his 2005 year-end appraisal that he does not embrace change positively.

I remember that around July 2004, he approached his line manager, the head of his team, and me together and requested a meeting with us. In the meeting, he said he is not happy with the reporting line and wants to know whether voluntary redundancy is available for him to leave the bank. I discussed the matter with Simon. We did not want him to leave. So, I informed him that we want him to stay and that there would be no offer of voluntary redundancy. I believe this was a genuine approach by him for voluntary redundancy. It was not a situation where he made a comment in the heat of the moment as a reaction to something I had said.

Towards the end of 2005, we were under pressure to cut costs. So, I asked Simon whether I could approach Ranjit to check whether he would be interested in taking up voluntary redundancy because he previously requested it and is still unhappy about the team's reporting line. Although the bank does not have a formal policy regarding voluntary redundancy, it is keen to avoid compulsory redundancies where possible. I approached Ranjit because he had once indicated he would be interested in voluntary redundancy. Because Katia had never given any such indication, the lack of a formal voluntary redundancy policy at the bank meant that I could not approach her. Hence, I did not approach her. My approach to Ranjit was in no way motivated by race.

Around October 2004, the head of the team, into whom Ranjit and Katia reported, left the bank. Simon reset their reporting lines directly into me. Thus, I became their line manager.

Around the middle of 2005, we hired two junior team members, the Market Risk Associates, Anthony Grenfell and Mary Richardson. Anthony reported into Ranjit and Mary reported into Katia.

In August 2005, the bank's legal department confirmed to me that I did not have the power to overrule decisions made by Ranjit and Katia because Simon delegated his risk authorities to them directly, bypassing me.

In September 2005, Simon announced that the delegation of authority is to include me. That is, it is to flow from him to me and then, from me to Ranjit and Katia. Simon and I confirmed to both of them that this change is in no way any reflection on how they carried out their responsibilities and duties, and that there is no change to their roles. The only change is that the delegation of authority will flow to them via me, to be consistent with the management reporting line.

Katia did query Simon and me on whether this change is anything to do with the way she performed her role. However, Ranjit made it clear that he is unhappy with the change and is not clear why business practice needs to be modified thus. He queried why he was not consulted? He raised various concerns. He felt that the Controller role is being relegated and demoted. This is a clear example of Katia embracing a change in a much more positive way than Ranjit. She did not query whether the change is necessary or why she was not consulted before the decision was made. Her only concern was whether it is a reflection of her performance. When assured it is not, she did not query any further.

I suggested to Ranjit that he seek clarification from Simon as the change came from him. He did indeed take up the matter with Simon. He challenged whether there is a business need for the change, or whether it is driven by desire. This is in direct contrast to how Katia responded. Clearly, he was not accepting of the change. Katia distributed the revised departmental procedures to notify relevant parties about the change.

These are the reasons why I scored Katia up and Ranjit down regarding the change in the line of delegated authorities. She was more accepting of changes than he was.

Another example is where I once suggested a change to the bank's New Product Procedures. Ranjit responded that the procedures represent good practice that has been developed over time and is signed-off by senior management and relevant stakeholders. He said the procedures should not be changed unnecessarily. I believe a change should be incorporated if it improves the procedures, whether or not it is necessary. I believe he considered the change unnecessary while I considered it an improvement. I marked him down for this. But, he thinks the marking down is for another situation, the Risk Limits Policy, where he, Katia, and I all agreed to reject a proposed change. That is not the situation for which I marked him down.

On 17th October 2005, Simon, in his weekly heads of teams meeting, informed us there will be significant redundancies in the bank and that our department will not be immune. He asked us to review our teams for costs and efficiencies and to consider possible redundancies. I knew that the Market Risk Control team had operated well and without any detriment for three months while Ranjit was off sick or working from home with a broken leg. I also noted that some of the projects that we staffed the team up for by building it up to four people had not materialised. Whilst I appreciated that Ranjit worked from home for a period of his absence from the office due to his broken leg, I did consider how the team coped with just three people while he was fully off sick. Although he received emails at home from fairly early on, I did not consider this to be working from home. His official sick note is for eight weeks. So, I told Simon we could lose one Controller without any impact on the work and save costs. At this point, I had not made the decision as to which of the two Controllers would be selected to go.

Simon and I considered the option of losing the two junior Associates instead of one senior Controller. But, I decided it is not a viable option because it is very difficult to operate with a team of fewer than three people. In a team of just two people, if one person is out on leave and then the other becomes sick and goes off work, then there is no cover at all in the team. This is less likely to be the case with a team of three people.

Simon and I also considered the option of a team of two Controllers and one Associate, of losing just one Associate rather than both. However, I did not feel this is an effective or efficient team structure because it means having two managers and one subordinate. It would not work because it means either both managers manage the one subordinate or one manager retains management responsibility while the other loses it.

At this point, no decision had even been made that a Controller role would be made redundant in case there were other teams in the department where greater efficiency savings might be made.

If someone who wants to leave the bank voluntarily could be found, then it would save me having to make a compulsory redundancy. I raised the topic to Simon that Ranjit had enquired about voluntary redundancy once and that I assume he is still unhappy about the team's reporting line. Simon decided to take these things up with HR. Subsequently, he advised me that I could approach Ranjit informally to see if he is interested in voluntary redundancy. I approached him. He told me he is not interested.

Soon after, Simon told me that a reduction in the number of Controllers is required after all and asked me to carry out a compulsory redundancy exercise. I commenced it. Veronica Cotton, our department's HR Business Partner, guided me. I drafted up the redundancy rationale in time for the meeting with the union on 9th December 2005. I carried out the redundancy selection exercise. I picked the selection criteria that I thought reflect the work carried out by the Controllers. I performed the scoring to identify which of them is at risk of redundancy. Ranjit scored 18/24 and Katia scored 22/24. Ranjit, having the lower score, was selected for redundancy.

I attended the first collective consultation meeting with the union on 9th December 2005. The union was concerned that the redundant Controller's work cannot be re-allocated effectively between the remaining members of the team. So, I attended a second collective consultation meeting with the union on the 15th December where I provided further details on how the work will be re-allocated. The union was satisfied. It approved our decisions. Thus, we followed the bank's agreed process on collective consultation. We wanted to make the redundancy announcement before Christmas. But, the union told us to wait until after because it said it is not fair to put people at risk of redundancy before Christmas.

I performed Ranjit's 2005 year-end appraisal in time for the meeting with the union on 15th December. I communicated the appraisal results to him on 16th December.

When performing the redundancy scoring exercise, I scored Ranjit and Katia completely separately, on their own merits. I did not compare them to each other and score them relative to each other. I completed the scoring for one of them first, determining what score to award for each of the eight competencies, a 0, 1, or 2. Then, I closed down that person's scorecard and, later on, opened up the other person's scorecard to complete. Thus, not having both scorecards open simultaneously, I could not compare them to each other and decide what scores to award them relative to one another. I could not know until I finish the scoring exercise which of them has the lower score and is identified as redundant. When I finished, I opened up both scorecards and saw that Ranjit happened to have the lower score.

I commented on Ranjit's appraisal that occasionally he needs to take greater account of the regulator's requirements and embrace change more positively. This comment is with regards to the following: the issues in relation to the change in the team's reporting line in 2003; the issues of the line of delegated authority; and his attitude to changing the New Product Procedures.

When the change in the team's reporting line was implemented in 2003, Ranjit was critical of the change. He was still unhappy about it in the middle of 2004 when he enquired whether voluntary redundancy is available to him to leave the bank. This evidences that he does not embrace change positively.

To clarify, I am not saying Ranjit is a poor performer or a bad worker. It is merely that against some of the selection criteria it is appropriate to mark him down.

Although I set Ranjit an appraisal objective to develop his role to be an autonomous one and to make the team more self-reliant and autonomous, I do not believe that my criticism that he rarely discusses issues with me is inconsistent with this objective. By autonomous, I mean making decisions within the remit of his delegated authority and dealing directly with others rather than through me. I do not mean he does not need to discuss important decisions with me, his line manager. He did not need my authority to make decisions. But, on occasion, on critical issues, he should have involved me more than he did. This is why I marked him down. He usually informed me by email after the event. On one occasion, this resulted in a situation where if he had consulted me beforehand, then we could have discussed a decision to pre-notify or post-notify the FSA. Whereas, when I was not consulted beforehand, whilst I could stipulate there is a need to pre-notify, the best we could do after the event in one case was to post-notify. In contrast, Katia regularly ran important decisions past me as a sounding board. That is one of the reasons why I did not mark her down.

Another example is where a clause was added to the Single Equities Portfolio in April 2005 to permit the trading of more stocks and shares. This increase in scope is a pre-notification item. Ranjit post-notified the FSA on the basis that the change impacts Appendix 1 of the FSA's compliance document. In September 2005, the FSA said that all changes, including those to Appendix 1, should be pre-notified. This is different to our normal practice up to then of post-notifying on Appendix 1 matters, which was based on supplementary email correspondence from the FSA saying Appendix 1 matters may be post-notified. At this point, I became aware that the change was not pre-notified. Ranjit should have pre-notified, not post-notified. This is an error in judgement on his part for which I marked him down.

Regarding my criticism of Ranjit that he considers praise from me patronising. There is an occasion where I sent both Katia and Ranjit an email setting out my expectations of them. I copied other members of the department in on the email. Both Katia and Ranjit told me it is unnecessary for me to copy in others on this email. I can understand how they could perceive my action of copying in the others as being patronising, even though it was not intended to be. This is not what I marked Ranjit down for, though. I marked him down for considering praise from me patronising. I had asked him to carry out certain work. When it was done, I emailed him saying, well done. His email response clearly shows that he found my praise patronising. I never had a situation with Katia where she found praise from me patronising. Any time I praised her, she just thanked me. She never once said to me that she finds praise from me patronising.

In January 2005, Ranjit brought to my attention a matter on the Managed Income Portfolio that he and I agreed we would notify the FSA about. I thought this is a matter that should be pre-notified. But, Ranjit and others in the department, but not Katia, advised me they did not think it is a pre-notification matter. I therefore changed my view and asked Ranjit to post-notify the FSA. But then, he informed us that he has decided there is no need to tell the FSA at all about this. He said we could discuss it with the FSA at an upcoming meeting. Then, he informed us that he has decided the item is not material enough to be brought up at the upcoming meeting. After the FSA meeting, I discovered that he had changed my decision without consulting me. Both Katia and I thought this is a pre-notification item. My criticism of Ranjit on this is justified and is not discriminatory. It is only this year in July 2006, when Ranjit flagged up to Nathan Wilcox in his grievance hearing that I have never taken any corrective action myself to rectify the error that I had discovered, that I realised the FSA still has not been told. So, I immediately took it upon myself and notified the FSA.

On 11th January 2006, I informed Ranjit that he is at risk of redundancy. I then had a meeting with the rest of the team and informed them they are not at risk. Veronica and I held Ranjit's initial individual consultation meeting with him on 12th January.

I am satisfied that I followed the bank's standard redundancy process. Ranjit said he does not think the bank's process satisfies the legal requirements and that the union could not represent him because he is not a member of it. I told him there is a two-week consultation period, that he is merely identified as being at risk of redundancy at the moment, and that a definite decision has not yet been made. He expressed that he is shaken and distressed by what is happening. He said he does not believe the process complies with the legal requirements and he was not consulted with. He said the union confirmed to him that it does not represent him. He said he would be happy to be redeployed in a vacancy in another area of the bank. He said he disputes the appraisal score. At his request, Veronica and I agreed to hold a further consultation meeting with him. We had that on 18th January 2006. We then had two further consultation meetings with him, on 19th and 23rd January.

In the meeting on 23rd January, he suggested that rather than losing a Controller, we lose one or even both of the Associates. I rejected his suggestion for the reasons I have given already. I told him that I believe the way I have restructured the team represents the most cost effective and efficient use of resources. He disagreed with my answer, challenging whether it is something I merely believe in or whether it is an actual fact. Whilst I accept that it is possible to restructure the team the way he was suggesting and while I can see why he might suggest it, I did not feel it is in the bank's best interest to agree with his proposal.

Ranjit lodged a formal grievance on 23rd January complaining that the redundancy process is unfair. He did not make any mention in it of being racially discriminated against.

If he had gained full marks on the competencies scorecard and his appraisal score is increased to the same as Katia's, then his total redundancy score would be the same as Katia's. Then, there would be a tie situation between them. Then, we would look at their absence records to break the tie. He had a higher level of absence than Katia because he broke his leg in August 2005. Thus, he still would be the one selected for redundancy.

On 20th March, I attended Ranjit's grievance hearing about his redundancy, chaired by Jackie Monroe. The panel of judges questioned me about the redundancy process that I had followed. I was not involved in the decision-making regarding the outcome of the hearing.

On 6th April, I attended the hearing on his bonus grievance, held by Colin Marr. Ranjit had given his consent for me to be present.

On 4th July, I had a meeting with Nathan Wilcox regarding Ranjit's race discrimination grievance. I was not involved in deciding the outcome of the grievance. Then, on 21st August, Adrian Brent had a meeting with me regarding Ranjit's race discrimination appeal. This meeting ended my involvement with Ranjit's race discrimination issue.

My only involvement with Ranjit thereafter was to check the job market for vacancies that he is potentially qualified to undertake. I believe the job market in market risk is very buoyant. I am very surprised that he has not yet found alternative employment, especially because he was made redundant and hence, there is no issue surrounding the reason why he left the bank.

I am named personally as an individual respondent to his claim of race discrimination. I deny that I discriminated against him at all.

'Mr Hobson, is that your signature on the witness statement and is that the evidence you wish to give?' his counsel asks.

'Yes,' he answers.

Addressing the chairman, she says, 'Sir, I wish to bring up some supplementary issues'.

'Do so now so the claimant's counsel may have the chance to cross-examine the respondent on them,' the chairman replies.

'Thank you, Sir,' she says. Addressing Neil, she asks, 'what is the Single Equities Portfolio issue?'

'In April 2005, an amendment was made to an internal

policy allowing the traders to trade stocks that were previously not permitted,' he answers. 'Later, in September, during the FSA's visit to our office, I discovered that Ranjit had decided that the change in the policy is a post-notification item because it is in Appendix 1 to our agreement with the FSA, rather than being in the main body of the document. I thought it should be a pre-notification item'.

'How did the FSA become aware of it?' she asks.

'At its September visit,' he replies. 'There, the FSA clarified that it should be a pre-notification item. Subsequently, we amended the FSA's agreement document to reflect that changes impacting Appendix 1 should be pre-notification items'.

'What was Katia's view on this?' she asks.

'She thought it is a pre-notification item too,' he answers.

'Moving on to the Managed Income Portfolio,' she says. 'What was your understanding of what Ranjit would do?'

'He had decided not to notify at all,' he replies. 'But, he said that he would tell the FSA about it at its next regular visit, which was about a month away. I understood that he would discuss it with the FSA'.

The chairman interjects, 'you thought there is a need to post-notify. Did you accept his view?'

'I thought the FSA needs to be told about it,' he answers. 'I would be happy so long as they were told. It didn't matter if it was by a formal post-notification or an informal discussion'.

The chairman signals his counsel to continue.

'Moving on,' she resumes. 'Ranjit says that when he and Katia recommend Simon Ong to implement a change, they say, *"Market Risk Control recommends you approve the change"*. He says they omitted this phrase from the email regarding the change in the line of delegated authorities because they did not recommend the change be implemented. Is this true?'

'They are responsible for proposing any changes to the risk procedures that need Simon's approval,' he answers. 'I would not necessarily look out for the phrase. Its inclusion or omission does not mean they approve or disapprove of the change. Anyway, their attitude is what matters. In terms of attitude, Katia only asked me whether the change is due to any issue with her performance, whereas he raised issues with the change'.

The chairman interjects, 'Mr Singh says he and Miss Mykonola discussed the change over the phone and they both thought the same things'.

'If those phone calls happened, then I wasn't privy to them,' he replies. 'Katia only asked me whether the change is because she had done something wrong, that's all. As far as I am concerned, she was happy with the change and he was unhappy, raising issues like it is unnecessary and it creates inefficiencies'.

The chairman signals his counsel to continue.

'Moving on to your conversation with Ranjit regarding voluntary redundancy,' she resumes. 'Did you use the term *"quids in"*?'

'No,' he answers. 'It was a very brief conversation. I didn't use those words'.

The chairman interjects, 'did you say that a redundancy is about to happen in the department and you would rather avoid a compulsory redundancy if there is someone who wants to leave voluntarily?'

'Hmm,' he deliberates. 'Yes,' he answers. 'That's what I said, I'm sure'.

'This conversation happened on the 22$^{nd}$ November 2005?' the chairman asks.

'Yes,' he answers.

'Do you recall that date, or do you just agree it is the date because someone said it is?' the chairman asks.

'That's the date. I recall it,' he answers. 'He told me he isn't interested and that was the end of our meeting'.

'No further evidence in chief, Sir,' his counsel says.

The chairman signals my counsel to cross-examine the respondent.

Addressing Neil, she says, 'you say it is clear that the Single Equities Portfolio matter in April 2005 is a pre-notification item'.

'Yes. I stand by that,' he replies.

'Did Katia take the same view as you?' she asks.

'Yes,' he answers.

'The email correspondence on this matter, on which you and Katia are copied in, seems to show that you both agree with Ranjit's view,' she puts to him.

'Er, we're speaking generally there,' he answers.

'If it is clear to you that he made an error in April 2005, then surely there should be some comeback on him straight away,' she says. 'But there is no comeback on him until eight months later, during his appraisal meeting in December'.

'I didn't become aware until September that he hadn't pre-notified. That's when the FSA highlighted it to me,' he replies.

My counsel looks at him and waits for an explanation. But, he says nothing more.

The chairman interjects, 'Mr Hobson, you purposely avoided explaining why you didn't say anything to him in September. This is not a rebuke, we always warn each witness once. You need to answer the question properly. Otherwise, it may have an impact on the tribunal's ability to trust your evidence'. Addressing my counsel, he says, 'ask the question again'.

'The error is brought to your attention in September,' she resumes. 'You do not bring it to his attention at any time during the three months prior to his appraisal meeting in December,' she says.

'No,' he answers. 'Er, he was out of the office with a broken leg. December is the first time I saw him'.

'You do not make any criticism or take any disciplinary

action at all in the three months prior to the appraisal,' she says.

'No,' he replies. 'The place to bring it to his attention is in our weekly one-to-one meetings. But, he was out of the office. The first time I saw him is in December'.

'He is working from home,' she says. 'You do not raise it by phone or email?' she asks.

'No. The place to bring it up is in our weekly one-to-one meetings,' he answers.

'He returns to the office in November. If it is so clearly an error, then you could have raised it with him in November,' she puts to him.

'I raised it as soon as I could, which was in December,' he replies adamantly.

'The reason you did not raise it at any time before his appraisal is because it is not an error,' she says.

'It is an error,' he replies.

'Moving on to the Managed Income Portfolio item,' she says. 'You say you understood that he would discuss it with the FSA at the April meeting. But later on, after the meeting, you discover that without telling you he changed his mind and did not discuss it at all with the FSA'.

'That's correct,' he replies.

'But in an email that you and Katia are copied in on, dated the 21st of February, he says quite plainly that this item will not be highlighted to the FSA'.

'Yes,' he replies.

'He tells you what he is going to do and you do not reply on it,' she says.

'No,' he says. 'I didn't need to reply because I had already expressed my view in earlier emails'.

'If you disagree with what he tells you he is going to do, then you would shout out, as he put it in his testimony yesterday,' she says.

'Not necessarily,' he replies. 'He had the delegated authority to decide what to do. I had expressed my views already. He, Katia, and I are the collective consciousness of the department and we think we should always err on the side of caution. We think it's better to notify the FSA than not,' he replies.

'You cannot always err on the side of caution,' she says. 'It is not efficient to pre-notify when there is no need because the FSA could take up to thirty days to respond, which would hamper business activity unnecessarily'.

'That's correct,' he replies.

'He tells you openly what he is going to do. You have the chance to say something if you think he is doing the wrong thing. You do not say anything because you do not think he is doing anything wrong,' she says.

'I didn't say anything because it was his decision. He had the delegated authority to make the decision,' he replies.

'You had weekly one-to-one meetings between February and June. You do not give him any comeback on his decision in all that time?' she says.

'No,' he replies.

'At the end of June, you conduct his 2005 mid-year appraisal. You give him no comeback in it,' she says.

'No,' he replies.

'If it is clearly a pre-notification matter to you, you would give him comeback in his mid-year appraisal. You clearly do not,' she says. 'Your emails show that you initially consider it to be a pre-notification matter. Later, you change your view and consider it to be a post-notification matter. Then, later on, you change your view again and think it is not a notification matter at all, but that it should be discussed with the FSA. Then, on the 21st of February, he tells you clearly in his email that there is no need to discuss it with the FSA'.

'I was happy for him to discuss it with the FSA, but he went back on his agreement with me to do that. He knew what my view was. He should have made the FSA aware of it in some way. He didn't give due care to the FSA's requirements. So, I raised that in his year-end appraisal'.

The chairman interjects, 'he told you clearly that he will not discuss it with the FSA at the upcoming April meeting. You said nothing about the appropriateness of that. If you thought it is wrong, then you would have said something'.

'I thought it's an error of judgement on his part. But, it was his decision to make,' he answers. 'I think the FSA would have wanted to know about it. He should give more attention to the FSA's requirements'.

My counsel resumes, 'Katia is copied in on the email in which he says the item will not be discussed with the FSA. You say Katia is part of the department's collective consciousness. Why does she not shout out?'

'The Single Equities Portfolio is his responsibility alone, not Katia's as well. Although they cover for each other, it's not for Katia to overrule him,' he answers.

'But, if one member of the team makes a mistake, it reflects badly on the whole team, right?' she asks.

'Yes,' he replies.

'Would an FSA sanction reflect badly on the whole team?' she asks.

'Yes,' he answers.

'So, you or Katia would shout out if he is making a mistake,' she says.

'Not necessarily,' he replies. 'We both receive about a hundred emails a day. Just because we're copied in on them doesn't mean we agree with what's in them'.

'Either Katia does not see anything wrong with what he said he is going to do, or she also has a lax view of what needs to be reported to the FSA,' she puts to him.

'It was his responsibility, not Katia's,' he asserts.

'Moving on to the mater of embracing change,' she says. 'Ranjit went with you to a meeting with the bank's legal department to help you understand what the delegation of authority means'.

'Yes. It's a subject that was important to both of us,' he answers. 'We both had different views of it. So we both went to seek clarification'.

'The legal department clarified that you had misinterpreted what the line of delegated authority means,' she says.

'Hmm, it clarified that Ranjit's understanding is, er, more accurate than mine,' he replies tactfully.

'Part of his job is to challenge, correct?' she says.

'Yes,' he replies.

'One of his appraisal objectives for the year is to develop the Controller role to be autonomous, correct?' she asks.

'Yes,' he answers.

'Another of his appraisal objectives is to give challenge and feedback, correct?' she asks.

'Yes,' he replies.

'That's what he does when considering proposed changes,' she says.

'Yes. He provides a view,' he replies.

'He challenged the need to change the line of delegated authorities to include you in it,' she says.

'Yes. He opposed the need for me, his line manager, to be included,' he answers. 'He had the right to do that,' he adds.

'It was his job to challenge and protest if things do not make good sense to him,' she says. 'Especially, if he is concerned risk procedures will become weaker or inefficient'.

'I'm not sure what his concerns were,' he replies. 'There was no change to his role. He should not have been concerned. Raising concerns is not the problem. The problem is the way he raised them. Katia's only concern was whether the change is due to her acting wrongly in anyway. Simon and I confirmed to both of them that the change is in no way any reflection of how they perform their roles. It's to make the line of delegated authority consistent with the management reporting line'.

'Katia also expressed the same concerns as he. Otherwise, she would not comment in her year-end appraisal that she gave detailed feedback on the change to the delegated line of authority,' she says.

'No, she didn't,' he replies. 'Her only concern was whether the change is due to her having done anything wrong'.

'That doesn't sound like giving *"detailed feedback"*, as she puts it in her appraisal,' she says.

'Objection!' his counsel interjects. 'Mr Hobson cannot answer why Miss Mykonola wrote that in her appraisal'.

The chairman interjects, 'Mr Hobson, is Miss Mykonola still working for you?'

'Yes,' he answers.

Addressing his counsel, the chairman says, 'am I correct in thinking the respondents have chosen not to adduce evidence from her directly?'

'Yes, Sir,' his counsel replies.

'Hmm,' the chairman muses and then, signals my counsel to continue.

'Was Katia supportive of the change?' she continues.

'Once she understood that it isn't due to her having done anything wrong and that her role isn't changing in anyway, then she had no objections,' he says. 'But supportive is too strong a word. She had no objections'.

'On the 12th of September, Ranjit writes to you while working from home. He assures you that whilst he flags up concerns about the change, he and Katia are both working together on implementing the change as instructed,' she says.

'Yes. But, he was still unhappy and did not accept the change,' he replies.

The chairman interjects, 'he did not act in any way contrary to the change, correct? He did not protest for any longer than he should, correct? He complied with the change when it became effective, correct?'

'Correct,' he replies. 'But, my feedback is about his mental attitude to change, not his behaviour. He didn't personally accept the change'.

'Mr Hobson,' the chairman says, 'do you agree that there is a difference between accepting something personally and getting on practically with doing the job. For example, there are parts of the law that I do not like personally. I think they are unjust. But, it is the law and I get on with my job of applying it as it stands'.

'Yes, I do,' he answers.

My counsel continues, 'you reply to him confirming that you appreciate he is working with Katia to implement the change as instructed even though he has concerns and while he is working from home with a broken leg'.

'Yes,' he replies. 'He took a professional attitude and I appreciated him doing so'.

The chairman interjects, 'so, he went along with the change even though he did not agree with it?'

'Er,' he mumbles. 'Yes,' he admits reluctantly.

My counsel continues, 'in the period from September, when the change arose, up to his appraisal meeting in December, you raise nothing with him about his attitude to the change. You make no criticisms of him regarding it'.

'That's correct,' he answers. 'Er,' he mumbles. 'I don't think there were any one-to-one meetings in that period. But, this aspect about him not embracing change stretches back to previous years. He and I have different opinions about the team's reporting line. He thinks it should report directly into Simon. It was quite clear to me what he thinks. I knew what he thinks. I didn't need to discuss it with him any further,' he replies.

'He is in hospital for a week only,' she says. 'He is out and working from home by the 16th of August. He works at home till the 11th of November. You do not raise anything about his attitude to him over the phone or via email prior to his appraisal. You say his attitude stretches back over the years. Yet, you did not record it as an issue in any of his previous appraisals'.

'No,' he answers.

'You never tell him at anytime that he is failing to embrace change,' she says.

'Not in those exact words,' he replies.

'You never say anything to him remotely like: you have a poor attitude to change and need to change it,' she puts to him.

'Not in so many words,' he answers.

'Moving on to the patronising comment,' she says. 'It is true, is it not, that Katia also has the view that you are patronising? You send her an email that she thinks is telling her something very obvious. She comes and speaks to you about it, does she not?'

'Yes. I remember her coming and speaking to me on one occasion,' he replies.

'Does she express herself very passionately and angrily?' she asks.

'On one occasion, yes,' he answers.

'She tells you she finds you patronising,' she says.

'I'm not sure she used that exact word,' he answers.

'You do not mark her down for it,' she says.

'I didn't mark Ranjit down for that either,' he replies. 'I marked him down for something different. I marked him down for finding praise from his line manager patronising'.

'The praise is not strictly from his line manager. You do not mange him on the SPAYN business, Simon does. Simon holds one-to-one meetings directly with him on SPAYN,' she says.

'I disagree,' he replies. 'He was working on SPAYN as a project for Simon. But, Simon was not his line manager, I was. He only had one line manager, that was me'.

'The SPAYN work is something he finds trivial and easy,' she says.

'I didn't think it's an easy piece of work,' he replies.

'You send him an email saying well done on something that he thinks is easy,' she says.

'I didn't think it's easy,' he replies. 'He did a good job. I was saying well done for that'.

'That occurs in November 2004,' she says.

'Yes,' he answers.

'You do not criticise him there and then that he finds praise from his line manager patronising,' she says. 'Nor do you raise it on his 2004 year-end appraisal in December'.

'No,' he confirms.

'You do not raise it six months later on his 2005 mid-year appraisal in June,' she puts to him.

'No,' he confirms.

'So, how can it be important enough to appear over a year later, in December 2005, in the redundancy selection exercise?' she asks.

'Er,' he mumbles. 'I mentioned it to him in our one-to-one meetings,' he replies. 'Er, anyway, I didn't mark him down specifically for this. It's just one of the factors that contributed overall to marking him down because it told me that he's unhappy with me being his line manager'.

'Katia is also unhappy with you as her line manager,' she asserts.

'But, he didn't respect me as his line manager,' he replies nervously.

'Neither does Katia,' she asserts. 'You do not mark her down similarly'.

'It's different with her,' he replies, his voice croaking and his legs trembling. 'I shouldn't have sent her that email. I shouldn't have copied in all those people. I apologised to her'.

'Both Katia and Ranjit make similar accusation at you, that you are patronising. You hold it against one, but not against the other,' she says.

'With Katia, I made a mistake. I didn't make a mistake with Ranjit,' he replies.

'Moving on,' she says. 'You criticise that he rarely discusses issues with his line manager'.

'That's right,' he replies. 'He didn't discuss matters until after he'd decided on them. He's very confident'.

'You set him the appraisal objective, *"to be autonomous and self-reliant"*,' she says.

'That doesn't mean not to discuss things with his line manager,' he replies.

'You had regular weekly one-to-one meetings with him. Did he not discuss things with you in those meetings?' she asks.

'Yes, he did,' he answers. 'But, during the rest of the week, he didn't seek my opinions'.

'We do not have available here at the tribunal all of the email correspondence that he ever had with you. But, we do have emails relating specifically to this case. They evidence that he discusses things with you regularly,' she says.

The chairman interjects, 'Mr Hobson, Mr Singh had a certain level of authority delegated to him, did he not?'

'That's right,' he answers. 'But, that doesn't mean he shouldn't discuss things with me'.

'If a subordinate is not discussing matters with his superiors that he really ought to be,' the chairman says, 'then one would expect there to be situations that go wrong or fail. Can you give the tribunal examples of such failures?'

'Er, hmm,' he mumbles. 'Well, there's the failure to pre-notify the FSA about the Single Equities Portfolio,' he replies.

'Yes. Do continue,' the chairman says. 'We are listening. I have my pen poised to note them down'.

'Er, hmm, there must be some others,' he mumbles, his voice croaking and his hands trembling uncontrollably. 'But, I can't think of any off the top of my head'.

Resting his pen down on his notepad, the chairman says, 'Mr Hobson, I am looking for examples from you to justify the criticism you make of Mr Singh. If you cannot think of examples, then clearly your criticism is very subjectively made. Another manager can quite reasonably think instead that Mr Singh gets on with his job and praise him for it. Subjective comments need to be justified. Can you think of anything else, other than the Single Equities Portfolio item?'

'Well, Katia had the same level of authority,' he replies, 'but, she checked with me first before making her decisions, in case I know something relevant that she isn't aware of. He didn't do that'.

'Why is that necessarily something to mark him down for?' the chairman asks.

'Because there is the Single Equities Portfolio notification failure,' he replies.

'Just one failure?' the chairman says. 'If you give someone the authority to act autonomously and be self-reliant, then you have to accept that there are bound to be a few mistakes now and then, and you have to be willing to tolerate them. It is wrong of you to mark him down in this way,' he asserts.

'Well, I regularly tell my line manager what I'm doing. I expect my subordinates to do the same to me,' he answers back.

The chairman signals my counsel to continue.

'Another manager could quite reasonably mark Katia down for not being autonomous,' she says.

'Huh,' he snorts. 'A manager who doesn't want to be consulted, then maybe yes,' he replies in sarcastic tone.

'There are at least fifty emails here evidencing that he discusses matters with you regularly, both orally and by email. It is not the case that he rarely discusses things with you,' she puts to him.

'Fifty isn't a lot,' he replies.

'When the tribunal asked you for examples of things that he did not discuss with you beforehand which then went wrong, you could only put forward one example,' she says.

'One example where there is a failure,' he replies. 'There are many other times he didn't discuss things with me but which did not result in failures. He should have come to check with me a lot more often than he did whether I know things that he might be unaware of'.

The chairman interjects, 'clearly, the number of interactions a subordinate needs to have with his superior depends on the nature of the work, would you agree, Mr Hobson?'

'Yes,' he replies.

'He did not come to you every five minutes. But, he also did not shut himself up for the whole week until your weekly one-to-one meeting with him, correct?' the chairman asks.

'That's right,' he answers.

'When did you become his line manager?' the chairman asks.

'In October 2004,' he answers.

'When is the first time you formed the view that he rarely discusses things with you,' the chairman asks.

'Within a couple of months,' he replies. 'He had delegated authority and was very confident. He kept me updated after making his decisions. Others asked me questions regularly. I didn't get that from him. He rarely sought my advice or checked with me prior to making his decisions. Ninety-nine per cent of the times, there were no negative consequences of his decisions. But, occasionally, there were'.

'Is the issue that there was a lack of face-to-face interaction on his part,' the chairman asks.

'He tended to communicate via email while others would communicate in person too,' he replies.

'Did that concern you?' the chairman asks.

'Not specifically,' he answers. 'I'm happy with communication by either method. He just didn't communicate as often as others did'.

'At your weekly one-to-one meetings, did you tell him you expect more interaction from him?' the chairman asks.

'Er, I told him to keep me updated on things,' he replies.

'Did you instruct him to notify you of things in advance of his decisions?' the chairman asks.

'Er, I told him he needs to consult me just as he would consult with Katia,' he replies.

The chairman signals my counsel to continue.

'You say occasionally his behaviour had serious consequences. You give just one occasion, the Single Equities Portfolio,' she says.

'Yes, one,' he replies.

'One is not occasionally,' she asserts.

'One in terms of where there is a negative consequence, where there is a failure,' he replies.

'You tell him to keep you updated. If he thinks updated means update you after he has made his decisions, then there is nothing wrong with that interpretation. Your instruction is open to both interpretations,' she asserts.

'That's not what I meant,' he replies. 'He couldn't have all the information relevant to decisions if he didn't talk to me beforehand and check whether I know something he isn't aware of'.

'You have no concerns about this in 2004 and the first half of 2005,' she says.

'I did have this concern during that time too,' he replies.

'But, it could not be a material concern because you do not record it on his 2004 year-end appraisal, nor on his 2005 mid-year appraisal,' she says.

'It wasn't material then,' he replies.

'But, it was material enough for you to raise in the redundancy selection exercise,' she says.

'Er, it became material from September 2005, when I discovered the Single Equities Portfolio error,' he replies.

'You give him a glowing 2004 year-end appraisal saying, *"he has performed well during a year of significant change and has successfully delivered on all of his accountabilities"*,' she says.

'Yes. I was pleased with him,' he replies.

'You do not record there your concern about his level

of interaction with you,' she says.

'It was something I was concerned about. But, I didn't record it on the appraisal,' he replies.

'And the appraisal prior to that one, the 2004 mid-year appraisal. He gets a glowing appraisal again. No concerns recorded on it about his level of communication,' she asserts.

'I didn't do that appraisal. I wasn't his line manager then. The then Head of Market Risk Control was his line manager at the time. He appraised him then, not I,' he replies.

'If his line manager at the time had concerns, he would have recorded them in the appraisal, correct?' she asks.

'I don't know,' he replies. 'I don't know what their relationship was'.

The chairman interjects, 'what do you mean by that, Mr Hobson?'

'Ranjit might have behaved differently towards him,' he replies.

'You recorded no adverse comments on the 2005 mid-year appraisal, which you conducted, correct?' the chairman asks.

'Correct,' he answers.

'Because there were no issues then,' the chairman asserts.

'No,' he replies, 'because he hadn't made any errors up to then'.

The chairman signals my counsel to continue.

'You are a manager,' she resumes. 'You do not wait for errors to occur. You manage proactively. You tackle concerns head on to pre-empt issues. You do not discuss any concerns with him and you do not record any concerns in his appraisal,' she puts to him.

'I agreed with him that he should inform me as and when needed,' he replies. 'That was fine until the Single Equities Portfolio error occurred'.

'Moving on,' she says. 'Where is your office situated in

relation to the HR department?'

'I'm on the first floor. They're on the fourth. We're a few minutes walk from each other,' he replies.

'On the 17th of October 2005, Simon Ong tells his direct reports, including you, to review their teams regarding redundancy. Your initial thought is that you can lose a Controller,' she says.

'It was the first option I thought of because the team had operated well with just one Controller while Ranjit was off ill. But, I considered other options too,' he replies.

'On the 22nd of November 2005, you approach Ranjit with an offer of voluntary redundancy,' she says.

'No,' he replies. 'I asked him if he is interested in me finding out from HR whether voluntary redundancy is a possible option'.

'You do that with a view to avoid a compulsory redundancy?' she asks.

'Yes,' he answers.

'If he were interested, would you have gone to HR?' she asks.

'Yes,' he replies.

'You do not make any similar approach to Katia,' she says.

'No. She hadn't ever expressed any interest in voluntary redundancy,' he replies.

'If you want to retain someone, you do not suggest voluntary redundancy to them, do you?' she asks.

'We were expecting to make a Controller redundant,' he replies. 'As only Ranjit had expressed an interest in voluntary redundancy, I asked only him if he is still interested'.

'So, you were not at all concerned about whom you wished to retain?' she asks.

'I'd rather someone who wants to go be the one who leaves,' he answers. 'I gave consideration to who wants to go, not to what I want to happen'.

'So, Katia and Ranjit are equally competent. It does

not matter to you which one of them remains?' she asks.

'They have different strengths,' he replies.

'You approach Ranjit exclusively because you want him specifically to leave,' she puts to him.

'No,' he replies. 'I asked only him because only he had previously expressed an interest in voluntary redundancy'.

'Why not ask everyone in the team who wants voluntary redundancy?' she asks.

'We didn't want to worry people unnecessarily,' he answers. 'I checked with Simon. He checked with HR that it's okay to approach Ranjit. Only after having obtained HR approval did I approach him'.

'If you would rather someone who wants to leave leaves, then is to ask everyone not the obvious thing to do?' she asks.

'No,' he answers.

'You wanted him to be the one who leaves,' she says.

'No,' he replies.

'He mentioned voluntary redundancy one and a half years prior to your approach,' she says.

'Yes,' he replies.

'Did he ever mention it again?' she asks.

'No,' he answers.

'His interest in voluntary redundancy was expressed in very specific circumstances, in an open team meeting and as a reaction to something you had said,' she says.

'No,' he replies. 'His line manger at the time approached me and said Ranjit wants a private meeting. Katia was not present at the meeting. It was not a general open team meeting. It was a private meeting specifically about voluntary redundancy'.

'That is not true,' she says.

'It is true,' he replies.

'It was an open team meeting where Katia was present and where you said that because no one in the team had resigned over an issue, the issue cannot be so bad,' she puts to him. 'The account you are giving here is untrue,' she says.

'My account is true,' he asserts.

'Moving on,' she says. 'You use the 2005 year-end appraisal in the redundancy exercise, correct?'

'Yes,' he answers. 'HR instructed me to use the year-end appraisal, rather than the mid-year one'.

'You have not disclosed any emails from HR instructing you to use the year-end appraisal,' she puts to him.

'Er,' he mumbles. 'There aren't any emails. I went to see Veronica in person,' he replies. 'She told me orally'.

'Ranjit has no notice or warning that the appraisal is being used in a redundancy exercise,' she says.

'I wasn't advised that I need to tell him that a redundancy is taking place,' he replies.

'He has ten days to appeal his appraisal,' she says.

'That's right,' he answers.

'You conduct his year-end appraisal on the afternoon of Friday the 16th of December. He has ten days from then to lodge an appeal,' she says.

'Yes,' he answers. 'But, he didn't appeal it'.

'Immediately after conducting his appraisal, you go on annual leave without giving him the information he needs to draft up and articulate his appeal. You return to the office sixteen days later, on the 3rd of January,' she says.

'Yes,' he replies. 'But, I genuinely forgot to send him the information. It was the end of the working day. I was rushing around trying to finish things off before I head off for my leave. I genuinely just forgot. It happens'.

'Immediately on your return, he presses you for the information. You wait a whole week before supplying it to him,' she says.

'It couldn't be helped,' he replies. 'It was the first week of the bank's new financial accounting year. There're a lot of urgent things to tend to at that time, like plans and budgets. It's an extremely busy time. I got back to him as soon as I could'.

'You wait ten days to pass from your return to the office before you tell him of the redundancy,' she says.

'Yes,' he replies.

'You intentionally wait for the appraisal appeal-time to expire before you tell him there is a redundancy,' she asserts.

'No, not intentionally,' he replies. 'The union told us not to communicate news of the redundancy until after Christmas. The minutes of the meeting with the union say the redundancy will be communicated from the 9th of January'.

'The minutes do not say explicitly to wait until after Christmas,' she says. 'They do not show that the union instructed you to wait until the 9th of January,' she clarifies. 'Did you think of extending the appeal-time, under the circumstances?' she asks.

'It's clear to everyone that they have only ten days to appeal,' he replies.

The chairman interjects, 'answer the question, Mr Hobson'.

'No, I didn't,' he answers. 'But, he still didn't appeal even after the appeal-time expired,' he adds.

'Because you and Veronica told him the redundancy consultation process takes over from the appraisal appeal process,' she says. 'Exactly when did you carry out the redundancy selection exercise?' she asks.

'On the 8th of December, in time for the collective consultation meeting with the union the next day,' he answers.

'The 9th of December is the date of the first of the two meetings with the union,' she says.

'Yes,' he replies.

'Who decided and chose the competencies that would be used in the scoring?' she asks.

'I did,' he answers. 'I selected them from a list of permitted competencies. I needed to select four competencies from the Technical category and four from the Behavioural category. I considered the list of available competencies and decided which ones are appropriate for the Controller role'.

'The minutes of the meeting with the union do not show that any discussions took place about the selection process,' she says. 'Does it follow that the union were told the results of the process only, but not given any details of the process itself or the selection competencies that you decided would be used for the scoring?' she asks.

'I told the union the result only. I didn't tell it any details about the process,' he answers.

'Why not?' she asks.

'I wasn't advised that I need to,' he answers.

The chairman interjects, 'Mr Hobson, we are trying to ascertain what the union knew about the methods by which you selected which Controller would be chosen for redundancy. Did you tell the union the details of the process that you applied?'

'They knew that I followed the bank's standard process and that I did the scoring,' he replies.

'The union expressed concerns about whether a Controller's work could actually be re-allocated fairly across the remaining members of the team,' the chairman says.

'Yes,' he replies. 'They wanted us to come back with a detailed breakdown of how the work would be re-allocated'.

The chairman signals my counsel to continue.

'So, for the first meeting with the union, who prepared the schedules showing how the workload would be re-allocated?' she asks.

'I did,' he answers.

'The schedule you present to the union labelled, *Current Duties*, lists the activities carried out individually by Ranjit and Katia, with estimated percentages assigned to each activity. Who created this list of activities and the percentages?' she asks.

'I did,' he answers.

'The other schedule, labelled, *Proposed Duties*, shows Ranjit with no duties and Katia with an increased workload. So, it is obvious to the union on the 9th of December that Ranjit, no longer having any duties allocated to him, is the one selected for redundancy,' she says.

'Yes,' he replies.

'You have a second meeting with the union on the 15th of December to allay their concerns about the re-allocation of the workload,' she says. 'Again, you do not tell the union any details of the process you applied, nor of the selection competencies you decided to use'.

'Er, hmm, I did go through all of that at that meeting,' he says.

'Really? The minutes of the meeting do not mention that you did,' she asserts.

'No, they don't. But, I did,' he replies.

'The end of this second meeting marks the end of the consultation with the union,' she says.

'Correct,' he replies.

'Did you do the scoring alone?' she asks.

'Yes,' he answers.

'Did anyone review or check the scoring you produced?' she asks.

'I talked it through with Veronica to check it is appropriate,' he answers.

'Did Veronica raise any issues?' she asks.

'She said I'm going into a lot of detail. She said my noting down that Ranjit had difficulty accepting the change in the team's reporting line in 2003 is unnecessary. She said it's unnecessary to note down that he thought the change in the line of delegated authorities amounts to a demotion of his role. She also commented that my noting down that he considers praise from me patronising is also unnecessary,' he replies.

'Even though she thinks some things are irrelevant, you

leave them in?' she asks.

'Yes,' he replies. 'The scoring represents my decisions and my words'.

The chairman interjects, 'what things did Miss Cotton want removed?'

'I can't remember,' he replies.

'Was it only the bits about the reporting line, demotion, and praise?' the chairman asks.

'I can't remember,' he answers.

'Did she say something that you do not want to tell us here?' the chairman asks.

'No, not at all,' he replies. 'She didn't give any specific feedback. She just checked if it seemed appropriate'.

The chairman signals my counsel to continue.

'You say you scored Ranjit and Katia separately, that you did not compare them to each other and score them relative to each other,' my counsel continues. 'You say you completed one person's competencies scorecard first, closed it down and then, some time later, you started and completed the other's. Thus, you say, you did not have open both scorecards simultaneously during the scoring, and hence, you could not compare them and score them relatively. You say you had no idea until the end of the scoring process, when you looked at both scorecards together to compare the bottom line results, which person is identified for redundancy'.

'Yes,' he replies.

'Looking at the comment you write on Ranjit's scorecard for the third competency, we see the first sentence reads, *"Internal controls are set and enforced appropriately through a series of mandates and limits, a number of which are under the direct delegated authority of the Market Risk Controllers",*' she says.

'Yes,' he answers.

'Would you agree that for the same competency on Katia's scorecard, the first sentence is exactly the same?' she asks.

'Yes,' he replies.

'It is rather a long sentence to write exactly the same across two scorecards when completing them separately and some time apart, as you say you did. Did you copy and paste that sentence from one scorecard to the other?' she asks.

'Er, hmm,' he mumbles. 'I can't remember,' he answers, strain showing across his face.

'Continuing reading,' she says, 'the second sentence you write for Katia says, *"Regulatory requirements are always given due attention"*. The second sentence you write for Ranjit reads, *"Regulatory requirements are not always given due attention"*. Exactly the same sentence, in the positive for Katia and in the negative for Ranjit, a mirror image'.

'Yes,' he replies.

'Did you copy and paste that sentence from one scorecard to the other and modify it to be positive or negative accordingly?' she asks.

'Er, hmm, I can't remember,' he answers. The strain across his face intensifies. 'I don't see what your point is'.

'I think you do remember and I think you know exactly what my point is, Mr Hobson,' she says. 'Let's continue looking at what you write,' she says. 'Looking now at the comment you write on both Ranjit's and Katia's scorecards for the sixth competency, we see that the comments start by saying exactly the same thing for both of them, that is, *"Sets high standards of control as evidenced by the unqualified Eurocredito Internal Audit Review and readily accepted additional maintenance recommended be migrated to the Market Risk Control team. Willing to stand ground resolutely defends the challenge role of Market Risk Control when questioned by other Market Risk teams. Willing to take a stand against the traders by refusing to grant"*. That is a very long comment indeed to write identically on two scorecards some time apart,' she puts to him. 'Clearly, Mr Hobson, you did not complete the scorecards separately, as you claim. Clearly, you had both scorecards open side-by-side and you completed them simultaneously, copying and pasting between them, comparing the two of them, intentionally marking Ranjit down relative to Katia to ensure he is the one selected for redundancy'.

'No, I did them separately,' he replies, but the strain across his face, now excruciating, betrays him.

'Let's continue and look at the comments you write for the eighth competency,' she says. 'On Ranjit's scorecard you write, *"Personal Development Plan highlights development needs focused on technical knowledge enhancement, recognising the need to continue to improve the technical knowledge that comes with the role"*. On Katia's, you write exactly the same thing up to the second instance of the word *"technical"*, where the sentence ends abruptly. The sentence does not make sense because the last six words, *"knowledge that comes with the role"*, are missing from it. Would you agree that this is a bit of sloppy copying and pasting on your part, Mr Hobson?'

'No. I know that's what it looks like, but I completed them separately,' he says, his voice croaking and his legs trembling.

'Then, you continue on that competency to write negative remarks on Ranjit's scorecard and reduce his score while awarding Katia full marks. You gave her full marks on every competency. The two scorecards are mirror images, Ranjit's being the negative and Katia's, the positive. Clearly, not coincidental, clearly, intentional, to ensure he is the one identified for redundancy,' she says.

'No, it wasn't intentional,' he replies, his hands also trembling now. 'That's just how they turned out. I completed them separately and objectively'.

'Not a single negative comment on Katia's scorecard,' she says. 'Does that not seem odd?'

'No,' he replies.

'Let's move on,' she says. 'Some of the competencies you decide to use in the scoring are highly subjective. You decide to use one competency called Conversion. Could you explain to us what Conversion means?'

'Er, hmm, I don't really know,' he answers.

'If you do not know, then why did you decide it would be one of the competencies that you would use in the scoring?' she asks.

'I don't know what it refers to. But, I know it concerns behaviour because the competency was listed under the Behavioural category. I think it means how an individual accepts change,' he replies.

'Look at the description the bank assigns to it,' she says pointing him to the description. 'Do you accept that the bank describes it to be about an individual's insight and capacity to learn?'

'Yes. But, I think that also means how the individual accepts change,' he replies.

'Having selected it, you praise both Ranjit and Katia under it for maintaining their technical knowledge,' she says. 'That seems consistent with what the competency is about. But then, for Ranjit, you criticise that he involves his line manager on a need-to-know basis only. That does not even have anything to do with accepting change, which you say is what you think the competency is about, let alone with insight and capacity to learn,' she says.

'I think it does,' he asserts.

'You are scoring him on how he works and interacts with his line manager. That is not scoring him on how he accepts change or on his capacity to learn,' she says.

'I disagree. I think it does,' he replies.

'You go on to note under this competency that he requested voluntary redundancy in the summer of 2004. That is irrelevant to this competency,' she says.

'I disagree,' he replies. 'It shows that he doesn't accept change'.

'You are taking into account things that are totally irrelevant to the competency because you decided beforehand that he will be the one to go,' she says.

'No,' he replies.

'Moving on,' she says. 'You do his 2004 year-end

appraisal. You give him a glowing appraisal. You record nothing negative in it'.

'Yes,' he confirms.

'You also do his 2005 mid-year appraisal. Again, you give him a glowing appraisal and record nothing negative in it,' she says.

'Yes,' he confirms.

'The first time you say anything negative is in his 2005 year-end appraisal, the one used in the redundancy. There you say, *"Occasionally, Ranjit needs to take greater account of the regulator's requirements and embrace change more positively",*' she says.

'Correct,' he replies.

'Is your negative comment the reason why his appraisal score is lowered?' she asks.

'It was taken into account,' he replies.

'The bank's policies state that there should be no surprises in the appraisal. They state that the manager should be monitoring the individual and providing feedback throughout the year, flagging up any performance concerns so that corrective action may be taken and so that there are no surprises in the appraisal,' she says. 'You do not flag anything to him prior to the appraisal meeting,' she says.

'I believe my emails to him throughout the year did that,' he replies.

'Never before the appraisal meeting do you say to him that he needs to take greater account of the regulator's requirements,' she says.

'I may not have used those exact words,' he replies.

'Not, may not, you did not,' she puts to him.

'I can't remember,' he replies.

'Your comment in the appraisal comes as a complete surprise to him,' she says.

'It was the first time I put it in writing,' he replies.

'It is the first time you put it in any form,' she says.

'I can't remember if I said it before,' he replies.

'You cannot remember because you did not say it,' she says.

'You can't say that,' he answers back.

The chairman interjects, 'Mr Hobson, if you cannot remember saying it, then you probably did not say it. Would you accept that is reasonable?'

'Er, yes,' he answers.

'You never prior to the appraisal tell him to embrace change more positively,' my counsel continues.

'Not in so many words,' he replies.

'So, the comment in the appraisal comes as a complete surprise to him,' she says.

'I wouldn't say it did,' he answers. 'I may not have said it to him during the year, but it's not as if there's no evidence that there's an issue'.

'It surprises him,' she asserts.

'I suppose it's possible it surprised him,' he replies in sarcastic tone.

'You knew the bank's policy, that there should be no surprises in the appraisal,' she says.

'Yes, I knew it,' he replies. 'But, he had concerns. I told him to accept things and get on with it'.

The chairman interjects, 'did you ever say to him anything like: I know you have concerns, but accept things with good grace and get on with it, otherwise it may be reflected in your appraisal?'

'Er, hmm, no,' he answers. 'Er, he was away a lot, I didn't have the chance'.

'He was working from home. You could have phoned him,' the chairman says. 'Do not tell me you do not have phones at the bank. I know you have them, I get enough annoying cold calls from your bank'.

'Er, hmm,' he deliberates. 'I didn't want to say that kind of thing over the phone,' he replies.

'But, you could have made it a priority on his return to the office,' the chairman puts to him.

'Yes,' he replies.

The chairman signals my counsel to continue.

'You do not raise any issues with him,' my counsel continues, 'because there are no issues'.

'No, that's not so,' he replies.

'But, when it comes to the redundancy, you make up these excuses,' she asserts.

'No. They're not excuses, they're legitimate issues,' he replies.

'You do not make a single negative comment on Katia's assessments. You do not look around for any reasons to mark her down,' she says.

'There weren't any issues regarding her. Besides, I scored Ranjit highly. It's just that Katia's score was even higher,' he replies.

'You mark him lower than you did in his two previous appraisals. You score him lower because of his race,' she puts to him.

'No, race never came into it,' he asserts.

'Can you offer any other explanation?' she asks.

'His performance just wasn't as good as it had been before. It was nothing to do with race,' he replies.

'You know he is protesting vigorously against his appraisal score,' she says.

'No, I didn't. He never appealed against it,' he replies.

'On the 10th of January, the day before you tell him he is at risk and while he does not know he is vulnerable, you know he is protesting his appraisal vigorously,' she says.

'No, I didn't. He never lodged any appeal against the appraisal score. All I knew is that he's a bit unhappy about my comment, but not seriously unhappy because he didn't appeal formally,' he replies.

'He is unhappy because he thinks the appraisal is unfair and unsupported,' she says.

'And I, his manager, thought the contrary,' he asserts.

'You make great play over his lack of formal appeal against the appraisal. But, you knew how strongly he felt,' she says.

'No, I knew no such thing,' he replies, 'because he didn't appeal'.

'On the 11th of January, you tell him he is at risk,' she says.

'Yes,' he confirms.

'Immediately after telling him he is at risk, you tell the rest of the team members that they are not at risk. He passes them on the stairs on their way to see you after he leaves you,' she says.

'Yes,' he confirms.

'If during the consultation period he convinced you to retain him, then you would have to tell the others that they are no longer safe, having already told them that they are safe,' she says.

'Yes,' he confirms.

'You would be reluctant to do that,' she puts to him.

'Yes,' he replies.

The chairman interjects, 'so, any proposal he came up with to avoid his redundancy that involved another redundancy would not be accepted. The only option he had was to convince you that no redundancy is necessary'.

'Er, hmm, I'm sure it was possible for something workable to be proposed,' he replies.

'Like what?' the chairman asks.

'If he came up with something that is cost efficient and better, then I would have considered it,' he answers.

'Tell us what you can think of that he could propose that does not involve making someone else redundant,' the chairman challenges him.

'Er, hmm, I can't think of anything off the top of my head,' he answers, his hands trembling.

'You told him he is at risk and you told the others they are safe. So, in what way is the two-week period that followed a consultation?' the chairman asks.

'He could have been redeployed elsewhere in the bank,' he replies.

'Redeployment, that was his only alternative to

redundancy?' the chairman asks.

'Yes,' he answers.

'In the first individual consultation meeting, on the 12th of January, he expressed to you how shocked he is,' the chairman says.

'Yes,' he confirms.

The chairman signals my counsel to continue.

'Moving on,' she says. 'Part of the reason why Ranjit is awarded a lower bonus for 2005 compared with 2004 must be because his 2005 appraisal score is lower'.

'Yes,' he replies.

'The size of an individual's bonus also depends on the size of the bonus pot allocated to the department. But, we do not know how big that is, do we?' she asks.

'No,' he replies. 'I'm not privy to that information'.

The chairman interjects, 'is there some method by which the size of the pot for the department is determined?'

'My understanding is that Simon decides how much each individual in the department should be awarded. He then sums the individual amounts to determine the total required for the department. Then, he makes a pitch to his superiors for the departmental total'.

The chairman signals my counsel to continue.

'Moving on,' she says. 'You've had no training in Diversity and Equal Opportunities, correct?'

'Correct,' he answers. 'I don't have the luxury of time to get away from my job to do courses. I've read some stuff on the Internet, though, but nothing specific. I'm not saying I'm not aware of the subject, though'.

'No doubt if someone asks you if you have any training, you would say no,' she puts to him.

'Correct,' he confirms.

'You say you have seen some stuff briefly. Do you remember seeing anything on race discrimination?' she asks.

'No,' he answers.

'Thank you,' she says. 'I have no further questions'.

Addressing his counsel, the chairman says, 'do you wish to re-examine your witness?'

'Yes, Sir, thank you,' she answers. Addressing Neil, she says, 'you say the issue is Ranjit's attitude. Could you expand on that?'

'His attitude, like highlighting issues about the change in the line of delegated authorities that Simon wanted implemented. It was Simon's decision. But, he couldn't accept the change is necessary. He thought it's being driven by desire,' he answers.

'I have no more questions,' she says.

The chairman gives way to the judge on his left to cross-examine him.

'Does Mr Singh's previous interest in voluntary redundancy have any bearing on him being selected for redundancy?' the judge asks.

'No,' he answers.

'But, you do note down his interest in voluntary redundancy on his redundancy scorecard,' the judge puts to him.

'Yes,' he confirms.

'Thank you, I have no more questions,' the judge says.

The chairman gives way to the judge on his right.

'When you received Mr Singh's email saying the Managed Income Portfolio item will not be brought to the FSA's attention, were you prohibited in any way from replying to it?' the judge asks.

'No,' he answers. 'But, er, I assumed he would tell the FSA. So, I didn't reply'.

'You could have replied saying something like: as your line manager, I instruct you to tell the FSA,' the judge puts to him.

'Er, no,' he answers. 'I didn't have the delegated authority at the time to tell him what to do. I only got such authority from September 2005, when the line of delegated authority was changed to include me'.

'But, you could have escalated it to Mr Ong, who did have the authority to instruct him what to do,' the judge puts to him.

'Yes,' he confirms.

'Did you do that?' the judge asks.

'No,' he answers.

'Thank you, I have no more questions,' the judge says.

'Mr Hobson,' the chairman resumes, 'what was your relationship with Mr Singh like?  Did you have any personal issue with him?'

'It was professional. There were no personal issues,' he answers.

'Hmm,' the chairman muses seeming unconvinced. 'Did you score him the way you did because of some personal relationship issue?' the chairman asks.

'No,' he answers.

'Hmm,' the chairman deliberates sitting back into his chair.

# 10

# SIMON ONG'S TESTIMONY

~ Thursday 7th December 2006, 3:00 p.m. ~

'Mr Ong, is that your signature on the witness statement and is that the evidence you wish to give?' the respondents' counsel asks him, he having just sworn in at the witness stand.

He has presented the tribunal his statement on the matters at hand. It says the following:

> I am the Director of the Market Risk Department at the bank. I report directly into the bank's Chief Risk Officer.
> 
> Up to December 2003, the Market Risk Control team consisted of three people, each separately reporting directly into me. In December 2003, I reorganised the team. I transferred one team member into another team in my department. Thus, the team shrank in size to two people, Ranjit Singh and the other member. I made the other member the head of the team, giving him the job title of Head of Market Risk Control. I reset Ranjit's reporting line into him, and his reporting line into Neil Hobson, who also managed another team for me.
> 
> Both Ranjit and the head of the team complained that they felt the team has been relegated as it used to report directly into me, the Director of the department. I was sensitive to their concerns. I ensured that I gave them every assurance possible that this is not a demotion of

their roles in any way, including continuing to have a weekly meeting with them to ensure they have direct access to me.

Then, in 2004, we recruited Katia Mykonola into the team alongside Ranjit. Later on, around October 2004, the head of the team left the bank. Neil and I agreed that to continue with a team of only two people is not viable in case of cover issues due to holidays and sickness. We decided we would hire two junior members, the Associates, to report into Ranjit and Katia. We wanted to over resource the team for two reasons. Firstly, there were plans to increase the amount of business. Secondly, Ranjit continued to express dissatisfaction with the team's reporting line being into Neil and expressed a desire to leave the bank if he were paid out. We wanted to allow for business growth and be ready for the risk of him resigning. This decision was taken prior to the bank being taken over by Eurocredito in September 2004.

Ever since the takeover by Eurocredito, there has been pressure at the bank to reduce costs and increase profitability. I understand 6,000 people have been made redundant. The redundancies programmes did not immediately impact my department because I took initiatives to combine teams to achieve efficiencies and benefit from natural attrition.

In July 2005, Ranjit was still unhappy with the team not reporting directly into me. He sent me an email on the matter.

He was also not happy later on, in September 2005, with the proposed change to the line of delegated authority. My impression is that he felt the change diminished his responsibility when, in fact, it did not. I had meetings with the team to reassure them.

From the middle of 2005, the Risk Division, of which my department is a component, was under pressure from senior management to look for ways to make cost savings. On 19th August 2005, senior management issued revised budgets for the remainder of the year. They involved a five per cent cost reduction in my department.

In the early part of October 2005, I held a meeting with all of my direct reports. I informed them that the Risk Division is under pressure and our department needs to achieve a small headcount reduction. I asked them all to consider their teams for possible staff cuts. Neil responded by coming to me with the proposal that the Market Risk Control team could function fine with one less Controller. He took me through his business rationale for his proposal. I accepted it as being rational. We agreed. I remember Neil explained that he also considered whether the team could function with two Controllers and no Associates. I believe teams of only two people do not work because there is a risk of both members being off work at the same time, like when one becomes sick while the other is off on holiday. Neil also considered the viability of a team with two Controllers and one Associate. However, we both thought this would not be viable because it means two senior members managing one junior member. Neil put forward what he thought is the most efficient and effective restructure, that is, to lose one Controller. This made more business sense than having a team of just two Controllers. I emphasise that at this time, the person who would be at risk of redundancy had not been selected. We had not even decided yet that a headcount reduction should be made. We had only determined how it could be made, if needed.

We discussed how, if we were to proceed, we would go about losing one Controller without affecting staff morale, as redundancies are an unpleasant experience for everyone. We discussed whether either Ranjit or Katia would feel less distressed by a redundancy. Hence, we discussed the fact that Ranjit had requested voluntary redundancy in the past and is still unhappy with the team not reporting directly into me. We thought about whether it would be appropriate to approach him with an offer of voluntary redundancy. We felt we would prefer to retain an employee who is happy and committed than one who is not. It was a delicate matter, as I did not want to damage our relationship with him with a wrong approach. I approached our HR department for advice. On their advice, we decided to approach him for an informal sounding out. I told Neil that he is permitted to approach him, which he then did on 22nd November 2005. Ranjit responded that he is not interested in taking up voluntary redundancy.

By this time, it was obvious that the Market Risk Control team is the area for a potential headcount reduction. I asked Neil to proceed to perform an objective compulsory redundancy of one of the Controllers. There was no pre-selection of Ranjit for redundancy. We had approached him informally only to determine if he might be happy to accept voluntary redundancy.

I was not involved in the redundancy selection process. I was aware Ranjit is being considered for redundancy. I was involved in reviewing the selection criteria with our HR advisor to ensure they are relevant, complete, and consistent with other processes. Neil consulted me on the individual scoring as a sense-check, but in no way did I influence or change his scoring.

On 6th February 2006, I heard Ranjit's grievance about his redundancy. Janet Shipley of HR was in attendance. He was unhappy about his selection for redundancy. He complained that the bank's redundancy procedure was not followed, that there had been no collective consultation with him because he is not a member of the bank's union, that his selection for redundancy was predetermined, and that the alternative team structures he proposed were not taken into account seriously.

I spoke with HR about the redundancy process. They satisfied me that the correct procedures were followed. The union has the ability to consult collectively for all employees of the bank, not only for those who are its members. I made it clear to Ranjit that I believe the union were effective in representing him.

Neil and Veronica Cotton had four meetings with Ranjit during the two-week individual consultation period to address his various concerns. I could not find any evidence to support his belief that Neil and Veronica were only paying lip service, as he put it, to the idea of consultation.

I am satisfied that he had requested voluntary redundancy in 2004 and that Neil acted wholly appropriately in approaching him exclusively regarding voluntary redundancy in November 2005. The bank does not have a formal policy on voluntary redundancy. But, we try to avoid compulsory redundancies where possible. I do not believe that Neil's approach indicates that Ranjit was preselected for redundancy. I found no evidence of the selection for redundancy having been prejudged.

The appraisal score is only one component of the overall redundancy selection score. I found no evidence that the redundancy scoring unduly influenced Neil in scoring the appraisal, or vice versa. Ranjit did not challenge his appraisal score through the normal formal process. I know he informally challenged the manager's comment on the appraisal, but not the appraisal score itself. I do not believe the appraisal score has any significant impact on his redundancy. Even if Neil had accepted his challenge to the comment, the removal of the comment would not alter the appraisal score and, therefore, the redundancy selection would be unaffected. Ranjit would still be selected for redundancy.

Regarding the alternative team structures that Ranjit proposed to avoid his redundancy, both Neil and I believe a team of two is not viable because it is vulnerable and inadequate, leaving us exposed to staff departures and absences. I am satisfied that Neil considered the levels of experiences in the team when identifying whether a Controller or an Associate should be made redundant.

For all these reasons, I did not support Ranjit's grievance that he is unfairly and less favourably treated. At no point during my conversation with him did he ever give any indication, allege, or even imply that he believes he is treated any differently on the grounds of his race or colour.

I had no further involvement in his redundancy grievance.

I was involved in the investigation of his grievance regarding his 2005 bonus award when I had a meeting with Colin Marr. Colin wanted clarification on how bonuses are allocated and awarded. I explained that it is wrong to compare one year's bonus with the next. The bank gives me a bonus pot. From it, I have to reward employees with higher appraisal scores the most. However, I also take into account an individual's bonus as a percentage of his salary. I also take into account the individual's market value. For example, in 2004, Ranjit was awarded an increased bonus because his team had a difficult year with the head of the team departing, leaving only him and Katia to continue with the work. I was mindful that not only had Ranjit made a considerable contribution that year, but also that it was vital to retain him at the time. If he left, then the team would reduce to just one person. So, his market value at the time was high.

I propose bonuses for individuals based on the following factors: the total bonus pot available for the department; the individual's absolute performance and performance relative to his peers; and market influences for the individual's role. I then discuss my proposals with the team heads. Thus, I discussed the bonus proposals for each individual in the Market Risk Control team with Neil. He had the opportunity to challenge my proposals and suggest amendments. If such challenges are justified, then I will make reallocations.

I explained how I allocate bonuses to Colin, but I had no involvement in the decision making process as to whether the 2005 bonus award is fair.

'Yes,' he replies.

Addressing the chairman, the respondents' counsel says, 'Sir, I wish to bring up some supplementary issues'.

The chairman signals her to do so.

Addressing Simon, she asks, 'what do you recall of the conversation between you and Neil in the summer of 2004 about Ranjit's interest in voluntary redundancy?'

'Neil approached me in my office and said Ranjit might be interested in voluntary redundancy. We couldn't manage without him. So, we couldn't offer it to him,' he answers.

'What about the conversation between you and Neil about approaching him about voluntary redundancy in November 2005?' she asks.

'Towards the end of a series of conversations with Neil about the downsizing of the Market Risk Control team to reduce costs, we discussed how people might respond to a redundancy situation,' he replies. 'We discussed Ranjit's history of having requested voluntary redundancy and the fact that he continues to be unhappy with the team's reporting line not being directly into me. We thought that there is the possibility that he's dissatisfied and looking for an opportunity to leave'.

'When you decided in September 2005 to change the line of delegated authorities to include Neil, Ranjit raised a number of concerns to you regarding the change. What did you think about that?' she asks.

'I was surprised by his confrontational tone,' he answers. 'It wasn't a case of him asking if we can please discuss the proposed change. It was very direct, saying there is no business need for the change and suggesting that it is being driven by desire'.

'How did that compare to Katia?' she asks.

'Katia didn't raise any concerns at all,' he answers.

The chairman interjects, 'you were not aware of any concerns from Miss Mykonola?'

'No,' he answers.

The respondents' counsel continues, 'Neil says he assessed Ranjit's and Katia's 2004 year-end, 2005 mid-year, and 2005 year-end appraisals. What was your involvement in these appraisals?'

'I didn't have any direct involvement,' he answers. 'Line managers perform their staff's appraisals. Neil was their line manager, not me. I do review appraisal scores across the department to ensure consistency. I don't want any of my people suffering at the hands of harsh managers and others benefiting from soft ones. Plus, I want to do a sense-check based on my own knowledge of the individuals'.

'Could you explain how the bonus is arrived at?' she asks.

'The bonus scheme is completely discretionary,' he answers. 'The amount isn't guaranteed and a bonus doesn't have to be awarded at all. The primary factor is the individual's performance, being the person's contribution to the department's success for the year as measured by his year-end appraisal score. I also consider what the individual's *total compensation* for the year will be. Total compensation is the individual's salary and bonus summed together. I set the bonus so that the total compensation is fair in relation to other teams and members of the department. My department has several teams. Each requires a different set of competencies. So, there are quite diverse levels of total compensation across my department, ranging from the tens of thousands to the hundreds of thousands of pounds. I also take into account the individual's market value'.

'Do you ensure year-on-year consistency of bonus?' she asks.

'No,' he answers firmly. 'We can't do that because each year we have a different amount in the bonus pot to distribute and because the number of individuals from one year to the next varies as staff join and leave the department'.

The chairman interjects, 'was Mr Singh's bonus adjusted downward because he was off work with a broken leg'.

'No,' he answers. 'He worked from home during that time'.

'Bonus documents disclosed to the tribunal show a list of Grade B and Grade C employees, and the bonuses allocated to each employee,' the chairman says. 'Do they include your bonus and the bonuses of the heads of your teams?'

'No,' he answers. 'The heads of my teams and I are not included anywhere on the disclosed documents. Only the bonuses of the people reporting into the heads are disclosed'.

'You are told what the size of the bonus pot is?' the chairman asks.

'Yes,' he answers.

'What was the total size of the pot for 2005?' the chairman asks.

'Er,' he hesitates. 'Do I really need to disclose that?' he asks back.

'Answer the question, Mr Ong,' the chairman orders.

'Er, hmm,' he deliberates. 'Three million pounds,' he answers reluctantly.

'That amount is entirely at the bank's discretion?' the chairman asks. 'It could have allocated less, if it wished?'

'Yes,' he answers.

'I appreciate that bonus setting is not a precise calculation. But, there must be some kind of method for it,' the chairman says.

'My starting point is the individual's base salary,' he replies. 'Then, I consider the individual's appraisal score. Then, the individual's market value, being the risk of losing the individual and how difficult it would be to replace him'.

'At what time of the year were the bonus figures for 2005 decided?' the chairman asks.

'Usually, they're decided in the first two weeks of December,' he answers.

'Mr Jai Khanna's appraisal score for 2005 is higher than for 2004. Why does his 2005 bonus decrease while others with decreasing appraisal scores do not experience any decrease in their bonus and some even get an increased bonus?' the chairman asks.

'This is awkward, but realistic,' he answers. 'In 2004, Jai worked on a special project. He performed well on it and so, got a high bonus, sixty-five per cent of his salary. The project finished and in 2005, he returned to his usual work. His regular duties didn't merit the same level of compensation as the special project work. Hence, he got a lower bonus in 2005, even though his appraisal score increased'.

The chairman signals the respondents' counsel to continue.

'Ranjit says he reported directly to you on the SPAYN and the Wealth Management businesses,' she resumes. 'He says you managed him directly on those'.

'Yes,' he confirms. 'I had him doing special project work for me on these businesses. But, I wasn't his line manager in respect of all of his duties. Neil was his line manager. I was concerned that there isn't a proper risk control framework around these businesses. I knew Ranjit could design and implement one. I had him work directly for me on that. But, Neil remained being his line manager'.

'What is your view of Ranjit telling Neil not to patronise him when Neil said well done to him regarding these businesses,' she asks.

'I was surprised,' he answers. 'I would've expected him to take it as a compliment'.

'Thank you, I have no more questions,' she says giving way to my counsel to begin her cross-examination.

My counsel starts, 'who sense-checked your bonus proposals for 2005'.

'Veronica Cotton, our department's HR Partner,' he answers.

'What kinds of things did she look for?' she asks.

'It's best if you ask her,' he replies.

The chairman interjects, 'answer the question, Mr Ong'.

'She asked how I decided the bonuses. She picked out example amounts that looked out of kilter to her and asked for explanations,' he answers.

'What matters did she raise with you?' my counsel

continues.

'I remember she picked up specifically on the reduction proposed for Ranjit,' he answers. 'She knew he's selected for redundancy. We discussed whether the reduction could potentially be an issue. If it were an issue, I could have easily re-allocated more to him. But, I didn't think it was'.

'Anything else?' she asks.

'No,' he answers.

'Did she pick up on any matters of race?' she asks.

'No,' he replies.

'Did you yourself pick up on any matters of race?' she asks.

'No,' he answers.

'Did anyone ever carry out a diversity audit of bonuses?' she asks.

'Not that I'm aware of,' he replies.

'Does it concern you that the only two people whose bonuses are reduced are both Asian?' she asks.

'No,' he answers.

'You say the size of an individual's bonus depends on the following factors: the size of the pot allocated to your department; the individual's appraisal score for the year; and the individual's market value,' she says.

'Yes,' he confirms.

'Does it depend on anything else?' she asks.

'No,' he answers.

'Could it also depend on your personal preferences, your like or dislike of the individual?' she asks.

'It's possible, but it didn't,' he answers.

'Do you have any records showing how you allocated the pot to individuals?' she asks.

'No,' he replies.

'So, you sit down with a list of names and apply in your head the process that you described to allocate to each individual. You then make adjustments in your head to ensure fairness. You do not write down or put on record anywhere how you arrive at each allocation amount, showing what adjustments you make and why you make them,' she says.

'Correct,' he answers. 'I've done it like that every year. Then, Veronica reviewed and checked my allocations'.

'No records whatsoever of the rationale for each figure?' she asks.

'No,' he answers.

'No notes of Veronica's review meeting?' she asks.

'No,' he answers. 'Bonuses are highly confidential. We discuss them orally only. We never write anything down about them, except the final figures'.

'So, if someone wants to check or audit your decision-making process, then there are no records available to be able to do that,' she says.

'Correct,' he confirms.

'Why not?' she asks.

'That's just how it is,' he answers.

'You must be aware that there are often legal cases concerning the allocation of bonuses?' she puts to him.

'Yes,' he replies.

'Yet, you did not think to maintain records of how you make your decisions?' she asks.

'No. I didn't think it was necessary,' he answers.

'You say the documents disclosed to the tribunal regarding the bonuses exclude some groups of people that you decide the bonuses for also,' she says.

'Yes,' he confirms.

'So, you do not make full disclosure to the tribunal,' she says.

'It's full disclosure in relation to Ranjit's peers,' he replies.

'But, you also decide the bonuses of other groups of people. You have not disclosed the information about them,' she says.

'Correct,' he confirms.

The chairman interjects, 'Mr Ong, how many people

have been excluded?'

'About ten,' he answers.

'Their bonuses come from the same three million pounds pot as Mr Singh's?' the chairman asks.

'Yes,' he answers.

The chairman signals my counsel to continue.

'Let us now look at the factor you refer to as an individual's market value,' she resumes. 'If you wish to retain someone in his role, then his market value is considered to be high. So, if someone is being made redundant, then his market value is low'.

'No,' he answers. 'It's the role that's being made redundant, not the individual'.

'There is no need to incentivise an individual occupying the redundant role. No need to incentivise him to stay,' she says.

'Er, hmm, that makes sense,' he mumbles.

The chairman interjects, 'is that a confirmation, Mr Ong?'

'Er, yes,' he confirms.

'The bank's policy document titled, *How Will My Bonus Be Calculated*,' my counsel continues, 'gives guidance to all employees on how their bonuses will be calculated'.

'That's correct,' he confirms.

'It does not mention anywhere that market value will be a factor in the calculation,' she puts to him.

'No, it doesn't,' he confirms.

'You yourself added in an extra factor, market value, being an incentive to stay,' she says.

'Well, I would only want someone to stay if the cost of replacing him is higher,' he says.

'If an individual's appraisal score goes down, will his bonus go down?' she asks.

'The appraisal score will have a significant bearing, but the key is that the bonus is fair relative to others,' he replies.

'You know before the bonus is finalised that Ranjit is

strongly protesting his appraisal score,' she says.

'No, I didn't,' he answers.

'No one tells you that he is protesting his appraisal score? No one says, do not finalise his bonus yet?' she asks.

'No, no one said that,' he answers. 'I knew he's protesting against the manager's comments that Neil made on his appraisal, but not the score itself'.

'But, the comments feed into and impact the score,' she says.

'It wasn't clear from his emails to me that he's protesting the score,' he replies.

'The manager's comments on the appraisal reflect the manager's view of performance,' she says.

'Er, hmm, possibly,' he replies.

'Do you not think it fair to take his protest into account before finalising his bonus?' she asks.

'There's a separate formal process for appealing the appraisal. He didn't initiate it,' he replies.

'If his appraisal is tainted with discrimination by Neil, then will that discrimination feed into your bonus allocation process?' she asks.

'Yes,' he answers.

'I suggest that the bonus is allocated irrationally,' she puts to him.

'No, it's not,' he rebuts.

'Those of Asian ethnicity are treated less favourably, especially Ranjit and Jai Khanna,' she says.

'I disagree,' he replies firmly.

'You agree that the only two people whose bonuses are reduced are both Asian,' she puts to him.

'Yes, but that's just coincidental,' he answers.

'You have no records showing how their bonuses are allocated. There are no independent diversity checks or audits. You have no Diversity and Equal Opportunities training,' she puts to him.

'Er, hmm,' he deliberates. 'No,' he answers.

'Moving on,' she says. 'You know in October that your department is being asked by senior management to make cost savings. So, you ask the heads of your teams to review their teams for potential cost savings'.

'Yes,' he confirms.

'Neil, on his own initiative, comes to you with the idea that the Market Risk Control team can function fine with fewer resources,' she says.

'That's right,' he confirms.

'You did not prompt or suggest to him that the team could function with fewer resources,' she says.

'No, it came from him,' he replies.

'He did not have to volunteer that the team can function with fewer resources,' she says.

'Correct,' he confirms.

'He is the one who suggests that a Controller should go rather than an Associate,' she says.

'Yes, and I agreed with his reasoning,' he replies.

'Who suggests that Ranjit be approached to take up voluntary redundancy?' she asks.

'Neil did,' he answers.

'You say you would prefer to lose someone who prefers to leave. Then, why not check with everyone in the team if they are interested in voluntary redundancy?' she asks.

'Because none of the others ever expressed an interest in voluntary redundancy, only Ranjit did,' he replies.

'How long ago did he express an interest?' she asks.

'I think about one and a half years earlier,' he answers.

'During that time, any of the others could have become interested too,' she says.

'Although it had been one and a half years, he continued to demonstrate that he's unhappy. None of the others demonstrated unhappiness,' he replies.

'Why not warn all four of them in October of the impending risk of redundancy?' she asks.

'That would unsettle all four of them. We didn't want

to worry everyone,' he replies.

'When did you know who is selected for redundancy?' she asks.

'I don't remember the exact date. Sometime in early December,' he answers.

'Was the redundancy scoring sent to you?' she asks.

'I can't remember,' he answers.

'You did not check the scoring Neil performed?' she asks.

'Possibly. I don't remember,' he answers.

'It does not sound like you did,' she puts to him.

'I don't remember,' he replies.

'Could it be that it was sent to you, but the communication has not been disclosed to the tribunal?' she asks.

'No,' he answers. 'Everything relevant has been disclosed'.

'The bank's document titled, *Job Security Policy*, states that it will let employees being affected by redundancy know as soon as possible, as soon as it knows it. You know in October that there will be a redundancy in the Market Risk Control team. You do not tell Ranjit until the 11th of January,' she says.

'We hadn't decided in October what the specific change would be,' he replies.

'But, you know there will be a change that will affect the Market Risk Control team, correct?' she puts to him.

'But, we didn't know which person it would affect,' he answers

The chairman interject, 'Mr Ong, who was it that communicated to you the need to make cost savings?'

'My line manager, the Chief Risk Officer of the bank,' he answers.

'How was it communicated to you?' the chairman asks.

'In an email, saying save five per cent of headcount. My headcount is fifty people,' he replies.

The chairman signals my counsel to continue.

'You know from October that a Controller will be made redundant,' she continues. 'You tell Ranjit about redundancy in January. During the whole of this time, from October to January, he has no knowledge and no opportunity to put forward his views,' she says.

'No, it doesn't seem so,' he confirms.

'The bank's policy does not seem to be complied with,' she says.

'We consulted the union,' he replies.

'You could let him know from October. You could tell him in November. But, you do not,' she says.

'We could, but the selection process wasn't finalised until mid December,' he replies.

'Did this not trouble you when you conducted and investigated his grievance against the redundancy?' she asks.

'No, it didn't,' he answers. 'I was comfortable we had followed the bank's policy. I believe we had constructive consultation with him. He had the opportunity to put forward his views in January, which he did'.

The chairman interjects, 'but he did not have the opportunity to put forward views before January, correct, Mr Ong?'

'We consulted the union. The union put forward views on his behalf,' he replies.

The chairman signals my counsel to continue.

'He has no chance,' she resumes. 'He cannot put his views forward until after the decision is made. He is told he is at risk and the rest of the team are told they are not at risk. When he puts his views forward, nobody takes them into account,' she says.

'I certainly took them into account,' he replies. 'I can't speak for others, but I took everything he said into account'.

'And you rejected it all,' she says.

'That was my conclusion,' he replies. 'He didn't convince me that his redundancy is unfair. If he had, then

I would have re-assessed the situation'.

'You could not re-assess the situation because then you would have to go back to the others, whom you had told were not at risk, and tell them they are at risk. That would be a very poor message for you to give to them, whom you were so concerned not to unsettle,' she says.

'We would only have had to go back to Katia,' he replies.

'You were so keen not to unsettle the team that you gave no warning in October,' she says.

'We didn't want to warn until we finalised the redundancy,' he replies.

'There is no way you would go back to the others and tell them they are at risk,' she says.

'We would, if it were necessary,' he replies.

'Did you even listen to what Ranjit was saying?' she asks.

'I certainly listened to him. I can't speak for the others,' he says.

'You say the union is consulted. You also say you do not know who is a member of the union and who is not,' she says.

'The union consults on behalf of all employees, whether they're its members or not,' he replies.

'The union supports its members only. Its website and documents clearly state that it acts for its members. You took the view that it supports non-members also,' she says.

'I didn't take that view alone,' he replies.

'If you are being represented, you want the representative to know what your views and interests are,' she says. 'The representative may not know what concerns and interests you most. The representative needs to liaise with you, take instructions from you, and get back to you with updates. You need to know that you are being represented,' she says.

'Yes,' he confirms.

'Ranjit does not know there is a redundancy situation

until the 11th of January,' she says.

'Correct,' he confirms.

'He does not know about the two meetings with the union on the 9th and the 15th of December,' she says.

'No,' he confirms.

'He has no idea he is being represented,' she says.

'No,' he concedes.

'He cannot liaise with the representative,' she says.

'I suppose not,' he replies.

'Did you read the bank's policy and process documents regarding redundancy?' she asks.

'Yes,' he answers.

'Did you see that they say that the basis of selection will be discussed with the union in every case?' she asks.

'Yes,' he replies.

'The minutes of the meetings with the union make no mention of the basis of selection being discussed. So, when you investigated his grievance, how did you check to ensure that they were discussed?' she asks.

'They were discussed. The discussions just weren't recorded in the minutes,' he says.

'How do you know?' she asks. 'You were not present at the meeting'.

'Veronica said they were. I accepted what she said,' he replies.

'Accepted it, just like that?' she asks.

'She's an independent source,' he says. 'I assumed it was discussed. It's part of the policy'.

The chairman interjects, 'Mr Ong, your assumption is going from the general to the specific. Just because it is a policy does not mean that they were discussed. Is there any record of your conversation with Miss Cotton on this point?'

'No,' he answers.

'When did you have that conversation with her?' the chairman asks.

'I can't remember the date,' he says.

The chairman signals my counsel to continue.

'One of the matters that Ranjit raises in his grievance letter,' she continues, 'is that he thinks his dismissal is predetermined because he was approached in November to take up voluntary redundancy. You were involved in the discussion and the decision to approach him. Did you not think that you might not be an independent person to hear his grievance?'

'I was involved in the discussion, but I didn't make the final decision that he should be approached,' he says.

'On reflection, someone else would be a better person to investigate his grievance, right?' she puts to him.

'I believe I remained independent,' he replies. 'And, the bank's policy is that his line manager's manager conducts the grievance, which is me'.

'The bank is a large organisation. Someone else could easily be found instead of you. You should not be a judge on something in which you are involved,' she says.

'I was only involved to a small extent. My only involvement was in the conversation with Neil about Ranjit having expressed an interest in voluntary redundancy,' he replies.

'You are not in the best position to decide on the appeal,' she says. 'Did it trouble you that the redundancy scoring is performed wholly by Neil alone?' she asks.

'No,' he answers. 'If the scoring is supported with examples, then it's fine'.

'Did it trouble you that the person doing the scoring also selected which competencies would be used in the scoring?' she asks.

'No,' he answers.

'It did not strike you that some of the things Neil scores Ranjit down for, another manager could score him up for instead?' she asks.

'I think not,' he answers firmly.

'You did not think there should be more than one person doing the scoring?' she asks.

'No,' he replies.

'Did it trouble you that the appraisal used in the redundancy is done by the same person who did the redundancy scoring?' she asks.

'No,' he answers.

'The selection process is not objective,' she says.

'I saw no evidence to suggest that it isn't,' he replies. 'The appraisal is a separate matter between him and his line manager. He could have challenged the appraisal score'.

'Challenging it, he was,' she says.

'I wasn't aware that he initiated any formal challenge,' he rebuts.

'And while he was challenging it, you told him, on the 11th of January, that he is selected for redundancy,' she says.

'Yes,' he replies.

'You say you are surprised by his reaction of viewing praise from Neil as patronising,' she says.

'Yes,' he replies.

'Is it not also surprising that Katia should go up to Neil and accuse him so angrily of being patronising?' she asks.

'Er, hmm, yes,' he mumbles reluctantly.

'Ranjit is a market risk professional. He has expertise and experience in market risk and it was his job to control market risks at the bank,' she says.

'Yes,' he confirms.

'If he raises concerns and issues about market risk at work, he is doing it because it is his job,' she says.

'Er, hmm, I assume so,' he replies.

The chairman interjects, 'Mr Ong, you were sitting in the public gallery behind Mr Hobson yesterday when I warned him to answer questions properly. The same warning goes to you. Answer the question properly!'

'Yes,' he answers.

'He raises concerns regarding the change in the line of delegated authority that you proposed in September 2005,' my counsel continues.

'Yes,' he confirms.

'He works to implement the change, as you instructed,' she says.

'Yes,' he confirms.

'When the change becomes effective, he complies with it fully,' she says.

'Yes,' he confirms.

'The same goes for Katia. She raises issues about this change too,' she puts to him.

'I'm not aware that she did,' he replies.

'In August 2005, you send both of them an email instructing them to implement the change in the line of delegated authority. A week later she forwards your email to the junior members of the team apologising for the week's delay because she had wanted to discuss the change with Ranjit first, and also with you and Neil,' she says.

'Her email just says she wanted to discuss the change, not that she wanted to discuss concerns,' he replies.

'She would not be wanting to discuss anything if she is perfectly happy, would she?' she puts to him.

'Someone can be perfectly happy but still want to discuss,' he replies.

'Thank you, I have no further questions,' she says.

The chairman gives way to the other two judges on the panel to question the witness.

The judge on the chairman's right starts, 'Mr Singh had the authority to decide which kind of notification be made to the FSA and Mr Hobson did not. Is this correct?'

'Yes,' he answers.

'Mr Hobson says Mr Singh did not make the correct notifications on the Managed Income Portfolio and the Single Equities Portfolio. Although he could not override him, he could say something like: I recommend you pre-notify,' the judge says.

'I think he did say that in one email, but discussions carried on thereafter,' he replies.

'He did not pursue what he believed in?' the judge asks.

'No,' he answers.

'So, he was on-board with what Mr Singh was doing,' the judge says. 'He does not say anything about it all year. Then, at the end of the year, in Mr Singh's appraisal, he criticises him for making the wrong notification and marks him down for it. Is this normal?'

'Usually, mangers discuss performance matters throughout the year,' he answers. 'I think Neil should have been firmer earlier. But, his style is very diplomatic. He would never say a bad word to anyone'.

'You did not say anything to Mr Singh during the year about these notifications?' the judge asks.

'No. Neil is his line manger, not me,' he replies.

'Thank you, I have no more questions,' the judge says.

The chairman resumes, 'Mr Ong, one of my jobs is grasping the nettle. What was the relationship between Mr Singh and Mr Hobson like, did you perceive there to be a problem between them?' he asks.

'Yes,' he answers.

'What was the problem?' the chairman asks.

'I think Ranjit didn't accept Neil as his line manager,' he replies.

'What did you observe that made you think this?' the chairman asks.

'I just think he thought he could do the job better than Neil,' he answers.

'Did you discuss that with Mr Hobson?' asks the chairman.

'Yes,' he answers.

'Right! I need to give Mr Singh's counsel a chance to cross-examine you on this,' the chairman says signalling my counsel.

My counsel starts, 'you were present here in the public gallery while Neil gave his testimony under oath'.

'Yes,' he confirms.

'You heard him say the relationship is professional,' she

says.

'Yes,' he replies.

'You heard him testify there are no personal issues,' she says.

'Yes,' he answers.

'You heard him deny categorically that his scoring is because of any relationship issue with Ranjit,' she puts to him.

'Yes, I did,' he confirms.

# 11

# VERONICA COTTON'S TESTIMONY

~ Friday 8th December 2006, 10:00 a.m. ~

'Miss Cotton, is that your signature on the witness statement and is that the evidence you wish to give?' the respondents' counsel asks her, she having just sworn in at the witness stand.

She has presented the tribunal her statement on the matters at hand. It says the following:

> I am a Senior Human Resources Partner at the bank. I have a degree in HR and seven years work experience in HR. I have been at the bank since November 2004. I have been involved in about thirty redundancies at the bank.
>
> I dealt with Ranjit Singh once when he called HR to query his role's position when the line of delegated authority was changed in September 2005 to include Neil Hobson. I confirmed that there is no demotion of his role. Simon Ong had meetings with Ranjit and Katia Mykonola to deal with the concerns that they had on this subject.
>
> I advised Neil regarding Ranjit's sickness absence when he broke his leg in August 2005. I told Neil that Ranjit could work form home while his leg recovers so that sickness absence can be kept to a minimum.
>
> The whole bank has faced cost challenges since Eurocredito took it over. We knew the Market Risk

Department would need to lose one person. Neil identified that a Market Risk Controller could be removed from the team as a way of saving costs. Neil spoke with HR on whether he could approach Ranjit about voluntary redundancy because Ranjit had previously expressed that he is interested in it. HR advised him that he could. Neil approached him. He was not interested.

I provided Neil with a blank form to complete with his business rationale for cutting one Controller role. He completed the form.

I talked Neil through the redundancy selection process to apply, which is agreed with the bank's union. If the scoring exercise results in a tie, then other selection criteria come into play.

I provided Neil with the redundancy competencies scorecards to complete. He performed the scoring and filled out the scorecards. I read through them, but I did not change them because I am not technically knowledgeable enough to be able to understand the Controller role because it is highly specialised.

On 9th December 2005, Neil and I submitted the business rationale for the redundancy to the union. The union was concerned that the redundant Controller's workload could not be re-allocated between the three remaining team members. It wanted us to return with more information on the breakdown of the tasks. Neil prepared the breakdown information. We presented it to the union at a second meeting, on 15th December. This is the collective consultation process that is followed at the bank for all redundancies. Hence, we followed the agreed procedure regarding collective consultation. The union instructed us to wait until after Christmas to announce the redundancy because it said it is unfair to put people at risk before Christmas. So, at the union's request, we delayed the announcement to 9th January.

I generated the At Risk and Not At Risk scripts for the announcement meetings. I gave the scripts to Neil and advised him on what he needs to do.

On 11th January 2006, I sat in on the At Risk meeting between Neil and Ranjit. Neil read out the At Risk script to Ranjit. I handed Ranjit the Redundancy Information Pack. Immediately after this meeting, I sat in on the Not At Risk meeting between Neil and the remaining team members. Neil read out the Not At Risk script to them.

On 12th January, Neil and I had the first one-to-one individual consultation meeting with Ranjit. I had told Ranjit that he could bring a union representative or an employee of the bank. He challenged the process that we had followed, saying it is unlawful. I asked why he thinks the process does not comply with the law. He believed we should have consulted him about the redundancy and the selection exercise, and that we should not have put him at risk before this happened. He did not believe the consultation with the union was effective because he is not a member of the union. He did not mention race as being an issue at any of the four one-to-one consultation meetings I attended, nor in his emails to me regarding the redundancy. The first I knew of his race discrimination allegation is from his solicitor's letter of 12th May 2006.

We had a further consultation meeting with him on 18th January to get back to him with answers on the questions he had raised in the previous meeting. Then, we had further meetings with him on 19th and 23rd January.

In the meeting on 23rd January, he proposed

alternative team restructures to avoid his redundancy. Neil rejected his proposals. The meeting was very short. He informed us he would be appealing the redundancy selection decision. I told him he is on his notice period effective immediately. Neil decided to place him on Gardening Leave for his entire notice period and took his security access pass from him, as per the bank's standard procedure. After the meeting, on the same day, he submitted a formal grievance about his redundancy.

If Neil had increased Ranjit's scores to the same as Katia's, then there would be a tie situation. We would then have looked at disciplinary records to break the tie. Both of them had clean disciplinary records. So, the tie situation would persist. Then, we would consider absence. Ranjit had more absence that year because he broke his leg. So, he would still be the one selected for redundancy.

'Yes,' she answers.

Addressing the chairman, the respondents' counsel says, 'Sir, I wish to bring up some supplementary issues'.

The chairman signals her to do so.

'Is the process applied in Ranjit's redundancy any different from that applied in other redundancies across the bank?' she asks.

'No,' she answers. 'It's exactly the same. It's the bank's standard process'.

'Where does the standard process come from?' she asks.

'It's designed by the bank's Employment Cost Optimisation Team. They're experts,' she answers.

'One of the scoring competencies Neil used in the redundancy selection is Conversion. Can you tell us what Conversion means?' she asks.

'Er, hmm,' she contemplates. 'I think it's for scoring

how an individual converts their capacity to learning their self-knowledge through, er, hmm,' she says and then trails off mumbling something inaudible.

'Did Neil discuss his scoring of Ranjit and Katia with you?' she asks.

'He sent me the scorecards by email on the 8th of December to review,' she answers.

The chairman interjects, 'when and how was the review performed?'

'We had a conversation,' she answers. 'I suggested minor tweaks to his comments'.

'How did you have the conversation? What did you suggest?' the chairman asks.

'It was a face-to-face conversation,' she replies. 'I suggested minor tweaks to the wording. I suggested he removes his comments from the Conversion competency about Ranjit finding praise from him patronising. I also suggested he removes his comment from the same competency from both Katia's and Ranjit's scorecards that they volunteered to design and deliver in-house education courses on risk management'.

'From Katia's too?' the chairman asks.

'Yes,' she answers. 'Those comments don't really relate to Conversion'.

The chairman signals the respondents' counsel to continue.

'You attended four consultation meetings with Ranjit during the two-week individual consultation period,' she resumes.

'Yes,' she confirms. 'The meetings were to go through the selection process and explore ways to avoid his redundancy'.

'You attended the consultation meeting with the union on the 15th of December,' she says.

'Yes,' she answers.

'The minutes of the meeting with the union say the redundancy will be announced from the 9th of January.

Whose decision is that?' she asks.

'The union's,' she answers. 'It told us to wait till after Christmas'.

'Why?' she asks.

'It doesn't like redundancies being announced before Christmas,' she answers. 'It doesn't look good'.

'You were involved in sense-checking the department's bonus allocations,' she says.

'Yes,' she answers. 'I sat with Simon in his office and we went through them on his computer screen'.

'No further evidence in chief, Sir,' the respondents' counsel informs the chairman.

The chairman signals my counsel to cross-examine the witness.

Addressing Veronica, my counsel says, 'Neil decides which scoring competencies would be used in the redundancy selection exercise. Does he involve Ranjit or the union in making his decision?'

'No,' she answers.

'From where does he select the eight competencies?' she asks.

'He had to have eight competencies, four behavioural and four technical,' she answers. 'He selected seven of them from the bank's standard list, which is quite large and wide. He created one technical competency himself because he couldn't find a suitable one in the standard list'.

'He creates one himself?' my counsel asks. 'Which one?'

'I don't know,' she replies.

'He writes up his own competency, even though he should select from the bank's standard list?' she asks.

'He's allowed to write his own if the standard ones don't fit,' she answers.

'Show me where in the bank's procedures it says he can write his own,' she challenges her.

'It's not written anywhere explicitly. It's implied,' she replies.

'Having created the competency himself, does he run it past Ranjit or the union?' she asks.

'No,' she replies.

'You say the redundancy process is agreed with the union. When? Where?' she asks.

'I don't know,' she answers. 'I'm told it's agreed and I believe it'.

'The bank discloses no documents evidencing the agreement,' she puts to her.

'I have faith that it's agreed,' she answers.

'You have never seen the agreement?' she asks.

'No,' she answers.

'Do you know the terms of the agreement?' she asks.

'No,' she answers.

'You are present at the two consultation meetings with the union, on the 9th and 15th of December,' she says.

'Yes,' she replies.

'You agree that the selection competencies are not discussed with the union,' she says.

'We presented the union only the redundancy results. If it wanted to know about the selection criteria, it could have asked us,' she answers.

The chairman interjects, 'the union did not delve into things like what process is being applied, what selection competencies are being used, why Mr Singh is selected and not Miss Mykonola?'

'No,' she answers.

'I'm amazed,' the chairman declares and signals my counsel to continue.

'No discussions with the union about the selection process or method?' my counsel resumes.

'The process is defined in the agreement with the union. It didn't need discussing,' she replies.

The chairman interjects, 'but, one scoring competency was created by Mr Hobson himself. Surely, that one needed to be highlighted and discussed?'

'It wasn't discussed,' she answers.

'Did you tell the union that one selection competency is not from the standard list, that it is created by Mr Hobson?' the chairman asks.

'No,' she answers.

'Did the union tell you not to announce the redundancy before Christmas?' the chairman asks.

'Yes,' she answers.

'The union was happy for someone to be unaware over the Christmas period that they are selected for redundancy, happy to let them continue to spend money over the festive period unaware of what is coming their way?' the chairman asks.

'I suppose so,' she answers.

'Would it not be fairer to let them know before Christmas, so they can moderate their spending to prepare for what is coming?' the chairman asks.

'I agree. But, I suppose the union thought otherwise,' she replies.

'You did not have to agree with the union,' the chairman says. 'You could have put your view to them'.

'It seemed like a standard request from the union,' she answers.

'You did not think to challenge it?' the chairman asks.

'No. I could see both sides of the argument,' she answers.

The chairman signals my counsel to continue.

'So, without any reflection, you simply agree to the union's request' she says.

'Yes,' she replies.

'Should a person who is at risk know as soon as possible, even if it is Christmas?' she asks.

'It depends on the person's circumstances,' she replies.

'You are present at the meeting where Neil tells Ranjit that he is at risk,' she says.

'Yes,' she replies.

'Ranjit expresses that he is shocked,' she says.

'Yes,' she replies.

'Does he appear shocked?' she asks.

'Yes,' she replies.

'He had no warning of what is coming to him,' she says.

'No,' she replies.

'You tell Neil to use the mid-year appraisal for the redundancy. But, he uses the year-end appraisal,' she say.

'Yes,' she replies.

'The mid-year appraisal is the objective one because it is performed outside of the redundancy situation. The year-end one is produced during the redundancy,' she says.

'Correct,' she replies.

'You want an objective redundancy exercise,' she says.

'Yes,' she answers.

'Personal biases regarding the redundancy can creep into the year-end appraisal because it is done during the redundancy,' she says.

'Yes,' she replies. 'But, the appraisal is just one of the inputs'.

'But, if the mid-year appraisal is used, then the process is more objective,' she puts to her.

'Yes,' she answers.

'You could have told the union that the mid-year appraisal should be used,' she says.

'I didn't think there was any risk,' she replies.

'Thank you, I have no more questions,' my counsel says.

The chairman gives way to the other two judges at the bench to question the witness.

'When did you know there would be a redundancy of one of the Market Risk Controllers,' asks the judge on the chairman's right.

'In November 2005,' she answers. 'Simon informed me'.

'First, Mr Singh is told that he is at risk. Immediately after, the rest of the team are told they're not at risk,' the judge says.

'Yes, that's correct,' she replies.

'So, where is the scope for consultation?' the judge puts to her.

'We began a two-week individual consultation period with him from the next day,' she answers.

'What would you have done if in the consultation period it became decided that Mr Singh should not be selected for redundancy? Would you have gone back to the people you had told are safe and tell them they are not safe now?' the judge asks.

'Yes,' she replies.

'Has such a thing actually ever happened?' the judge asks.

'I've never seen it happen before,' she answers.

'Thank you, I have no more questions,' the judge says.

'How many scoring competencies are in the bank's standard list that Mr Hobson could select eight from?' asks the judge on the chairman's left.

'Something like forty or fifty,' she answers.

'Who checked that the ones he chose are appropriate to the Market Risk Controller role?' he asks.

'I gave them a cursory review. But, I couldn't really check them properly. The Controller role is too specialised for me,' she replies. 'I'm an HR professional, not a market risk control expert as well'.

# 12

# JACKIE MONROE'S TESTIMONY

~ Friday 8th December 2006, 11:30 a.m. ~

'Ms Monroe, is that your signature on the witness statement and is that the evidence you wish to give?' the respondents' counsel asks her, she having just sworn in at the witness stand.

She has presented the tribunal her statement on the matters at hand. It says the following:

> I am the head of the bank's Employment Cost Management Unit. I have worked at the bank since May 2004. I have over seventeen years of experience in HR. I am Chartered Institute of Personnel Development qualified and have fifteen years of post-qualification work experience. I have considerable experience in redundancies and restructuring. I also carry out appeals against redundancies. In relation to all the appeals I have heard at the bank, in about half of the cases I overturned the decision to make the person redundant. I believe I hear appeals and determine the outcomes totally objectively.
>
> Since Eurocredito took over the bank in September 2004, there has been a huge cost optimisation programme with over 6,000 redundancies. All redundancies at the bank are subject to the agreement between the bank and its union, which covers collective consultation. Ranjit Singh's redundancy is part of the large-scale cost optimisation programme at the bank and therefore,

is subject to the collective consultation agreement with the union. I chaired the collective consultation meeting with the union on 15th December 2005, where Neil Hobson and Veronica Cotton presented the case for the redundancy. I was present in the capacity of a chairperson only and gave no substantive input to the proceedings.

The way the redundancy selection process works is that individuals are scored. If there is a tie situation, then the following criteria are looked at in this order: sickness absence, disciplinary records, and then, finally, length of service records. This applies across the whole of the bank.

I chaired Ranjit's grievance appeal meeting on 20th March 2006 with two other judges on the panel, who are both more senior than I am. The meeting lasted approximately one hour.

Ranjit's first complaint was that he is not consulted with until after he was identified as being at risk of redundancy. We conduct collective consultation only with those individuals who are identified as at risk because it is less unsettling on the other employees who are not. Ranjit is saying that for consultation to be effective we must individually consult with all employees within a redundancy pool prior to agreeing the selection criteria and prior to scoring. But, this would negate the purpose of collective consultation. It would be very time-consuming and unsettling for all employees in the pool. The process we apply ensures that only the individuals who are identified as being at risk are unsettled because only they are consulted.

I am satisfied that the individual consultation in Ranjit's case was effective. He had several meetings with Neil and Veronica, which in my opinion is effective individual consultation. Redeployment was discussed and he put forward various alternative restructuring suggestions to avoid his redundancy. I am satisfied that Neil considered them properly and rejected them for valid reasons. I am satisfied that had Ranjit put forward a suggestion that Neil viewed as a viable alternative, then Neil would have re-considered his selection for redundancy. If Neil had not, then I certainly would have at the appeal hearing and overturned his selection for redundancy. I am satisfied that all the points he raised were considered properly and rejected validly.

Also, HR and the union had already challenged and approved the redundancy and the restructure of the Market Risk Control team prior to Ranjit being told he is selected for redundancy. The decision was not arrived at lightly.

Regarding the timing of the announcement, we have a Christmas moratorium agreed with our union that no announcements be made in the two weeks prior to Christmas. I am satisfied the standard procedure was followed.

After the appeal hearing meeting, the panel members and I sat and discussed our views.

I was not concerned that Neil had approached Ranjit exclusively with an offer of voluntary redundancy because, although the bank does not have a formal voluntary redundancy policy to avoid compulsory redundancies, there is an unofficial policy to approach individuals who previously indicated they might be interested in taking up voluntary redundancy to discover if they are still interested. I did not see Neil's action as being untoward or indicating any prejudgement of the redundancy selection outcome. Neil simply followed the bank's normal procedure.

Although only one person was at risk in the

Market Risk Department, overall across four locations of the bank more than one hundred people were put at risk in a ninety-day period, meaning the bank had to carry out collective consultation with the union. We were also satisfied that the individual consultation Neil and Veronica carried out with Ranjit is effective consultation. They listened to the points he raised and considered them genuinely. We were satisfied that had he put forward viable alternative options, then Neil would have considered them genuinely and his redundancy would possibly have been avoided.

The focus of Ranjit's appeal really centred on what he perceives as lack of consultation, rather than his scoring. He did not challenge to any great extent the scoring that is given to him. Even if his scoring were increased, he would still be selected for redundancy. It was clear to us that he is not a poor performer but, rather, he is in a pool of two people in which the other person performed just slightly better. Unfortunately, the drastic cost cutting going on in the bank can lead to situations where good performers are made redundant.

For all these reasons, we did not uphold Ranjit's complaints and we did not overturn the decision to make him redundant.

At no point in the appeal process did he even hint that he believes his scoring or his redundancy is tainted by his race or colour.

'Yes,' she replies.

Addressing the chairman, the respondents' counsel says, 'I wish to bring up some supplementary issues, Sir'.

The chairman signals her to do so.

Addressing Jackie, she asks, 'the bank's two-page document titled, *Job Security Agreement*, is this the redundancy agreement between the bank and the union?'

'Yes,' she replies.

'It is not signed, not by the bank and not by the union,' she says.

'I've never seen a signed version. But, it is agreed,' she replies.

'When was it agreed?' she asks.

'Towards the end of 2004,' she answers, 'just after Eurocredito took us over. We knew there'd be a huge programme of redundancies, like never before. We put the agreement together to manage the volume'.

The chairman interjects, 'could you be more accurate on the date please?'

'I don't know the exact date,' she replies.

'Have you ever seen minutes of any meetings saying the bank and the union have made the agreement?' the chairman asks.

'No,' she replies. 'But, I believe the agreement is made and we have been complying with it'.

'Complying with an unsigned agreement document which you have never seen as having been agreed in any minutes of meetings?' the chairman puts to her in amazed tone.

'Yes,' she replies.

'Remarkable,' the chairman says and signals the respondents' counsel to continue.

'At the time of Ranjit's redundancy, how many other people were also being made redundant at the London Wall office, where he worked?' she asks.

'I can't tell you that,' she answers. 'I can tell you it was two hundred and seventy-five across all London premises plus Northampton'.

'Miss Cotton gave evidence that the union said not to announce the redundancy before Christmas. Do you have any comments on that?' she asks.

'It's never a good time to announce a redundancy. I appreciate that Christmas is a festive period where people tend to spend extra. But, I don't think before Christmas is a good time to announce a redundancy because of the practical difficulties due to a lot of staff tending to be away on annual leave around then, particularly the managers,' she answers.

'How many managers would normally be involved in a redundancy scoring exercise?' she asks.

'It depends on the area,' she answers. 'It can be just one manager supported by an HR person, it could be more'.

'You conducted Ranjit's appeal against his redundancy,' she says.

'Yes, that's right,' she answers. 'He felt there was a failure to consult him'.

'What possible outcomes could there have been from the appeal?' she asks.

'In some appeals, I've reinstated people. In others, I've sent the decision back for reconsideration. In one appeal, we created a new job for the wrongful redundancy. So, there are a variety of possibilities that might have applied,' she answers. 'In some cases, we've agreed financial compensation because the people felt they couldn't continue working at the bank'.

'How many appeals have you been involved in?' she asks.

'Twenty seven,' she answers.

'Of those twenty seven, what is your estimate of the different types of outcomes?' she asks.

'In about half of them, I upheld the appeal and rejected management's decision. The outcomes ranged from compensation to reinstatement and redeployment,' she answers.

'You were the chairwoman on a panel of three in Ranjit's appeal. Was it a unanimous decision?' she asks.

'Yes,' she answers.

'How did you decide the outcome?' she asks.

'Ranjit questioned the legality of the consultation process. So, we decided to take legal advice. We took the advice on board when deciding,' she answers.

'No further evidence in chief, Sir,' the respondents' counsel informs the chairman.

The chairman signals my counsel to cross-examine the witness.

'The consultation meeting Neil and Veronica have with the union,' my counsel starts. 'You chaired that meeting. Was there any discussion of the selection criteria used in the redundancy?'

'No,' she answers.

'You have never seen the agreement on redundancies between the bank and the union,' she says.

'No,' she replies.

'So, you could not check the agreement terms,' she puts to her.

'That's correct,' she answers.

'Ranjit asks the appeal panel if an employee can be selected for redundancy without being informed that there is a redundancy in progress,' she says.

'Yes,' she replies.

'He says he was selected without knowing a redundancy is happening,' she says.

'He feels that way,' she replies.

'Was he selected for redundancy before the 15th of December 2005?' she asks.

'Yes,' she answers.

'Is the 11th of January 2006 the first time he is told there is a redundancy?' she asks.

'Yes,' she answers.

'Therefore, he is selected without him knowing there is a redundancy in progress,' she puts to her.

'I can see how he feels that, but he was only put at risk,' she replies.

'But, he is selected for redundancy before he is told he is at risk,' she says.

'Yes,' she answers.

'So, your answer in your decision letter to his direct question is wrong,' she asserts.

'But, the redundancy was not confirmed when he was told he is at risk,' she answers. 'He could have challenged it'.

The chairman interjects, 'Ms Monroe, you wrote to him saying, *"the bank consults with the individual as soon as there is a possibility that the job will be put at risk"*. The possibility of a redundancy in Market Risk Control arose in October. Why were Ranjit and Katia not told then that they are both at risk? Is it the case that the bank does not actually do as it claims to do?'

'Er, hmm, by that logic, yes,' she replies.

'Please, Ms Monroe, do explain to me what is wrong with my logic,' the chairman challenges her.

'Nothing's wrong with it,' she replies.

'One of the purposes of consultation is to seek ways of avoiding any dismissal. So, the consultation needs to occur when it might actually be effective. Here, the person has already been selected before any consultation,' the chairman says.

'Yes,' she replies.

The chairman signals my counsel to continue.

'You and the panel are so consumed by your procedures and by what you always do that you stop listening to Ranjit,' she says.

'No,' she answers. 'We didn't stop listening to him. It's because we listened to him that we decided his concerns are important enough for us to seek legal advice'.

'With the hindsight of the answers you have given here today, would you decide the appeal differently?' she asks.

'No,' she answers, 'because we had legal advise that told us otherwise'.

'Did the legal advise make your minds up for you?' she asks.

'No,' she answers. 'It guided us'.

'You say there are practical problems in announcing redundancies around Christmas because staff tend to be off on annual leave,' she puts to her.

'Yes,' she answers.

'That would not be the case in October, November, and at the beginning of December,' she puts to her.

'No,' she replies. 'But, the redundancy process takes time to conclude'.

'The minutes of the meeting with the union say that the process is going on since October. Would you explain why Ranjit could not be told well before Christmas?' she asks.

'Although the process started in October, it hadn't completed until near Christmas,' she answers.

'If the bank's policy is to warn as soon as possible, then the warning could be given in October or November. Then, the Christmas problem would be irrelevant,' she says.

'The process hadn't completed then,' she replies.

'Did you bother to find out if anyone relevant to his redundancy is away around Christmas?' she asks.

'I can't remember,' she answers.

'So, no,' she says.

'Honesty, I can't remember,' she replies.

'The union did not request the announcement to be delayed to the 9th of January,' she puts to her.

'I can't remember,' she replies.

'The bank does not have a voluntary redundancy policy,' she says.

'No,' she confirms.

'No policy of asking people who in the past enquired about voluntary redundancy,' she says.

'No,' she confirms.

'Is it normal to sound people out?' she asks.

'Yes,' she answers.

'It is not agreed with the union, is it?' she puts to her.

'Not formally,' she replies.

'If it is normal practice to sound people out, then it would be written down in a policy or agreed with the union,' she says.

'Not necessarily,' she answers.

'Did it not trouble you that Neil approached Ranjit exclusively for voluntary redundancy?' she asks.

'No. I saw no problem with it,' she answers.

'Do you see any problem with Neil being the only person carrying out the scoring?' she asks.

'No, I don't,' she answers.

'Do you see any problem with Neil also being the only person carrying out the year-end appraisal that is used in the redundancy?' she asks.

'No. The appraisal has a separate appeal process applicable to it,' she answers.

'Ranjit was appealing against his appraisal vociferously,' she says.

'If he had raised a formal appeal, I would have taken that into account,' she replies.

'Does it not trouble you that Neil is the sole decision maker throughout the entire redundancy process?' she asks.

'That's not how I see it,' she answers. 'Veronica and Simon Ong sense-checked some of his decisions'.

The chairman interjects, 'Miss Cotton and Mr Ong say that they did not really challenge Mr Hobson's decisions'.

'I don't know, I wasn't privy to what they did,' she replies.

'You had no concerns,' my counsel continues, 'that Ranjit is preselected?'

'No,' she replies.

'Thank you, I have no more questions,' my counsel says.

## 13

# COLIN MARR'S TESTIMONY

~ Friday 8th December 2006, 2:30 p.m. ~

'Mr Marr, is that your signature on the witness statement and is that the evidence you wish to give?' the respondents' counsel asks him, he having just sworn in at the witness stand.

He has presented the tribunal his statement on the matters at hand. It says the following:

> I am the bank's Head of Trading Credit. I manage a team of eighteen people. I have been at the bank for over six years. I am comparable in terms of seniority to Neil Hobson.
>
> I worked with Ranjit Singh on various matters, from time to time. I had a very good working relationship with him. It was open, frank, and constructive. I had no involvement at all in his appraisal or in his selection for redundancy.
>
> I heard and judged his formal grievance about his 2005 bonus award. He was told that Neil would do it. But, he was not happy with that and requested an independent person does it. It is in the capacity of an independent person that I was involved.
>
> I heard his grievance on 6th April 2006. Before the hearing, I had an informal chat with Neil to get the background. He told me that all the relevant information is contained in Ranjit's grievance letter. I knew that Ranjit had been selected for redundancy. But, I did not know at the time that

he is appealing his redundancy also. I thought to myself, why bother challenging the bonus, why not challenge the redundancy itself? I now know that he was challenging the redundancy too.

Each department in the bank is allocated a bonus pot for the year. Each individual's bonus is totally discretionary. It is not guaranteed and a bonus does not have to be awarded at all. So, it is really up to the department head how to allocate the pot out to individuals. My department head includes me in a discussion to review the bonuses proposed for the individuals in my team. Line managers, like me, sense-check the bonus allocations proposed by our department heads. The bonus allocated to an individual is based on his performance for the year, as measured by the appraisal score, and on the bonus pot available for the department.

I asked Ranjit to outline the exact nature of his grievance. He did. I said I could not make a decision there and then, as I need to analyse the bonus allocations for the current and the previous year for the whole of his department. At no point did he even allege that he believes his bonus allocation is due to his race or colour.

After the hearing meeting, I received the bonus data from Veronica Cotton and I performed my analysis. I split the data between Grade B and C employees. Ranjit was a Grade C employee. Grade C employees get paid higher salaries than Grade B employees because it is the higher grade. I compared individuals' 2005 appraisal scores against their 2004 scores to see how they changed. I was looking for inconsistencies in the bonuses awarded. I identified a couple of anomalies that needed investigating. They did not concern Ranjit, though. I went to Simon Ong and asked him why they were slightly inconsistent from the rest. He gave me explanations that seemed reasonable to me. I was satisfied and agreed with his rationales.

Simon explained that to compare one year's bonus with the next is an incorrect way to look at bonuses. You have a bonus pot from which you have to reward the high performers the most. So, he looks at the bonus to salary percentage ratio for the year for each individual. He also looks at the individual's market value. Bonuses have to be considered this way. Comparing one year's bonus with the previous year's bonus doesn't work because the size of the bonus pot changes and the individuals in the pool change. So, you have to consider each year individually.

I was satisfied. It did not seem to me that Ranjit's bonus is materially out of kilter with other people's bonus awards.

Ranjit never said to me that he thought his bonus is based on his race or colour. Although he was unhappy with his appraisal score, he never said that he thought it is tainted with race or colour discrimination.

I was happy that he is not treated less favourably. Hence, I dismissed his grievance.

When Ranjit appealed against my decision, Adam Sirinathan was assigned to hear the appeal. I was involved again prior to the appeal hearing in talking Adam through the analysis that I had performed. It was a brief discussion. I had no further involvement thereafter.

I am surprised that Ranjit has not yet got another job. I made someone redundant around the same time as Ranjit was made redundant. He was not as good as Ranjit. But, he got another job really quickly. He got a job at another investment bank, a very good name, equal to, if not better, than us. He even got a better role with more responsibility. The job market is really hot at the moment, especially in market risk roles. I cannot see why Ranjit should have any problem getting another job quickly. The job market is really buoyant.

'Yes,' he replies.
The respondents' counsel gives way to my counsel to cross-examine him.
'When you are assigned to conduct Ranjit's bonus grievance,' she starts, 'do you know that he is selected for redundancy?'
'Yes,' he replies.
'Ranjit states in his grievance letter that he cannot help but link how he is treated on the bonus to the similarly unfair treatment he has received in his redundancy,' she says.
'Yes, I noted that,' he replies.
'How did you investigate if there is any link between his bonus and his redundancy?' she asks.
'I had a conversation with Neil. I asked him whether there's anything more that I should be aware of that isn't in his grievance letter,' he answers.
'Did you do anything else or ask anyone else anything to investigate the link?' she asks.
'No,' he replies.
'You know Neil selected him for redundancy,' she puts to him.
'Yes,' he replies.
'So, if you are investigating whether there is a link between the bonus and the redundancy, then Neil is not the best person to ask, is he?' she asks.
'Er, hmm,' he contemplates. 'No, he's not,' he concedes.
'Simon decided the bonuses, correct?' she asks.
'Yes,' he answers.

'You spoke to him?' she asks.

'Yes,' he replies.

'You brought to his attention the anomalies you found,' she says.

'Yes. They were minor matters,' he replies.

'What are they?' she asks.

'There were two. One concerned a decrease in a bonus and the other, an increase,' he answers.

'What did Simon say?' she asks.

'He gave me valid explanations,' he answers. 'The decrease is due to greater expectations of the individual, who was promoted into a higher role. The increase is due to the award being for a full year to someone who joined part way through the previous year. The previous bonus award was lower because it was for a fraction of the year'.

'Ranjit did not raise the issue of race to you,' she says, 'but, if someone had pointed out that the only people who suffered a reduced bonus are Asian, would you have probed it?'

'No,' he answers. 'My investigation methodology would be exactly the same. I'd identify and investigate exactly the same anomalies'.

'Did you investigate Simon's explanations further to check they are correct?' she asks.

'No,' he answers. 'They sounded totally plausible to me. I accepted them as being satisfactory'.

'You accepted them at face value,' she says.

'Yes,' he replies.

'If Simon discriminated, he would not just own up when asked and tell you, would he?' she puts to him.

'Er, hmm, no, I suppose not,' he replies. 'But, I've known him for a few years now. I have no reason to believe he'd discriminate against anyone'.

'Well, there is the fact that the only two people who received reduced bonuses are both Asian,' she says.

'But, he gave me plausible explanations for the anomalies I identified,' he replies.

'Does he keep any records evidencing the rationale of his bonus allocations?' she asks.

'No,' he answers.

'Would such records have helped you to investigate the explanations he gave you?' she asks.

'Er, yes,' he answers.

'What else did you discuss with him?' she asks.

'How the bonuses are allocated,' he answers. 'I wanted assurance from him that the allocation is fair and equitable. For that, I needed to know how they're decided. He told me how. I believed him'.

'Anything else?' she asks.

'No,' he replies.

'How long did your conversation with him last?' she asks.

'About half an hour,' he answers.

'Did you make any notes of the conversation?' she asks.

'Very brief notes,' he answers.

'Where are they?' she asks.

'Er, I couldn't find them,' he replies.

'Simon does not explain to you the precise rationale regarding Ranjit's bonus award,' she puts to him.

'No. It wasn't discussed specifically,' he answers.

'*It wasn't discussed specifically*,' she echoes his answer. 'You mean you did not ask and he did not mention'.

'No, not specifically,' he confirms.

'You ask him how bonuses are allocated in general terms only and he replies in general terms only,' she puts to him.

'Yes,' he confirms.

'Then, how do you know that the general process is applied specifically to Ranjit?' she asks.

'Because it's applied to everyone,' he asserts.

'You do not ask specifically how Ranjit's bonus is awarded and Simon does not tell you?' she puts to him.

'That's right,' he replies.

'The bank had a highly profitable year in 2005,' she

says.

'Yes,' he confirms.

'So, it is logical to conclude that the bonus pot must be bigger,' she says.

'Yes, that seems logical,' he replies.

'Simon considers an individual's market value when allocating bonuses, correct?' she asks.

'Yes,' he confirms.

'In other words, he considers how much to pay to incentivise an individual to remain in his role,' she says.

'Correct,' he confirms.

'Thank you, I have no further question,' she says.

# 14

# ADAM SIRINATHAN'S TESTIMONY

~ Friday 8th December 2006, 4:00 p.m. ~

Adam Sirinathan is nowhere to be seen in the courtroom. He has presented the tribunal his statement on the matters at hand. It says the following:

> I started working at the bank in April 2006 as its Chief Credit Officer. I was equivalent to Simon Ong in terms of seniority. My employment at the bank ended amicably by mutual agreement on 30th September 2006. I am now employed in a similar role at another bank.
>
> I never had any dealings with Ranjit Singh prior to being involved in his 2005 bonus grievance. I had never even met him before the appeal hearing on 3rd July 2006.
>
> Janet Shipley of HR was also present at the hearing meeting. The meeting was very cordial. I explained that I am relatively new in the bank, I am unaware of the personalities and circumstances involved, and that places me in a completely impartial position.
>
> I asked Ranjit what his concerns are. By the end of the meeting, I was satisfied I had identified and understood the specific issues he raised. His complaint is that there does not seem to be any correlation between his performance appraisal score and his bonus.

After the meeting, I investigated the method by which bonuses are awarded at the bank. On 10th July, I had an investigation meeting with Simon Ong in the presence of Janet Shipley. I established from my investigation that it is incorrect to look for a correlation between appraisal scores and the year-on-year change in the bonus. Simon confirmed that what a person may have gotten in the previous year is irrelevant in calculating the bonus for the current year. The starting point is the size of the bonus pot allocated to the department for the year. Then, he looks at the individual's performance for the year in comparison to the performances of other individuals in the pool. A comparison with the previous year's bonus is completely irrelevant. Relative performance is the critical factor because it is important for the bank to reward and retain its high-calibre staff. Then, he factors in the individual's market value. This is a significant factor. If an individual is perceived as being highly marketable, such that there is a significant risk of the individual leaving and creating a hole for the bank that would be difficult to fill, then the individual's market value increases. Simon gave the example that after the Head of Market Risk Control left the bank in October 2004, the team was left with just two members, Ranjit and Katia. If one or both of them left, it would put the bank in a very difficult position. Thus, their market values increased.

I have worked at several large institutions. The bank's approach is very similar to that of other banks.

I did not find Ranjit's complaint well founded in any way, shape, or form. I was happy that his bonus is awarded in accordance with the bank's approach and that there is no unfairness. I was satisfied that his bonus is awarded fairly and so, I dismissed his appeal.

At no point did he complain to me that he believes his bonus is reduced due to any act of race discrimination. In fact, he was not complaining about what he is awarded in comparison to Katia Mykonola, but rather that he is being paid less in comparison to what he received for the prior year. There was no way to tell from his complaint that he believes race discrimination is a possibility. He certainly did not complain of any racial prejudices to me.

Addressing the chairman, the respondents' counsel says, 'the respondents apologise to the tribunal that Mr Sirinathan is unable to appear before you to give evidence in person. It is because he left the bank's employment and is now employed at another bank. His commitments to his new employer prevent him from attending here to testify before you'.

'How are we supposed to cross-examine him?' the chairman asks.

'The respondents apologise, Sir. Mr Sirinathan tried his best to appear in person, but his commitments do not permit it. The respondents request that you accept his statement as read, at face value,' she answers.

'We cannot place much reliance on it if we cannot probe him on it,' the chairman asserts.

# 15

# NATHAN WILCOX'S TESTIMONY

~ Monday 11th December 2006, 10:30 a.m. ~

'Mr Wilcox, is that your signature on the witness statement and is that the evidence you wish to give?' the respondents' counsel asks him, he having just sworn in at the witness stand.

He has presented the tribunal his statement on the matters at hand. It says the following:

> I am the bank's Head of Fraud in its Financial Crime Division. I have been at the bank since February 2005. I am similar to Neil Hobson in terms of seniority.
>
> I had never met Neil and Ranjit Singh prior to my involvement with Ranjit's grievance on race discrimination. I had met Simon Ong previously at business meetings, but we never discussed any issues regarding Ranjit.
>
> I have carried out a number of redundancies in my department due to the cost savings drive put in place by Eurocredito since it took us over. Hence, I am fully aware of how the bank's redundancy process should work. I had no information about the other grievances Ranjit had raised. I did not want to know about them because I did not want to be influenced by previous decisions. I did, however, know that he had appealed the decision to make him redundant.
>
> I held the race discrimination grievance hearing on 4th July 2006. There, I went through the issues

with Ranjit. I found him to be very likeable, articulate, and clearly well educated.

He never complained to me at the hearing that his bonus allocation is tainted with race discrimination. Although he raised it in an email after our meeting, he did not mention it during the meeting. I was aware he had raised a separate grievance regarding his bonus. So, I did not think the bonus matter is within my remit to investigate.

Ranjit worked at the bank for four and a half years. Initially, he worked alongside Neil. A few years later, he worked under him, when Neil became his line manager. He described the relationship as a professional one, although challenging at times due to the highly complex and responsible nature of the work. Having talked with both of them, I got the impression there were at times professional conflicts, but no sense that they were based on race. I was conscious that both of them worked at a senior level and in a complex area where, of course, there would be professional disagreements and conflicts from time to time. However, nothing they said gave any indication of race discrimination. The first time Ranjit mentions race is when he cannot think of any other reason why he would be selected for redundancy over Katia. I believe he is unwilling to accept that he could be selected for redundancy over Katia and is trying to find justification.

I asked him specifically whether there was any hint of race discrimination prior to his redundancy. He said no. I also asked him if there are any independent witnesses on whom I could call to corroborate his complaint of discrimination. He said no. Besides saying that he would not be selected for redundancy if the process is applied in a non-discriminatory fashion, he could give no evidence of any race discrimination.

He said that he did not raise any complaint of race discrimination earlier in the redundancy consultation and grievance process because he did not realise until later on, in the redundancy appeal hearing on 20th March, that race is an issue.

He brought along to the hearing a file containing printouts of emails. He said they evidence what he is saying. He showed me the file and offered it to me for my investigation. I declined it.

I asked him about the scoring and why he perceives it to be racially motivated. I was trying to identify what exactly it is he is challenging. Basically, he does not agree with the reasons that Neil gave to justify the lower scores he awarded him. He believes the criticisms Neil made of him are equally applicable to Katia, but only he is criticised and marked down and that the reason for this is due to his race.

After the hearing, I held a meeting with Neil to discuss the issues Ranjit raised. Janet Shipley of HR was present. I explained the purpose of the meeting and that I have already interviewed Ranjit and gotten his version, and that my role is to be independent.

I asked Neil how long the two of them had worked together and to describe how their relationship was. I asked him whether Ranjit would have any evidence of race discrimination. I also asked him to explain the business rationale for making a Controller redundant. I wanted to be sure the restructure is not a sham merely to remove Ranjit. I also got him to describe why he decided on the redundancy pool of Ranjit and Katia. I asked him to talk me through the scoring and whether the scores are close. I tried to pull apart why the scoring of Ranjit and Katia is different. I was trying to challenge whether the explanations sound plausible, reasonable, and objective. I was looking for any hint of racial discrimination, whether conscious or unconscious. Neil explained everything satisfactorily.

After the meeting with Neil, later on the same day, I decided I need further clarifications from him on one point. We had a telephone conference call on it that same day. It was regarding an issue of not notifying the FSA of a perceived reportable matter. Neil gave me an explanation with which I was satisfied.

Then, I took some time to consider my decision. Neil's explanations and reasons for the scoring all seemed plausible to me, and the bank's process was followed. I made my decision and drafted the grievance outcome letter. I sent it to the bank's legal and HR departments to double-check that I followed the process correctly and that my letter is drafted appropriately.

Having considered everything, I could find no evidence of any racial prejudice. I was not only looking for overt racial discrimination, but also whether Ranjit believes there is any underlying racial reason for any decision that was taken. However, he had confirmed to me that he had no reason to think that his working relationship with Neil was anything other than professional and that he had no reason to think that there are any issues regarding race discrimination prior to his selection for redundancy. I do not believe the bank's redundancy procedure is inherently tainted with race discrimination. I am satisfied that Neil followed the standard procedure. The only issue I could see is that Katia is of a different race, colour, and ethnic origin to Ranjit. I accepted every business rationale Neil gave for the need to make a Controller redundant. I therefore had to consider whether the process was carried out fairly and consistently. I am satisfied from the explanations Neil gave that the scoring is justified. Neil is not saying Ranjit is underperforming, but rather that Katia is performing better than him in certain areas, which is why he awarded her full marks and marked him down. I was satisfied that there is no hint of any race discrimination anywhere. Hence, I dismissed his grievance.

I was involved again on this issue when Adrian Brent, who heard Ranjit's appeal against my decision, telephoned me. We discussed what I had done and the process I had followed. Thereafter, I had no further involvement.

I would like to point out that if I thought the redundancy is racially motivated, I would have found in Ranjit's favour and asked HR to discipline Neil. I am comfortable that I have the authority to do that. There is no place for discrimination in the workplace. However, I found absolutely no basis to uphold his claim.

'Yes,' he replies.

The respondents' counsel gives way to my counsel to cross-examine him.

'How many grievances have you conducted?' my counsel asks.

'This is my first,' he answers.

'Did the bank give you any training on grievances?' she asks.

'No,' he replies.

'Has the bank given you any training on Diversity and Equal Opportunities?' she asks.

'No,' he answers.

'You say the first time Ranjit mentions a race issue is

when he can think of no other reason why he would be selected for redundancy over Katia,' she says.

'Yes, that's correct,' he confirms.

'So, what do you believe his motive is to claim race discrimination occurred?' she asks.

'He couldn't find any other reason to justify his redundancy. So, he concluded it could only be race discrimination,' he answers.

'Do you think he jumped to that conclusion because he cannot accept being selected for redundancy?' she asks.

'Yes, I do. From reading his grievance letter and from meeting him, yes, absolutely,' he asserts.

'You meet him before you have your two meetings with Neil?' she asks.

'Yes,' he confirms.

'Neil does not suggest an unfair selection in anyway?' she asks.

'No,' he answers. 'He explained his business rationale, the process, and the scoring'.

'He tells you he was fair?' she asks.

'Yes,' he replies.

'His explanations seem plausible to you?' she asks.

'Yes,' he answers.

'Did you see the email where Ranjit tells him not to patronise him?' she asks.

'Yes, I saw that one,' he confirms.

'Did you see any other emails?' she asks.

'No, only that one,' he answers. 'Ranjit brought a file containing email printouts to the grievance hearing. He said they evidence and support his grievance. But, I declined to look at them and didn't take them from him'.

'You do not ask Neil to back up what he says with any documentary evidence?' she asks.

'No,' he answers.

'You simply accept what he tells you?' she asks.

'Yes,' he replies.

The chairman interjects, 'Mr Wilcox, why did you not

take a look at the email evidence that Mr Singh brought along with him for you to consider?'

'I didn't think it necessary,' he answers.

My counsel continues, 'He lodges the grievance on the 14th of June. The hearing meeting is held on the 4th of July. Then, later on the same day, you have meetings with Neil. Then, on the 18th of July, you send your outcome decision by letter'.

'That's correct,' he confirms.

'Did you read the bank's policy and procedures beforehand on how to conduct grievances, especially the section on those of a complex or sensitive nature?' she asks.

'Yes, I did,' he answers firmly.

'Did you conduct the grievance in accordance with the policy?' she asks.

'Yes, I did,' he replies firmly.

'Did you decide a formal investigation is needed?' she asks.

'Yes, I did,' he answers.

'Whom did you assign to perform the formal investigation?' she asks.

'What do you mean?' he asks back. 'I decided I need to speak with Ranjit and with Neil, and I spoke with them'.

'Mr Wilcox, did you actually read the policy and procedures beforehand?' she asks.

'Yes, absolutely,' he answers firmly.

'Did you see that the procedures clearly state that if a formal investigation is needed, the person conducting the grievance, which is you, will ask an independent senior member of staff to perform the investigation for him. Did you consider whether a formal investigation is needed?' she asks.

'Yes,' he replies.

'Did you decide that a formal investigation should be performed?' she asks.

'Yes,' he answers.

'You think speaking with Ranjit and Neil constitutes a formal investigation?' she asks.

'In my view, yes,' he asserts.

'You do not assign another member of staff to perform the investigation. You perform it yourself,' she says.

'That's correct,' he replies.

'Did you agree a timetable for the investigation and give all parties involved a copy?' she asks.

'Er, what timetable?' he asks back.

'The procedures, which you said twice that you read, clearly state you will agree a timetable and make sure all parties involved get a copy. Did you actually read the procedures, Mr Wilcox?' she asks.

'Yes, I read them,' he asserts.

'So, you do not assign someone independent to carry out the formal investigation and you do not agree a timetable?' she puts to him.

'No,' he replies.

'But, you still claim you read the policy?' she asks.

'Yes,' he answers.

The chairman interjects, 'Mr Wilcox, if you read the policy, then why did you not do the things it says to do?'

'I didn't think they mattered,' he answers.

The chairman signals my counsel to continue.

'Did you meet the key people, as per the policy?' my counsel continues.

'Yes,' he answers.

'Did you write up what they said and get them to sign it, as per the policy?' she asks.

'Er, hmm, no,' he concedes.

'Did you write up a formal report, as per the policy?' she asks.

'Hmm, no, only my decision letter,' he answers.

'Are you still suggesting that you conducted the grievance according to the policy?' she asks.

'Er, hmm,' he deliberates. 'No, not as it's written down,' he concedes.

'Why not?' she asks.

'I didn't realise the significance,' he answers.

'But, race is a complex and sensitive issue, correct?' she puts to him.

'Yes, it is,' he replies.

The chairman interjects, 'Mr Wilcox, why did you deal with it the way you did? Is it because you did not read the policy properly? Is it because you did not think there is any substance to the grievance? Is it because you did not have the time, or thought there already have been redundancy and bonus grievances? What is the reason?'

'I just hadn't read the policy properly,' he answers.

The chairman signals my counsel to continue.

'You do not hold the hearing meeting and you do not send your decision letter within the time limits the policy states,' she resumes.

'I take your word for it,' he replies.

'Ranjit has to chase you and the bank repeatedly because of the excessive delays,' she says.

'Yes,' he confirms.

'I suggest your dealing with the grievance is unreasonable and not compliant with the bank's own policy,' she puts to him.

'Er, yes, I have to agree,' he concedes.

'Because you had made up your mind beforehand that he is looking for an excuse for his redundancy,' she puts to him.

'I categorically deny that!' he protests.

'You do not follow proper procedures because you do not take his allegation of race discrimination seriously,' she puts to him.

'I refute that allegation!' he replies.

'No independent investigation suggested,' she says.

'Er, no,' he confirms.

'No sense of urgency, Ranjit having to chase repeatedly,' she says.

'Er, hmm, yes,' he concedes.

'No one in the bank taking it seriously,' she says.

'I believe we all took it seriously,' he protests.

'Normally a grievance would be dealt with quickly?' she says.

'Yes,' he confirms.

'Not this grievance though, because Ranjit is Asian and is complaining of race discrimination,' she says.

'That's not true, and it's not fair!' he protests.

The chairman interjects, 'Mr Wilcox, why is it not fair to suggest that?'

'Because I believe race discrimination matters to the bank,' he replies.

The chairman signals my counsel to continue.

'Did HR ask you if you are trained in Equal Opportunities?' my counsel continues.

'No. But, I told them I'm not, and I said I'd conduct the grievance anyway,' he replies.

'HR was fine with that?' she asks.

'Yes,' he answers.

'Did you really even read the procedures and policy on how to conduct the grievance?' she asks.

'Er, I checked some parts of it on the intranet, but I can't categorically say that I read it all,' he concedes.

'If you thought the matter is important, you would have read it properly,' she puts to him.

'I beg your pardon!' he objects.

'If you truly consider the matter to be serious and important, as you say you do, then you would read the policy thoroughly,' she puts to him.

'Er, hmm,' he deliberates. 'Yes,' he concedes.

'In terms of looking behind what Ranjit and Neil told you, all you look at is the one email about the patronising comment,' she puts to him.

'I also looked at the scoring,' he replies.

'But, the scoring is the thing that is being disputed. You do not look into the scoring, you do not investigate it independently,' she puts to him.

'I had two meetings to investigate it. I looked at whether the difference in the scores is reasonable and whether the explanations are plausible. I also looked at whether the difference is motivated by race,' he asserts.

'How did you make a judgement on those things?' she asks.

'By speaking to Neil about them,' he answers.

'He tells you he is fair,' she says.

'Yes,' he replies, 'he gave me reasonable and plausible explanations for everything'.

'What else did you do?' she asks.

'Nothing,' he replies. 'I believed him'.

'Thank you, I have no further questions,' she says.

# 16

# ADRIAN BRENT'S TESTIMONY

~ Monday 11th December 2006, 1:00 p.m. ~

'Mr Brent, is that your signature on the witness statement and is that the evidence you wish to give?' the respondents' counsel asks him, he having just sworn in at the witness stand.

He has presented the tribunal his statement on the matters at hand. It says the following:

> I am the Head of Compliance across the whole of the bank. I joined the bank at the start of 2006. I am responsible for a team of seventy people.
>
> I never had any dealings with Ranjit Singh or Neil Hobson prior to my involvement in investigating Ranjit's grievance regarding race discrimination. I had, however, worked with Simon Ong. He and I share the same line manager, the bank's Chief Risk Officer.
>
> I have had training at my previous employers on how to chair disciplinary and grievance hearings, and how to consider cases on appeal. I have also at my previous employers had briefings on discrimination in the workplace. But, I have not had any such training and briefing at my current employer. Ranjit's hearing is the first one that I carried out at this bank.
>
> Janet Shipley, an HR Business Partner, assisted me with the appeal. I had no involvement with Ranjit's selection for redundancy or with his appraisal scores. Therefore, I was an independent

person, appropriate to hear the grievance appeal.

I decided in consultation with HR that it would be appropriate for me to hold a meeting firstly to hear his appeal and to consider his evidence. Then, I would investigate and interview the relevant witnesses. Then, I would give him the outcome result.

Although he had put down a lot of evidence in his appeal letter, I wished to speak with him directly in order to be sure what are the issues that need to be determined. I also wished to hear his complaints from him directly, without any preconceived ideas. For these reasons, I did not interview any witnesses prior to the hearing meeting. My primary objective was to ensure his concerns and grievances are investigated as fully as possible.

At the appeal hearing, on 10th August 2006, I went through all of the points he listed in his appeal letter. I started off by asking him whether he could give me any examples of where he believes he was discriminated against whilst working at the bank. He said that he does not believe he is discriminated against other than during the redundancy process. Then, I talked through the various issues that he had raised. I ended the meeting by asking him whether there are any further questions that he has. He wanted clarification on the timeframe of when I planned to talk to witnesses, investigate his grievance, and get back to him with an outcome decision.

I approached the meeting as a complete re-hearing of all his concerns. I was not relying on any records from the previous stage conducted by Nathan Wilcox. I wanted to hear what Ranjit had to say first and then, conduct my own investigation and form my own conclusions. I am satisfied that

I acted in the utmost appropriate manner.

After the hearing meeting, on the same day, Ranjit sent me an email enclosing the evidence that he referred to during the grievance process. I printed off the documents he sent me and read them. From an evidential point of view, I did receive a lot of information from him after the meeting.

I had a meeting with Neil on 21st August. I also had a telephone conversation with him.

During my investigation, I found no evidence of race discrimination. Actually, I do not believe the evidence Ranjit put forward supports his claim of race discrimination. He says that from the way he feels he was treated, the only conclusion he can reach is that he is discriminated against on the grounds of race. But, he has no evidence of direct race discrimination. So, essentially, because he does not accept his redundancy, he concludes he must be the subject of race discrimination.

Having reviewed all of the information Ranjit gave me, and having spoken with Neil too, I did not form the same conclusion as he. I do not believe he is treated any differently from anyone else. He is not a poor performer. It is merely that Katia is a better performer and therefore, scored higher.

The subjective view of the managers is always taken into account in a redundancy scoring process. From the information I had, I could not see that Neil treated Ranjit less favourably than Katia. I was satisfied the bank's standard process was followed. Consequently, I dismissed his appeal. I sent him a letter on 7th September 2006 informing him of my decision and the reasons, and that my decision is final and the bank considers the matter closed.

'Yes,' he replies.

The respondents' counsel gives way to my counsel to cross-examine him.

'Did you receive any Diversity and Equal Opportunities training from the bank?' my counsel asks him.

'No,' he answers.

'What experience did you have of the banks redundancy process prior to being involved in Ranjit's appeal?' she asks.

'None,' he answers. 'There wasn't any reason to have had any'.

'So, what research did you do to familiarise yourself with the banks procedures?' she asks.

'I went on to our intranet site and read up on them,' he answers.

'What about at your previous employers, any experience in redundancies there?' she asks.

'Yes, lots,' he answers.

'So, you know what a fair redundancy involves?' she asks.

'Yes, I do believe I do,' he answers in cocky tone.

'When Ranjit comes to see you, he brings along a file containing printouts of emails,' she says.

'I can't remember,' he replies.

'He offers it to you,' she says.

'I can't remember,' he repeats. 'But, I did ask him to supply me emails after the meeting, which he did promptly'.

'You did not seek out to establish the full set of evidence for yourself?' she asks.

'I don't know what a full set would look like,' he answers.

'Did you produce an investigation report?' she asks.

'I don't know what that means,' he replies.

'Did you assign anyone to do an investigation and produce a report?' she puts to him.

'Did I need to?' he asks back.

'Mr Brent,' the chairman interjects, 'you are here to answer questions, not to ask them. Answer the question!'

'No,' he answers.

'Did you check whether Mr Wilcox's investigation is appropriate?' my counsel continues.

'No, it wasn't my responsibility to do so,' he replies.

'The bank's policies state that you should complete your investigations and communicate your decision on the appeal within four weeks of it being lodged. You took much longer than that,' she says.

'It depends when you consider the start time to be,' he replies.

'The policy clearly states the time starts from the date the appeal is lodged,' she says.

'But, the clock stops when I'm not actually working on it. It doesn't run continuously,' he replies.

'The policy says within four weeks,' she says.

'The policy doesn't say the clock can't stop,' he replies. 'Therefore, the clock can stop and start as necessary'.

'The policy says within four weeks,' she repeats.

'No, I don't accept that,' he answers. 'It doesn't say the clock can't stop and start'.

'Do you accept that the time period between the date the appeal is lodged to the date you give your decision is greater than four weeks?' she puts to him.

'Er, hmm, factually, yes,' he answers.

'*Factually, yes,*' she echoes his answer. 'Moving on, then,' she says. 'You speak with Neil. He tells you the selection is fair'.

'Yes,' he confirms.

'You accept it?' she asks.

'Of course,' he asserts. 'He is his manager'.

'In your witness statement you say, *"The subjective view of the managers is always taken into account in a redundancy scoring process"*. Is this what you mean to say?' she asks.

'Yes,' he confirms.

'Is Ranjit's selection for redundancy fair?' she asks.
'Yes, absolutely,' he asserts.
'How do you know?' she asks.
'Because Neil says it is,' he answers.
'Thank you, I have no more questions,' she says.

# 17

# RESPONDENTS' CASE

~ Monday 11th December 2006, 3:00 p.m. ~

'Mr Singh would be selected for redundancy even if his redundancy scores are increased,' the respondents' counsel submits to the tribunal. 'His absence in 2005 is greater than Miss Mykonola's, due to a broken leg. This becomes relevant in the redundancy exercise because if his scores are increased to match Miss Mykonola's, then there is a tie situation. Then, the bank looks at disciplinary records, which for both of them are completely clean. Then, absence is looked at. On this criterion, having the greater absence, Mr Singh loses and is the one selected for redundancy'.

'Moving on to collective consultation,' she says. 'More than twenty people are being affected by redundancy within a ninety-day period at the same premises as Mr Singh. Therefore, the bank is under a duty to engage in collective consultation with its union. This duty displaces the statutory procedural duty upon it to consult Mr Singh directly'.

The chairman interjects, 'where is the evidence of that number?'

'In Ms Monroe's testimony,' she replies.

'No, it is not,' the chairman clarifies. 'Ms Monroe says she cannot tell us how many at London Wall'.

'She says two hundred and seventy-five across four premises,' she replies, 'which implies more than twenty in each office'.

'That does not prove more than twenty at London Wall,' the chairman rebuts. 'Besides, that number is across a lot more than four premises,' he clarifies. 'It is across all London premises plus Northampton. Where is the evidence that the bank was proposing to put at risk more than twenty people over a ninety-day timeframe at Mr Singh's premises when it put him at risk?'

'Ms Monroe also says that although only Mr Singh is at risk in his department, over a hundred people are at risk over a ninety-day period across four locations,' she answers.

'But, I do not recall her saying over twenty at Mr Singh's location,' the chairman asserts. 'I recognise this is a highly technical point of law,' he says. 'But, it does matter. If the bank wishes to take advantage of sections of the law to displace statutory procedures that are designed to protect employees, then it needs to prove that it displaced them properly,' he asserts. 'Besides, an employer should possess all the information necessary to be able to evidence the numbers precisely'.

'Yes, Sir,' she concedes. 'Moving on then to whether the dismissal is automatically unfair,' she says. 'The bank gives warning of Mr Singh's impending redundancy to the union, if not specifically to Mr Singh himself,' she submits. 'The union is consulted twice on the matter, on the 9th and the 15th of December. This amounts to good warning,' she submits. 'In fact, at the first meeting, the union challenges the redundancy. It is not satisfied that a Controller's workload can be re-allocated to the remaining team members. Whilst there are some failures in complying with the law in consulting the union,' she concedes, 'this is not a situation that amounts to a complete outright failure of compliance. The bank followed the same standard consultation process that it follows in all of its other redundancies. The question that needs answering is: is the consultation with the union so inadequate that it renders the redundancy unfair? I submit that it is not so inadequate'.

'On the matter of delaying the redundancy

announcement till the 9th of January 2006,' she continues. 'Mr Hobson, Miss Cotton, and Ms Monroe were all present at the meeting with the union. They all say the union instructed them to wait until after Christmas. Ms Monroe explains the practical difficulties of announcing before Christmas, due to it being a period when many managers are on annual leave'.

'Although the specific redundancy criteria and the redundancy process are not brought to the union's attention and are not discussed with it,' she continues, 'they are taken from the standard process, which is agreed with the union'.

'Albeit after he is selected for redundancy and informed he is at risk,' she goes on, 'in the two-week individual consultation period that ensues, there are four meetings with Mr Singh. These meetings give him the chance to challenge his redundancy and put forward alternative proposals to avoid it. The period also gives him the opportunity to explore redeployment. He does all of these things. Hence, the individual consultation is effective,' she submits. 'Furthermore, Mr Singh brings his grievances to Mr Ong and Ms Monroe, both of whom are in a position to overturn his redundancy and would overturn it if it were unfair'.

'Regarding notification errors on the Single Equities Portfolio and the Managed Income Portfolio,' she says, 'Mr Hobson is Mr Singh's superior officer and he says Mr Singh is remiss'.

'Moving on to the matter of whether the dismissal is prejudged,' she continues. 'On the matter of Mr Singh being approached about voluntary redundancy, his and Mr Hobson's accounts of the conversations in 2004 differ considerably,' she says. 'However, it should be noted that when Mr Hobson gets back to Mr Singh with an answer, Mr Singh accepts that he does not tell Mr Hobson that what he said was not a genuine request for voluntary redundancy'.

The chairman interjects, 'do you accept that there is a difference between someone taking the initiative to ask for voluntary redundancy and someone asking about it as a reaction to something someone said that caused frustration?'

'I do accept there is a difference,' she replies. 'But, I dispute the situation is as Mr Singh says. I submit that it is as Mr Hobson says, that is, a cold request for voluntary redundancy initiated by Mr Singh'. She pauses a moment to check the chairman's reaction and then, continues, 'although the bank has no formal policy on voluntary redundancy, you heard from witnesses that it is common practice to approach people who previously expressed an interest in leaving. Hence, Mr Hobson's approach to Mr Singh does not mean his redundancy is prejudged'.

'Moving on to the matter of race,' she says. 'Section 54a of the Race Relations Act applies to discrimination on the grounds of *ethnic origins* and *national origins* only. It does not apply on the basis of *skin colour* also. In his witness statement, Mr Singh alleges that he is discriminated against because of the colour of his skin. He defines his race by the colour of his skin, not by his ethnic or national origins,' she asserts. 'Hence, the protection afforded by section 54a of the law on discrimination in employment is not available to him,' she submits.

What! No way! I need section 54a. It's the part of the law that recognises that smart employers are cautious not to leave behind any evidence of their discriminatory acts. They do not express that they are firing you because you're black, or that they are passing you over for promotion because you're a woman. They just decide it mentally without breathing a word of it and see to it surreptitiously that you suffer. Section 54a recognises this. It says that if the claimant can prove that the difference of treatment can only be due to race discrimination and nothing else, then the tribunal will have to infer that race discrimination occurred. Then, the respondents will have to prove that the treatment is not due in any way to race discrimination. If they can't prove it, then the tribunal must rule that discrimination occurred. I need section 54a to deal with the respondents' stealth. My race discrimination case will have no basis in law if section 54a is disallowed. My heart sinks at the thought that section 54a will be disallowed due to a wording technicality of defining race in legal terms by colour instead of ethnicity and nationality, when they all mean race anyway in layman's terms.

The chairman interjects, 'how does Mr Singh define his race on his Employment Tribunal application form?'

'Of *Indian origin* and of *Indian ethnicity*,' my counsel interjects.

'But, he supersedes that definition by repeatedly referring to his race by the colour of his skin and by referring to his comparator as white,' the respondents' counsel rebuts.

'He also defines his race in his witness statement as Indian and Asian,' the chairman points out. 'It seems that whenever he refers to colour, he means both colour and ethnicity because colour is a visible racial difference between people. Their ethnicities and nationalities are invisible. If you stand Mr Singh and Miss Mykonola side-by-side, the differences visible are their sexes and their colours. The fact that one is male and brown and the other is female and white is plainly visible. But, the fact that one is Indian and the other is Greek is invisible. Would you agree that colour is often used in society to refer to people's race?'

'It is not critical to our case,' the respondents' counsel replies. 'But, we say he defines his race by his colour and therefore, the section 54a protection is not available to him'.

'I also submit,' she continues, 'that just because someone is treated unreasonably, it does not necessarily mean that the unreasonable treatment is racially motivated. Mr Singh's dismissal is completely fair. There is no unreasonable treatment, whatsoever. The respondents followed the same process as they do for all their other redundancies. Mr Hobson denies that there is any relationship issue between himself and Mr Singh. However, I urge the tribunal to reject his denial because I say he is not impartial on the matter and is unlikely to admit there is an issue,' she submits. 'Mr Ong, on the other hand, says there is a difficult relationship between them. I urge the tribunal to accept Mr Ong's view as the impartial view. The basis for the difficult relationship is Mr Singh's personality, not his race,' she asserts. 'His race is irrelevant. Even if he were of another race, the relationship would still be difficult. Any unreasonable treatment is adequately explained by a clash of personalities. Therefore, it does not follow that it is motivated by race'.

'Yes, tribunals take great care not to attribute to race that which is adequately explained by matters of sense and judgement,' the chairman says. 'But, what about the treatment by others, the lack of care exercised by Mr Wilcox and Mr Brent in dealing with Mr Singh's grievances relating specifically to race?' the chairman asks.

'Er,' she mumbles. 'Mr Brent's handling of the grievance is not as lacking as Mr Wilcox's,' she replies.

'What about the bank's refusal to answer Mr Singh's Race Relations Act Questionnaire properly?' the chairman asks.

'Answers are provided where the bank has the information necessary to provide them,' she replies. 'There is not a complete failure to provide answers,' she replies.

'But, some of the ignored questions are critical to the issues at hand,' the chairman says. 'It is not as though they are peripheral. Furthermore, they concern matters that it is unreasonable for the bank not to have the information for,' he asserts. 'Also, the bank took over eight weeks to answer, far beyond what is reasonable, and has not given a plausible explanation for the delay. The bank fails to answer the questionnaire in good time. The questions it omits to answer are crucial. It continues to leave them unanswered, despite Mr Singh chasing it for answers. Do you agree?'

'Yes,' she replies. 'But, unfortunately, the bank does not have the information necessary to answer those questions'.

'That sounds highly unlikely and unbelievable,' the chairman rebuts. 'An established business the size of the bank has a duty to comply with codes of practices and regulations which require it to maintain databases with information of the sort Mr Singh requested in the questionnaire'.

'Er, I submit the bank does not comply with those codes of practices,' she replies.

'Really?' the chairman says rolling his eyes. 'Move on,' he orders.

'Turning to the matter of the bonus,' she says. 'The bonus is discretionary. The bank recognises it has a duty not to exercise that discretion irrationally or perversely. Mr Ong makes clear that the method is wholly rational'.

'Mr Ong explains the general method only as being rational,' the chairman clarifies. 'He does not provide any records to show that the specific awards are made rationally'.

'There is no documentary evidence of his thought process because it is all performed electronically,' she replies.

'He could have saved down his electronic files,' the chairman rebuts.

'Mr Ong gives very cogent evidence,' she replies. 'He only takes into account those matters that are permitted to be included, according to the bonus scheme policy. He does not act irrationally or perversely. There is a cogent reason for the calculation and allocation of all bonuses, including Mr Singh's,' she submits.

'The explanation needs to be cogent for sure,' the chairman says. 'But, it also needs to be capable of being elucidated and explained,' he clarifies. 'Mr Ong did not show us how he arrived at his numbers. He only told us what he does and what he takes into account. He did not show us what he actually did and what he actually took into account. Someone else might very well arrive at he same numbers but be able to show us how he arrived at them. Mr Marr is satisfied with Mr Ong merely telling him what he did regarding the few anomalies he identified. But, he did not identify Mr Khanna as an anomaly, we did and we are left without an explanation for him,' the chairman asserts.

'In terms of Mr Singh's bonus history,' she continues, 'he received an increased bonus every year at the bank except his final year, on which he experienced a reduced bonus. Mr Ong explains that he takes into account an individual's market value. Although the bank's primary case is that Mr Singh's selection for redundancy has no impact on his bonus, I say it does have a bearing. Having been selected for redundancy, his market value drops. Mr Ong does not need to incentivise him to stay. This explains the reduction in the size of his bonus,' she submits.

'One problem with your argument,' the chairman points out, 'is that Mr Ong tells us he allocated the bonuses before the redundancy selection was completed. So, he could not know that Mr Singh's market value is low'.

'Right you are, Sir,' she replies.

'Another problem,' the chairman continues, 'is that your argument can run the other way. That is, Mr Singh's redundancy is predetermined, that it is known about before the selection exercise is carried out'.

'That is why it is not the bank's primary case,' she replies.

'Finally, moving on to the matter of individuals'

credibility,' she continues. 'Where there is a conflict between what Mr Hobson and the witnesses on behalf of the respondents say and what Mr Singh says, and there is no other corroborating evidence, we say the tribunal must accept the witnesses' words, especially Mr Hobson's, over and above Mr Singh's'.

# 18

# CLAIMANT'S CASE

~ Tuesday 12th December 2006, 10:00 a.m. ~

'Starting with whether Mr Singh's dismissal is automatically unfair,' my counsel says. 'The bank fails to prove that more than twenty people are being put at risk of redundancy within a ninety-day period at the London Wall premises, where Mr Singh works,' she submits. 'Therefore, it does not prove that it can displace the individual consultation with Mr Singh by the collective consultation with the union. He is not consulted with when he should be. This renders his dismissal unfair'.

The chairman interjects, 'Ms Monroe says one hundred people across four locations'.

'That does not prove categorically more than twenty at London Wall,' she replies. 'We cannot simply divide one hundred by four and, because the result is more than twenty, say there are more than twenty at London Wall. It is necessary to know with absolute certainty that there are more than twenty there. No information specifically about London Wall is presented. Ms Monroe tells us she cannot say how many at London Wall'.

'One hundred divided by four gives the mathematical average, twenty-five,' the chairman says. 'So, it could be that there are more than twenty at each location'.

'But, it also could be that there are fewer than twenty at some locations and many more at others,' she replies. 'No information specifically about London Wall is presented. We simply do not know what the actual number at London Wall is. We know Mr Singh is at risk there. So, all we know for certain is that the number is at least one.

Hence, the bank does not prove categorically that it can displace the individual consultation with Mr Singh by the collective consultation with the union. He is not consulted when he should be. This renders the dismissal unfair'.

'Moving on,' she continues. 'The decision to make Mr Singh redundant is made around October and November. It is then that Mr Ong tells Mr Hobson and the other heads of his teams that there is a need to make redundancies and asks them all to review their teams. From then on, all of the activity is initiated and lead by Mr Hobson alone,' she highlights. 'It is he who volunteers to lose a Controller, but not an Associate. It is he who suggests that Mr Singh be approached for voluntary redundancy. It is he who approaches Mr Singh about voluntary redundancy. No one else in the team is approached. When Mr Singh says no to voluntary redundancy, it is again Mr Hobson who does the redundancy scoring and the appraisal. It is hardly surprising that Mr Singh is identified as the one selected for dismissal. It is because Mr Hobson wants to get rid of him,' she submits. 'Mr Hobson only approaches the person he is happiest to lose with an offer of voluntary redundancy' she says. 'The feebleness of his excuse, that he approached Mr Singh exclusively because only he, one and a half years earlier, had expressed an interest in voluntary redundancy, makes it even clearer that he wants to get rid of him,' she says. 'Mr Singh never repeated his interest. So, why would Mr Hobson think he still wants to leave?'

'If my suspicions are correct,' the chairman interjects, 'Mr Hobson wants to get rid of Mr Singh because, as Mr Ong says, he has a difficult relationship with him and does not want to work with him'.

'If that is true,' my counsel says, 'then the dismissal is blatantly unfair, in which case the respondents would plead unfairness but not racial discrimination. But, they do not plead unfairness,' she highlights. 'They plead this is a completely fair dismissal. Although Mr Ong suggests that Mr Hobson has a relationship issue with Mr Singh, Mr Hobson himself denies it'.

'Perhaps Mr Hobson's sense prevents him from admitting it himself,' the chairman puts to her. 'Perhaps he feels fear and embarrassment to admit it before his manager and colleagues sitting in the public gallery'.

'He would indeed admit it himself if it were true,' she replies, 'because he is well aware of what the stakes are here and possesses the good sense and judgement to admit it. Yet, he denies it under oath'.

'Hmm,' the chairman muses seeming unconvinced. 'Do continue,' he says.

'As I was saying, Mr Hobson approaches Mr Singh exclusively about voluntary redundancy because he wants to get rid of him,' she continues. 'From a business perspective, it is highly unlikely that a manager would simply allow the person who wishes to leave to be the one who goes because this might result in the loss of skills that are critical to the team's proper performance. A manager is far more likely to retain control over his resources proactively and rule out voluntary redundancy. If it genuinely is the case that a manager is happy to lose the person who wants to leave, then he would ask everyone in the pool, not a single member exclusively,' she submits. 'Mr Singh's remark about voluntary redundancy is a spontaneous, off the cuff reaction out of frustration to what Mr Hobson said at a team meeting,' she says.

The chairman interjects, 'whether Mr Singh's remark is the way he says or the way Mr Hobson says, Mr Hobson took it seriously enough to get back to him and let him know that voluntary redundancy is not available'.

'Mr Singh accepts that Mr Hobson gets back to him,' she says. 'But, he thinks nothing of it and he never again expresses any interest in voluntary redundancy'.

'Do you accept that this is a genuine redundancy situation?' the chairman asks.

'No, I do not. It is a sham,' she answers.

'Why?' the chairman asks.

'How can it be a genuine redundancy situation when trying to cut costs by five per cent but at the same time paying out a wholly discretionary amount of three million pounds in bonuses?' she answers.

'Hmm, it is difficult to disagree with your point,' the chairman says.

'The respondents rely heavily on an agreement with the union,' she continues. 'However, the bank does not produce any agreement signed by itself and the union'.

'Ms Monroe says she has never seen a signed agreement,' the chairman interjects, 'although she honestly believes in the agreement'.

'Yes,' my counsel replies. 'But, the bank is expected to evidence the agreement with a signed document so the terms it relies on can be scrutinised. Without a signed agreement, we do not know what is agreed with the union. We do not know how the union is to be consulted, what criteria are to be used, whether absence and length of service matter, and how sickness is to be measured. So much is left obscure without an agreement document,' she says.

'Mr Singh has more sickness absence than Miss Mykonola due to a broken leg,' the chairman says.

'A reasonable employer will not only look at the number of days absent, but also consider the circumstances and the nature of the absence,' she replies. 'A fair consultation at the correct stage would allow agreement to be reached on what criteria are to be used, including what kind of absence to take into account and which to omit'.

'The respondents' case is also predicated on the assumption that all employees of the bank are members of its in-house union,' the chairman says. 'But, Mr Singh is not a member'.

'That is correct,' she replies. 'No one checks whether

he is a member. When he contacts the union, it says it does not represent him. The only safe thing for the respondents to do is to assume he is not a member and check with him directly. In other words, consult him'.

'Moving on to the matter of the lack of warning,' she continues. 'In October 2005, Mr Hobson knows a redundancy is possible. In November, he knows it is certain. The union is consulted on the 9th and 15th of December, unbeknown to Mr Singh. No mention is made to Mr Singh during the redundancy scoring exercise. He has no opportunity to give input on the selection process. He might want to say Mr Hobson should not do the scoring, or that more people should be involved. He might want to speak to representatives. But, he cannot give such input because he does not know. He does not know how important it is for him to appeal his year-end appraisal. On the morning of the 9th of January, two days before he is told he is at risk, he sends Mr Hobson an email saying he does not agree with the appraisal. He says the negative manager's comment is not supported by evidence. He urges Mr Hobson to remove it from his appraisal because it is important and will impact his prospects. He does not know how right he is. He has no idea that the appraisal is being used to dismiss him'.

'Mr Hobson replies to Mr Singh's email at 5:45pm that day,' the chairman interjects, 'saying, *"I see no reason to remove the criticism and I believe it is important that I provide feedback to one of my subordinates to guide him to improve his behaviour appropriately"*. What do you make of that?' he asks.

'It is utterly inconsistent with warning him of the redundancy,' she answers. 'It is misleading him into believing his employment is continuing'.

'Yes, it seems very disingenuous of Mr Hobson,' the chairman says. 'There is nothing in his email that implies Mr Singh's employment will not continue'.

'Mr Singh is not told until after the redundancy decision is made and until after it becomes too difficult to change the decision,' she continues. 'Also, and this is a minor point, there is no excuse for not telling him before Christmas. Just because the union requests it, it does not mean it is fair,' she submits.

'Ms Monroe says staff can often be away over Christmas, which makes it difficult to announce redundancies around that time,' the chairman says.

'True,' she replies. 'But, each situation should be looked at individually. Mr Hobson was not away'.

'Was he not away over Christmas?' the chairman asks.

'I do not recollect any evidence that he was on leave at the time,' she replies.

'Me neither,' the chairman says.

I rise up from my seat, much to everyone's notice, take a step forward towards my counsel, bend down, and whisper in her ear.

'We stand corrected,' my counsel says. 'Mr Singh just referred me to paragraph 32 of his witness statement, where he himself evidences that Mr Hobson was away from the 17th of December and returned to the office on the 3rd of January'.

'Noted,' the chairman replies.

'Mr Hobson does the redundancy scoring on the 8th of December,' my counsel continues. 'He is around then. Mr Singh could be warned then, while Mr Hobson is around to deal with any concerns'.

'Not only is there a lack of warning,' she submits, 'but also, there is a lack of consultation with the union. The bank says the criteria are agreed with the union. But, it produces no signed agreement showing what is agreed. The union is not consulted about the specific criteria used in Mr Singh's redundancy. Not all the criteria are standard, Mr Hobson creates one himself,' she highlights. 'That deviation is not disclosed to the union. The union is not consulted about which appraisal should be used, the mid-year or the year-end,' she says.

'Mr Singh seems to be hit with a double-whammy,' the

chairman says. 'His scores on the redundancy scorecard and on the appraisal are reduced for the same reasons. So, if he does badly on one, then he also does badly on the other. This magnifies any negative marking, which seems inherently unfair and it was not agreed with the union'.

'The mid-year appraisal is done months before the redundancy situation. So, it is objective,' she replies. 'It provides some protection in the redundancy. But, the year-end appraisal is done during the redundancy by the same manager who does the redundancy scorecard. If the manager is factoring in personal likes and dislikes, then it is a double-whammy, the prejudices get magnified,' she says. 'The union might be interested in this. But, the union is not told'.

'Regarding individual consultation,' she says. 'There is none. Mr Singh is selected for redundancy by the 8th of December and it is set in stone by the time he is told,' she submits.

'It cannot be said that there is none,' the chairman interjects. 'There is a possibility still that Mr Singh might be redeployed elsewhere in the bank'.

'As soon as he is told he is at risk, the rest of the team are told they are not at risk,' she replies. 'Redeployment is the only possibility of avoiding redundancy. Therefore, he is at risk only in this limited and improbable sense. Mr Hobson accepts that the decision is made and he is disinclined to go back to the others and tell them they are at risk. Mr Ong and Ms Monroe are unwilling to overturn the redundancy. Ms Monroe insists that Mr Singh cannot be selected without him knowing there is a redundancy situation despite the fact that he is selected without him knowing it. Their minds are made up and closed off,' she submits. 'It is too late for individual consultation. It is consultation in name only, a rubberstamping of a decision already made. They are happy with their procedures. They are not interested in what he has to say, even though the things he is saying are so blatantly correct'.

'Ms Monroe concedes that there is no consultation about the specifics of the redundancy,' the chairman says.

'Yes. But, she clearly does not take that on board at Mr Singh's appeal,' my counsel replies. 'If she does, she ought to take some action. Mr Ong clearly fails to check the process is fair. Mr Hobson is never going to overturn his own decision'.

'Turning to the matter of the redundancy selection criteria,' she continues. 'The criteria are highly subjective. Miss Cotton says that the manager must support his assessment with evidence. But, with highly subjective criteria, the manager can select and disregard the evidence according to the outcome he desires, according to whom he wants to get rid of. Mr Hobson carefully selects the evidence and chooses how to interpret it according to his objective. He chooses to criticise Mr Singh as being someone who does not consult him enough. Another manager can just as easily interpret the same evidence differently and praise Mr Singh for being autonomous and self-reliant'.

'Mr Hobson does not know,' she continues, 'what the competency called Conversion even means. When asked by their counsel what it means, Miss Cotton does not know either. She is a Human Resources professional. It is her job to know. She says it is, *"how an individual converts their capacity to learning their self-knowledge through"*, and then, she hesitates and mumbles, and trails off inaudibly. She is the HR advisor to Mr Hobson and she does not know. Conversion is actually about self-development. It is not the place to score how a worker and his manager relate to each other. Yet, Mr Hobson comments under this competency that Mr Singh finds him patronising'.

'Turning to the appropriateness of the criteria,' she continues. 'Mr Singh is marked down on two FSA notification matters, the Single Equities Portfolio and the Managed Income Portfolio'.

'On the Single Equities Portfolio,' she continues, 'it is

alleged that there is a failure to pre-notify. The minutes of Mr Brent's meeting with Mr Hobson show that Mr Hobson clearly tells Mr Brent that pre-notification should be done because changes to Appendix 1 of the FSA's document need to be pre-notified. But, Miss Mykonola, in her email on the matter to Mr Hobson and others, clearly says, *"Changes to Appendix 1 are not necessarily pre-notification"*. Mr Singh did not do anything culpable. Mr Hobson's spin in Mr Singh's appraisal is that he is casual with the regulator's requirement. If he were culpable, then why is he not disciplined before the appraisal?' she submits. 'There should be no surprises in the appraisal meeting. But, the first Mr Singh hears of this is during the appraisal meeting. It is unfair to criticise him and mark him down'.

'On the Managed Income Portfolio,' she continues, 'Mr Hobson says that Mr Singh went against his advise without consulting him. But, Mr Singh's emails clearly show that he tells Mr Hobson all along what he is going to do. He is not doing anything behind Mr Hobson's back. Mr Hobson does not disagree with what Mr Singh tells him he is going to do. He does not criticise it. He does not protest'.

The chairman asks, 'why is that not explained by Mr Ong's comment that Mr Hobson does not say a bad word about anyone?'

'Mr Hobson does not proffer that explanation himself,' she answers. 'Mr Ong proffers it, in an attempt to protect Mr Hobson. Mr Hobson's explanation is a very poor excuse for the appraisal being a complete surprise. No reasonable manager would score Mr Singh down,' she submits.

'On the issue of Mr Singh's alleged failure to embrace change, Mr Hobson's account changes,' she continues. 'At the beginning, he says that Mr Singh raised issues regarding the change in the line of delegated authorities while the change is in its proposed stage. He does not say that Mr Singh failed to accept the change once it is implemented and effective,' she clarifies. 'It is Mr Singh's and Miss Mykonola's job to flag up issues. Their appraisals show that one of their set objectives is, *"to give challenge and feedback on proposed changes"*. They both do this. If this were culpable behaviour, Mr Hobson would mention it to Mr Singh before his final appraisal. He would mention it on the job or record it in the earlier appraisals, the 2004 year-end and the 2005 mid-year appraisals, which he himself performed. To the contrary, he praises Mr Singh in his earlier appraisals for challenging the department set-up by flagging up the inherent inefficiencies and risks, and for proposing reasonable solutions. Then, here at the tribunal, having conceded under the scrutiny of cross-examination that it is Mr Singh's job to raise such matters, he changes his criticism of Mr Singh to say he fails to accept the change when it becomes implemented and effective. But, what he says is utterly inconsistent with Mr Singh's email to him expressing that he accepts the change and is complying with it. Under further cross-examination, Mr Hobson admits that Mr Singh does not act in anyway contrary to the implemented change. The facts are simply not as Mr Hobson says. Mr Singh's behaviour is a credit to him. He should not be scored down'.

'On the allegation that Mr Singh rarely discusses things with his line manager, we have clearly seen lots of email correspondence showing that he often and regularly discusses things with Mr Hobson,' she continues. 'It is clear from the emails that he not only discusses things with Mr Hobson during his weekly one-to-one meetings with him, but also that he does so throughout the week'.

'Perhaps that is not as often as Mr Hobson would like,' the chairman interjects.

'That comes back to the unfairness of leaving it completely up to Mr Hobson to interpret the evidence how he likes,' she replies. 'Another manager might interpret the same evidence otherwise. The highly subjective scoring process is inherently unfair. It allows for Mr Hobson's personal tastes and wishes'.

'Moving on to the patronising comment,' she continues. 'This is an unfair criticism in the sense that Miss Mykonola reacts in the same way but is not criticised and is not scored down. She tells Mr Hobson very angrily to his face that he is patronising. Mr Singh witnesses it. Mr Hobson admits that he remembers it. Of course he remembers it. No manager would forget that. He says Miss Mykonola is right, he is patronising. It is unfair to score Mr Singh down here'.

'Moving on to the scoring exercise,' she continues. 'Mr Hobson says he did not compare Mr Singh and Miss Mykonola against each other. He says he scored them individually and separately, some time apart. But the copying and pasting across their scorecards clearly evidences otherwise, that he scored them simultaneously, comparing them against each other. He selects examples where he can score Mr Singh down, but he awards Miss Mykonola full marks. He does not cast around for reasons to score Miss Mykonola down. He does so because he wants Mr Singh to be the one who is selected for redundancy. Otherwise, we would see some criticism and down scoring of Miss Mykonola too. This is the *smoking gun*,' she submits. 'This is the incontrovertible incriminating evidence that he performed the scoring with one eye on the outcome he desires'.

'Mr Singh's dismissal is so deeply unfair,' she continues, 'that if it comes to a stage of asking what would have happened instead, then it just is not possible to say. The process is unfair in every respect, procedurally and substantively. No warning is given. Mr Hobson conducts it alone. There is no union agreement, which becomes important if Mr Singh's and Miss Mykonola's scores tie neck and neck. In a tie situation, the bank says sickness absence will be considered to make the selection. This is where the agreement with the union and consultation with it is critical. Aside from his absence in relation to his leg break, both Mr Singh and Miss Mykonola have five absence days. So, they continue to tie neck and neck. The bank says the next criterion will be length of service. Miss Mykonola was last in. Hence, she will be selected for redundancy'.

'Turning to the race issue,' she says. 'Mr Hobson and the bank have consistently denied the hostility of race discrimination. They consistently pleaded and made the case that Mr Singh is selected for redundancy through a completely fair process. Courts recognise that aggressors rarely admit their hostilities. They recognise that their hostilities must be inferred from the evidence. The evidence in this case is compelling,' she asserts. 'Firstly, there is unfair treatment. Secondly, there is less favourable treatment than the comparator. Thirdly, there is a difference of race. Fourthly, race discrimination can be inferred. Fifthly, the respondents have not disproved race discrimination. The selection process is not simply unfair, it is grossly unfair because it is used by Mr Hobson specifically to remove Mr Singh,' she submits. 'He blatantly does the scoring in a way to remove him. He says nothing at all negative about Miss Mykonola'.

'What if Mr Hobson does all this, not out of any racial motivation,' the chairman interjects, 'but, simply because, as Mr Ong suggests, he has a relationship issue with Mr Singh?'

'If that were true, then Mr Hobson would have admitted it himself by now,' she answers. 'He is an intelligent, conscientious man. He is well educated and experienced. It is clear that he is capable of speaking up for himself, not least by the fact that the bank employs him in a senior, highly responsible position in which he needs to be able to consider matters conscientiously and speak his mind. He is not naïve. He is aware of what the stakes are here. He denies there was any relationship issue. The case he consistently puts forward is that the dismissal is completely fair. Mr Ong proffers the difficult relationship explanation on his behalf to try to save him'.

'Hmm,' the chairman reflects on her submission. He leans back into his chair, muses for a moment, and then, sitting up again, signals her to continue.

'The bank does not provide Equal Opportunities training to its staff,' she continues. 'It does not investigate race discrimination properly. Mr Wilcox accepts that, having heard Mr Singh and before carrying out any investigation, he believes Mr Singh raises the race issue only because he can think of no other reason why he would be selected for redundancy over Miss Mykonola. He believes Mr Singh is not willing to accept it is conceivable that he could be selected over Miss Mykonola. He believes Mr Singh is trying to find justification for being selected. When pressed under the scrutiny of cross-examination, he admits that he did not even take the trouble to work out what the correct procedure is to investigate the allegation of race discrimination. He admits he did not seek out the evidence and challenge Mr Hobson. Mr Hobson acts in an environment where Mr Wilcox can casually prejudge that Mr Singh is only trying to use race as an excuse. A culture where an accusation of race discrimination is not taken seriously and the facts are not enquired into. A domain that provides opportunity for racially motivated hostility, where Mr Hobson need not say Mr Singh's face does not fit because he can get away with removing him without giving a plausible explanation'.

'Let us consider for a moment that Mr Hobson removed Mr Singh because he would not accept him as his line manger,' she continues. 'Mr Hobson is an intelligent man. He would at some stage in the grievance process tell someone that the real reason is non-acceptance as manager. This would be a plausible explanation. Mr Singh gave him every opportunity to give a plausible explanation. He has had ample opportunity to give a plausible explanation. But, never has he given one, not even here before the tribunal'.

'Although the respondents have consistently denied race discrimination throughout,' she continues, 'the evidence that it is race discrimination is there. Just like Mr Singh, Miss Mykonola also expresses concerns about the change in the line of delegated authority. Just like Mr Singh, Miss Mykonola also tells Mr Hobson not to patronise her. Just Like Mr Singh, Miss Mykonola also says there is no need to pre-notify on the Single Equities Portfolio. Just like Mr Singh, Miss Mykonola thinks no notification is needed on the Managed Income Portfolio. She thinks and does the same as Mr Singh. They are both accepting of Mr Hobson as their line manager to the same degree. Yet, Mr Hobson scores only Mr Singh down for all these things, and it has nothing to do with not accepting him as his line manager'.

'If anything,' the chairman interjects, 'if he has animosity towards Mr Singh, then the bank provided him with a good opportunity to vent it'.

'Yes,' she agrees. 'The fact that he gives no plausible explanation but denies the hostility of race discrimination is the reason the hostility should be inferred,' she submits. 'Additionally, Mr Wilcox and Mr Brent not treating Mr Singh's grievance of race discrimination as seriously as it deserves is another reason the hostility should be inferred. Furthermore, the bank's refusal to answer Mr Singh's Race Relations Act Questionnaire as properly as it deserves to be answered is yet another reason the hostility should be inferred'.

'If the hostility of race discrimination is inferred,' she continues, 'then look at the explanation the respondents proffer. They say the redundancy is fair. This explanation must be rejected because it clearly is not fair. Mr Hobson selected Mr Singh for reasons best known only to himself. But, the reason is not that Mr Singh does not accept him as his manager, because this is a reason he would have declared by now. Never have the respondents pleaded or said this. They cannot plead it now and thereby, move the goalpost and deny the tribunal the chance to hear and investigate the pleading,' she asserts. 'Both Mr Singh and Miss Mykonola accept Mr Hobson as a manager to the same degree. Had the respondents run the non-acceptance case instead, then the tribunal would have had the chance to investigate whether Mr Hobson's motive is that an Asian person is non-accepting of him,' she submits.

'Your point being that Mr Singh has met and answered the case the respondents pleaded,' the chairman says.

'Yes,' she replies. 'Their explanations must be rejected and race discrimination must be concluded,' she submits.

'Moving on now to the matter of the bonus,' she says. 'The bonus is a matter of race discrimination and also of a breach of contract'.

'Firstly, let us look at it from the race perspective,' she says. 'There is no transparency on how Mr Ong set the bonuses. He produces no records evidencing his thought process. The appraisal score is the primary factor in the bonus calculation. If the appraisal score is tainted by race discrimination, then the discrimination feeds into the bonus allocation process. The only two people in the department to suffer a reduction in their bonuses are both Asian,' she asserts. 'They are Mr Khanna, despite his appraisal score increasing, and Mr Singh. Everyone else is non-Asian and none of them suffer a reduction, even if their appraisal scores reduce,' she highlights. 'The explanation Mr Ong proffers for Mr Khanna's reduced bonus is not backed up by records. On these facts alone, race discrimination must be inferred,' she submits. 'The bank cannot prove there is no discrimination because Mr Ong does not maintain any records showing his thought process. There is no transparency at all'.

'Now, let us look at the bonus from a breach of contract perspective,' she continues. 'The term in the employment contract between the bank and Mr Singh that is breached is the implied term of trust and confidence between them. Mr Ong does not follow the bank's bonus allocation procedures. He incorporates a factor of his own, being market value, an amount incentivising an individual to remain in the role. Market value does not feature anywhere in the bank's bonus allocation procedures and policies. There is no need to incentivise Mr Singh to remain in the role, he is selected for redundancy and will be gone anyway,' she says. 'The bank's procedures state clearly that the bonus is a reward for past performance. But, come the end of the year, Mr Ong introduces and applies market value, a forward-looking factor that incentivises future behaviour rather than reward past performance, and Mr Singh's bonus is reduced. This makes perverse the fact that Mr Singh worked the year in good faith believing his bonus will reward him for his past performance. Mr Ong breaches the implied trust and confidence Mr Singh has that the bonus will be allocated on the basis the bank's procedures say'.

'Finally,' she says, 'let us consider individuals' credibility. On matters that Mr Hobson scores Mr Singh down, his accounts change. He says different things during the grievances to what he says contemporaneously at the time of the redundancy exercise. Then, here at the tribunal, under cross-examination his accounts change again. His explanations and his versions of events not only change, but also are inconsistent with the evidence. You witnessed the immense strain he showed he is suffering under the scrutiny of cross-examination. If this is not a genuine redundancy situation and is an exercise driven out of his personal reasons, then he has never admitted it. The tribunal should reflect all of this on his credibility,' she submits.

'In contrast,' she continues, 'you witnessed Mr Singh today highlight evidence against himself by drawing the tribunal's attention to the fact that Mr Hobson was on leave over the Christmas period. Under cross-examination, he demonstrates complete calm and total ease. He demonstrates that he knows his case intimately. He is reasonable. He backs down where it is appropriate, unlike Mr Hobson and some of the respondents' other witnesses. He is slow to conclude and suggest race is an issue. When Mr Wilcox and Mr Brent ask him if he has ever experienced any race issues at the bank before his redundancy, he says, no. He acts entirely straight the whole time. Where there is a conflict between what he says and what the witnesses for the respondents say, especially Mr Hobson, and there is no other corroborating evidence, the tribunal should accept his word'.

# 19

# JUDGMENT DAY

~ Friday 15th December 2006, 11:30 a.m. ~

Preparing mentally for the worst while hoping for the best is what I've spent the past two days doing over which the tribunal deliberated its decision behind closed doors. The risk analyst in me mulled over the likelihoods of the possible outcomes. Unfairness, being the simple and linear matter, I feel quietly confident about. Race discrimination, a complex and multidimensional matter with vast room for the tribunal to exercise discretion, I dare not try to predict.

Today is judgement day. We are all gathered before the tribunal to receive its verdict. I sit in my regular spot in the public gallery immediately behind my counsel on the far right hand side of the courtroom. As usual, Neil, Simon, Veronica, and a number of the bank's other officers sit together in the public gallery immediately behind their counsel on the far left hand side of the room. The public gallery is full with spectators.

'All stand,' the courtroom attendant cries out.

We rise to our feet. From behind the platform at the head of the room, the three judges emerge from their chamber's door. They file in, take up their seats at the judges' bench on the platform, and gaze down authoritatively on their courtroom.

'Be seated,' the attendant cries out.

I brace myself to receive their rulings. I try to calm my nerves by being grateful for personal circumstances that allowed me even to stand up for myself against such a powerful adversary. I recognise that merely in having been able to attempt to set the record right means I'm fortunate.

Pure chance placed me in the privileged position of being able to stand up for myself while everyday countless others suffer far worse injustices and their circumstances deny them the ability to do anything about them. I remind myself to keep things in perspective because they could easily be miles worse.

The chairman begins, 'on the 7th of July 2006, Mr Singh presented a complaint to the tribunal alleging the following: he is dismissed from his employment unfairly; his contract of employment is breached; and he is the victim of race discrimination. He brought all of these claims against the bank and also against Mr Hobson, his line manager, personally'.

'His case is that he is dismissed unfairly when the bank purported to dismiss him for the reason of redundancy,' he continues. 'He alleges that both respondents discriminated against him racially in his 2005 year-end appraisal and in the redundancy selection exercise, which leads to him being selected for dismissal. He alleges that the bank did not follow the statutory disciplinary procedure. He alleges the bonus awarded to him is an act of unfairness and race discrimination, as well as being a breach of his contract of employment'.

'Both respondents deny the claims of unfairness and race discrimination,' he continues.

'The tribunal heard evidence from Mr Singh on his own behalf,' he continues. 'On behalf of the respondents, it heard evidence from Mr Hobson and five other officers of the bank, and received only a witness statement from a sixth'.

'Mr Singh's primary case,' he continues, 'is that his selection for redundancy is predetermined by Mr Hobson for the following reasons. Mr Hobson approaches Mr Ong and offers to lose one of his staff. Mr Hobson suggests Mr Singh be approached with an offer of voluntary redundancy. Mr Hobson makes the approach himself. He would not do these things if he were not personally content for Mr Singh to be dismissed. He does not approach anyone else with a similar offer of voluntary redundancy. His reason for approaching Mr Singh exclusively, that Mr Singh requested voluntary redundancy one and a half years earlier, is implausible. Mr Singh was speaking out of frustration on behalf of his team regarding what he thought is an inappropriate comment by Mr Hobson and one and a half years had passed since. Therefore, this is unlikely to be the reason why Mr Hobson approaches him exclusively. When Mr Singh declines the offer, Mr Hobson does the redundancy scoring exercise alone, in which he marks Mr Singh down relative to Miss Mykonola'.

'The respondents' primary case,' he continues, 'is that the reason for his dismissal is redundancy and the dismissal is fair'.

'Moving on now to the tribunal's findings,' he says.

'On the matter of whether the dismissal is automatically unfair,' he continues, 'no letter is sent to Mr Singh informing him of the redundancy and the reasons for it before he is told that he is selected for dismissal. Nor is any such letter sent to him before the bank serves him his notice of the termination. The bank fails to follow the statutory dismissal procedure. Therefore, the dismissal is automatically unfair,' he rules.

Phew! The ruling gives great relief to my nerves. At the very least, I am right that my dismissal is unfair.

'Moving on to the matter of collective consultation with the union,' the chairman continues. 'Mr Singh receives no warning at all that he is selected for dismissal. There is no evidence that Mr Hobson and Miss Cotton even attempt to find out whether he is a member of the union. He has no say in what the selection criteria should be and how they should be applied. He has no say in who should carry out the redundancy process or the method by which it should be performed. He cannot discuss the situation with the union because the union is not willing to talk to him. He has no knowledge and no reason to appeal his scoring. The failure to warn him and the passage of time rob him of the critical chance to appeal. No reasonable employer would fail to warn an individual of an impending redundancy prior to Christmas, a festive time associated with additional expenditure'.

'The bank fails to prove with hard evidence of the sort that is reasonable to expect from it that it has even agreed the redundancy selection criteria with the union,' he continues. 'No meaningful consultation with the union is conducted. Mr Hobson is left alone to his own methods to choose how to carry out the redundancy'.

'Moving on to the matter of individual consultation,' he says. 'For individual consultation to be fair, it has to be done at a stage when it can be meaningful. In this case, it is not done until a long time after Mr Singh is selected for dismissal. It is not meaningful. Therefore, it is not fair,' he rules. 'The suggestion that Mr Singh could overturn his selection for dismissal is implausible. Neither Mr Ong nor Ms Monroe, who conduct the appeal process in a *repeating the party line* manner, is likely to overturn it'.

'Moving on to the selection criteria,' he continues. 'The criteria are highly subjective. Mr Hobson marks Mr Singh down for being self-reliant and not consulting him. Another manager can easily think that, for a person occupying the senior and responsible office of Market Risk Controller, being self-reliant and not consulting his manager unnecessarily are positives and score him highly instead'.

'Mr Hobson's evidence regarding the Single Equities Portfolio issue changes,' he continues. 'During the grievance process, he tells Mr Brent that there is a clear need to pre-notify. But, neither he nor Miss Mykonola thinks so on the job at the time the issue arises. If he thinks there is a clear need to pre-notify, one would expect him to challenge Mr Singh. He makes no such challenge. In fact, no mention is made of it until Mr Singh's redundancy appraisal, being some eight months later. It is unjust to lower Mr Singh's score for this'.

'Regarding the Managed Income Portfolio,' he continues, 'Mr Hobson's evidence again changes. First, he complains the failure is not pre-notifying the FSA contrary to his advice. Then, he says that Mr Singh changed his decision without consulting him. Then, he says something else. The email evidence contradicts both his earlier statements. It is clear that Mr Singh keeps him informed of what he intends to do. Yet, he does not disagree or protest. It is unjust to lower Mr Singh's score for this'.

'Regarding the failure to embrace change,' he continues, 'again, Mr Hobson's evidence changes. Firstly, he complains that Mr Singh highlights issues concerning the change to the line of delegated authorities while it is in a proposal stage. Having conceded that it is Mr Singh's job to highlight such matters, he then changes the complaint to suggest that Mr Singh does not accept the change after it becomes effective. Yet, he accepts that Mr Singh works to implement the change as instructed and complies with it once it becomes effective. Some criticisms Mr Hobson makes of Mr Singh regarding embracing change relate to 2003, a time long before the period in which the redundancy is being assessed. But, never had any such criticisms been made of Mr Singh before. It is unjust to lower Mr Singh's score for this'.

'These are just the most striking and dramatic examples of the changes and inconsistencies in Mr Hobson's testimony and of his excessive criticisms of Mr Singh,' he clarifies. 'The tribunal acknowledges there are many more such examples, like overstating that Mr Singh fails to discuss things with his line manager, and overplaying Mr Singh's comment about finding him patronising'.

'As for Mr Hobson's testimony that he did not score Mr Singh and Miss Mykonola relative to each other,' he continues, 'it is clear from placing their scorecard assessments side-by-side that he completed them simultaneously and in a similar way, copying and pasting from one to the other while marking Miss Mykonola up and marking Mr Singh down'.

'Under the competency of Conversion, which concerns an individual's personal development,' he continues, 'Mr Hobson criticises and scores Mr Singh on matters that are irrelevant to the competency, like, to mention a few, finding praise from his line manger patronising and raising issues regarding the team's management reporting line'.

'For all these reasons, Mr Singh's selection for redundancy is substantively unfair,' he rules.

Thank heavens! I've managed to put right my employment record. The ruling gives me a great sense of relief.

'Turning now to the issue of race,' the chairman says. 'Mr Singh claims three detriments regarding his race discrimination claim. First is the selection for redundancy. Second is the dismissal of his race grievance by Mr Wilcox and Mr Brent. Third is the failure to pay him a proper bonus'.

'Mr Singh defines his race not only by his colour, but also by his ethnic and national origins,' he clarifies. 'Hence, the full protection of the law, including section 54a, is applicable to him contrary to what the respondents say. Clearly, there is a difference of treatment; he is selected for dismissal whereas Miss Mykonola is not. Clearly, there is a difference of race between them. Furthermore, there is evidence from which the tribunal may draw the inference of race discrimination'.

'The dismissal is not simply unfair, it is grossly unfair,' he continues. 'However, gross unreasonable treatment does not of itself necessarily mean the existence of racial discrimination,' he cautions. 'But, combine it with the strong evidence of the following. Mr Hobson uses the selection process to remove Mr Singh by reducing his redundancy score unreasonably with unjust, illegitimate criticisms of which he gives him no prior warnings. The bank provides no Equal Opportunities training for any of the managers involved in the selection. Mr Wilcox and Mr Brent demonstrate a corporate culture of denying and refusing a complaint of race discrimination. They believe that because there is no overt racial prejudice, then there cannot be any racial discrimination at all. The bank gives evasive answers to Mr Singh's Race Relations Act Questionnaire. For some of the questions, it bluntly responds that it does not know the answer or is unable to obtain the necessary information. In addition, the bank is in breach of the Code of Practice on Racial Policy in Employment regarding monitoring. It does not take Mr Singh's allegation of race discrimination seriously. It does not investigate it properly and promptly. It does not provide managers with training on Equal Opportunities. It does not conduct any monitoring of employees' performances by racial groups. It does not monitor workers' grievances by racial groups. It does not use monitoring and disciplinary data to see if there are any disparities between racial groups. Based on all of this, Mr Singh proves successfully that the unreasonable treatment can only be based on race. The tribunal is satisfied that the inference of racial discrimination be drawn and, per section 54a of the Race Relations Act, the burden of proof be upon the respondents to prove that there is no racial discrimination whatsoever regarding Mr Singh's dismissal'.

'Their explanation,' he continues, 'is that the dismissal is on the grounds of a genuine redundancy that is carried out reasonably and fairly. The tribunal rejects their explanation. The dismissal is unfair. Mr Singh's selection is predetermined by Mr Hobson. The respondents fail to prove that the dismissal is in no way on racial grounds. However,' he says, 'an alternative non-racial explanation is put forward by Mr Ong. That is, Mr Hobson simply has a relationship issue with Mr Singh. But, Mr Hobson himself does not accept this explanation. Hence, the tribunal cannot place any reliance on Mr Ong's suggestion. The tribunal rejects Mr Ong's explanations. Having put forward no non-discriminatory explanations, the respondents fail to discharge the burden upon them of proving that the reason for Mr Singh's selection and dismissal is in no way on racial grounds,' he rules.

'There are total failures on the parts of Mr Wilcox and Mr Brent in dealing seriously and properly with Mr Singh's grievance of race discrimination,' he highlights.

'For all of the reasons given, Mr Singh's dismissal is motivated by race and is on racial grounds,' he rules.

Thank heavens again! The tribunal confirms that my highly serious allegation of race discrimination, which I did not bring lightly, is properly conceived and rooted in good faith. I can hold my head up high.

I look over at Neil to check his reaction. He maintains a poker face. Simon, sitting beside him, leans towards him to say something.

'Oh, well. So, we lost. It's no big deal,' I read Simon's lips say.

'Turning to the matter of Mr Singh's bonus award,' the chairman continues. 'There is a failure to provide detailed notes and records of the reasoning for the allocation of the bonus. Mr Ong gives the tribunal general evidence only, nothing specific. The appraisal is contaminated with race discrimination. The bonus depends partly on the contaminated appraisal. Hence, the bonus is contaminated by race discrimination and is lowered on racial grounds,' he rules.

The tribunal upholding every single one of my claims adds to my overall relief.

'Although the bonus scheme is discretionary,' the chairman continues, 'the discretion must not be exercised irrationally or capriciously. The appraisal is contaminated by Mr Hobson's racial motive to predetermine Mr Singh's selection for dismissal. It feeds as a determining factor into the bonus allocation process. Thus, the discretion exercised by Mr Ong is tainted by the racial motive and is rendered irrational and capricious. This constitutes a breach of the implied term of trust and confidence in the employment contract between the bank and Mr Singh. Therefore, the reduction in the bonus is a breach of contract,' he rules.

'To summarise,' he continues. 'Mr Singh is dismissed unfairly. Both the bank and Mr Hobson discriminated against him racially in dismissing him from his employment. The bank discriminated against him racially in his grievances regarding his selection for redundancy, which it dismissed out of hand, and also in the allocation of his 2005 bonus, which it lowered. Additionally, the bank is in breach of contract regarding the bonus award. The tribunal's decision is unanimous. All of Mr Singh's claims are upheld'.

I am grateful my employment record is restored. I feel no sense of jubilation, though, only relief. After all, I have gained nothing really over the past year with the immense amount of energy and money I expended. All I have done is held people to account for their wrongdoings against me and achieved the restoration of something that should not have been taken from me in the first place. There is no gain. I am worse off than where I should have been a year ago because now I'm also jobless and out of pocket by the huge legal fees I incurred in seeking justice. I have gone through a yearlong ordeal that I should not have had to go through. An ordeal that could have been cut short if even only one of the bank's officers had demonstrated the personal integrity necessary to uphold my grievances. But, not one did. Rather than stand up to wrongful conduct and call it out, they all supported it and perpetuated my ordeal.

Addressing the respondents' counsel, the chairman asks, 'do you wish to make any statement on behalf of the respondents?'

She turns around and confers with Neil in private whispers. I wonder what they're saying. I recall a week ago I witnessed him swear solemnly to testify truthfully and thus, place himself under a fundamental obligation to serve the tribunal with an honest and accurate testimony. Then, I watched him give a cringeworthy testimony in which he would not give up the truth voluntarily. Under cross-examination pressure he brought upon himself, his face strained and his body trembled involuntarily in agony as he tried to hold on to the truth from being extracted from him by giving what the tribunal, in its technical legal language, refers to as a changing, inconsistent, and contradictory testimony. I believe in layman's language that is tantamount to saying he lied under oath. Perhaps he will apologise now.

Upon finishing conferring with Neil, the respondents' counsel replies, 'no, Sir'.

Remarkable! No apology from Neil or the bank, despite their wrongdoings and the basis for an apology being formally established by the tribunal. Surely, the reasonable thing to do now is to acknowledge without reservation that they did wrong. But, they choose not to express any form of remorse for their unlawful conduct, or even acknowledge that they are guilty of it. They react as though they have done nothing wrong whatsoever. I'm astonished how they continue to act like they are innocents following the tribunal's ruling against them on every count. I don't need their apologies or confessions to assuage my feeling or to be able to proceed with a responsible attitude myself. Their lack of remorse is irrelevant to me in that sense, but it gives me cause for concern that they do not care for behaving reasonably and facing up to their responsibilities in the forthcoming matter of remedy.

'Mr Singh,' the chairman says addressing me directly, 'we now proceed to the matter of remedy. Two remedies are available. They are *reinstatement* and *compensation*. You must choose one. Reinstatement is the primary legal remedy. It is non-monetary. It entails the bank re-employing you in your original Market Risk Controller role or, if that is not practical, in some other capacity. Compensation, on the other hand, is the secondary legal remedy. It is monetary, entailing financial indemnity. Do you understand the difference?'

'Yes, Sir,' I answer.

'Mr Singh,' the chairman says, 'do you choose reinstatement or compensation?'

Printed in Great Britain
by Amazon

23299496R00148